# TAMING THE VULTURE

*Brides By Chance
Regency Adventures
Book Ten*

## Elizabeth Bailey

SAPERE
BOOKS

# TAMING THE VULTURE

Published by Sapere Books.

20 Windermere Drive, Leeds, England, LS17 7UZ,
United Kingdom

saperebooks.com

Copyright © Elizabeth Bailey, 2021
Elizabeth Bailey has asserted her right to be identified as the
author of this work.
All rights reserved.

No part of this publication may be reproduced, stored in any
retrieval system, or transmitted, in any form, or by any means,
electronic, mechanical, photocopying, recording, or otherwise,
without the prior written permission of the publishers.
This book is a work of fiction. Names, characters, businesses,
organisations, places and events, other than those clearly in the
public domain, are either the product of the author's
imagination, or are used fictitiously.
Any resemblances to actual persons, living or dead, events or
locales are purely coincidental.

ISBN: 978-1-80055-329-3

# CHAPTER ONE

The brass plaque beside the worn front door announced the identity of those within: *Beardsley & Beak, Publishers*. Miss Latimer ignored the upsurge of blood in her veins and turned to the maid who had insisted on coming with her and was waiting upon the flagway.

"This is the place, Peg. Come along."

The girl hesitated. "You'd best ring, Miss Silve. What if they ain't there?"

"Of course they are there. Or someone will be. These are business premises."

Peg wrung agitated hands. "You had ought to have written for an appointment first, Miss Silve."

"But then Mr Beak might not have given me one. He cannot refuse to see me if I'm here in person."

Peg sighed. "I ought to have told madam what you meant to do."

That was precisely what she had wished to avoid. Aunt Angelica would have vetoed the expedition, counselling her to wait for a response, but Silvestre could not endure the suspense. All well and good when it had been the gothic tale. She had not minded waiting to hear from the publishers then. But this manuscript was altogether different. She had poured heart and soul into the story and it mattered too much to allow for patience.

She came down the single step and set a hand on the hovering maid's back, pushing her up into the porch. "You would come, Peg. Try not to look as if you disapprove, if you please."

She had lost no time in getting upon terms with the maid designated by her godmother to serve her while she was staying with Mrs Summerhayes in George Street. It was such a joy to have a maid at all, now she no longer had her twin. When the bulk of the servants had been turned off to save expense, she and Hetty had helped each other with the complexities of female dress. But Hetty was the Duchess of Charlton now and had been whisked off to Devenal Castle, leaving her twin bereft. Writing became Silvestre's solace and *Emmeline* was born of the unexpected agony of her loss. She'd had no notion of how much she would miss her sister, but it had proved hard indeed to lose her.

Shaking off the thoughts, she lifted her hand and tugged on the brass bell. The jangle it made, echoing within the building, mirrored the one in her bosom. She thrust it down. *Come, Silvestre Latimer, this is not like you.* She was in general far too insouciant, taking life as it came. But this business was making her as volatile in spirits as her twin. Not that Hetty's happiness was in doubt.

Footsteps beyond the closed door took her attention and she braced. It opened, revealing a young lad who must be a page or clerk. He did not look surprised to find a lady on the doorstep. "May I help you, ma'am?"

Silvestre drew herself up, determined not to buckle under her own anxiety. "Yes, indeed. I wish to see Mr Beak, if you please."

A crease appeared between the lad's sandy brows. "Mr Beak does not see anyone, ma'am. Would you be wanting Mr Christy?"

She had no notion who Mr Christy might be, but if it got her into the place, so be it. "Certainly. I will be happy to talk to Mr Christy in his stead. Would you tell him Miss Latimer is here?"

The lad opened the door wide. "Please to come in, ma'am, and I'll see if he's free."

Feeling relieved, if a trifle apprehensive, Silvestre threw a triumphant glance at Peg and walked through, beckoning the maid to follow. She entered upon a room like a wide vestibule, furnished with a counter at the far end and a series of bookcases set down one side, shelved with leather-bound volumes and forming alcoves. "Gracious, are these all your published books?"

The page was heading for the counter, but he halted. "That's right, ma'am. You can browse if you like. Or there's a chair, if you prefer to sit."

He gestured to the other half of the room, where two round tables were set with a couple of chairs to each. At one of them, a gentleman was seated, his elbow on the table, one hand supporting his brow as he studied a batch of papers. He did not look up, apparently fully engrossed.

"I'll go and ask Mr Christy, ma'am. What was the name again?"

Silvestre turned from contemplation of the lone gentleman. "Latimer. Miss Silvestre Latimer. He has a manuscript of mine."

The lad nodded, looking more resigned than surprised. "Right you are, ma'am."

He went off towards the counter, disappearing through a door behind it. Silvestre stood irresolute for a moment, and then walked to the nearest bookcase and cast a glance across the volumes in the shelf at eye level. It appeared to be devoted to books of verse and historical treatises. Of the latter, she noted one on Elizabeth Tudor's effect on Protestantism, another about the revival of the monarchy with Charles the Second. Having no present interest in such matters, she turned away to look for evidence of novels. She knew through Aunt Angelica's good offices that Beardsley & Beak published them.

Peg was standing to one side of the front door, wearing a look of resigned boredom. Amusement lightened Silvestre's anxiety. Was the maid regretting foisting herself into this excursion? Well, too bad. Although she did lend it respectability. At least this Mr Christy could not fault her on that. She had taken care to look the part too, choosing, with a hazy idea that an authoress ought not to be a model of fashion, a modest old gown of green stuff with a matching spencer atop and a plain bonnet adorned only with a riband.

She wandered along the shelves, and at last came upon a collection of three-volume novels. An exclamation escaped her. Mrs Fossebridge? They published her gothic novels? Heavens above! Silvestre had read her and judged her work overly sentimental and ridiculous in its exaggerated plots of lustful villains and kidnapped maidens who had to be rescued by unlikely heroic knights. No wonder the publishers had rejected her own effort in that direction. It had been a good deal tamer by comparison and, if she was honest, Silvestre had written it with her tongue in her cheek. But if this was the sort of thing Beardsley & Beak liked…

"Well, really! I have chosen ill, then."

She had not realised she spoke aloud until the gentleman at the far table abruptly dropped his hand from his brow with a bang and looked up, a startled expression in a countenance that struck Silvestre at once as extraordinary. Its planes looked sculpted, the cheeks sunken under prominent bones. Eyes fiercely black raked her from below a pair of frowning eyebrows, dark as the raven hair untidily framing the whole.

Becoming aware she was rudely staring, Silvestre dredged up a smile. "I disturbed you, sir. I beg your pardon."

He blinked, giving his head a small shake, as if he sought to bring himself back from some other plane. With relaxation, a little of the vulture look left him and he fluttered long fingers. "No matter." The fingers tapped the pages sitting on the table. "Mistakes. Proofing, you see. Have to concentrate." With which, he returned his attention to the task and became absorbed.

Intrigued, Silvestre studied him, confident he would not notice. Proofing? Then he must be a writer. No doubt these were his publishers. Now she had leisure to take him in, she recalled the sight of his fingers, now hidden by his hair as it fell forward about his bent head, the hand once more supporting his brow. Inky fingers. The inevitable stains that plagued the writer, as Silvestre had discovered. Although she had changed to writing in pencil for *Emmeline*, the speed of her thoughts proving too swift for the scratching with a pen to keep up. But she'd stained her fingers while copying it out in preparation for submission to the publishers. She'd done it herself this time, tedious though it was to do, unwilling to ask Aunt Angelica to pay again for a copyist. Or was that true? Was it not rather that this manuscript mattered so much more? Both her godmother and Mama remained in ignorance of its existence. Silvestre had pretended she was writing another gothic story and that it was not yet finished.

Why she was reluctant to confess to this very different sort of tale she knew not. Yet she hugged the secret to her bosom, which was why she had to come here without Mrs Summerhayes knowing anything about it.

While she pondered, she found she was still studying the gentleman going over his proofs. A thread of excitement ran through her. If she was lucky enough to be successful here, would she also be obliged to do as much? Without thinking, she walked directly to the table where he sat.

"Sir?"

He looked up and started, dropping a pencil which rolled across the table. Silvestre deftly seized it as the gentleman pushed back his chair and rose in haste, eyeing her with a touch of anxiety, she thought.

"Ah … you wanted?"

Conscious of an odd patter in her breast, Silvestre held out the pencil. "Forgive me, I did not mean to startle you."

He looked at the pencil, frowned and then reached out, almost snatching it back.

No word of thanks? She would persist in spite of him. "I wanted to ask… You are a writer? This is your work?"

He drew back a little, chin dropping as he appeared to withdraw into himself, fiddling with the pencil. "Such as it is." His voice was gruff. Grudging?

She drew a tiny breath. "You see, I am very new to all this. At least, I hope I may —" She broke off, feeling foolish. What was she about to be accosting the man? Disturbing him in his work too.

He raised his brows and the gaunt look was back. "You hope you may be published." He gestured to the pages. "Work. No pleasure in it, you see. Needs passion if you mean to keep it up." He hesitated, glancing from the pages to Silvestre's face, fiddling now with the chair as well as the pencil, making its legs scrape across the floorboards.

Dismayed by his attitude and highly embarrassed, Silvestre shifted back a couple of paces. "I've disturbed you again. I'm sorry." She indicated his work. "Pray continue."

She turned away, crossing with deliberation to the bookcases once more, keeping her back to him as she glanced along the spines of the volumes without seeing them.

What an odd creature! The way he spoke, as if he shot arrows from a bow. So terse. So intense. Such words too! Discouraging in the extreme. She stiffened her spine. She would not allow his dismissive attitude to intimidate her. She meant to succeed at this. Indeed, she must. It began as a means to help Papa by making a little income on her own account. But that was no longer its chief intent. Besides, Papa was not in quite such desperate straits any longer.

Silvestre did not know what arrangements had been made, but Mama told her a little. Their lawyer, who had thrashed out the marriage contracts for Hetty's joining to the duke, had said the settlements were generous. In addition, the duke had insisted upon provision for Hetty's parents during their lifetime. Mrs Latimer had confided all this to Silvestre in a spirit of anxiety, knowing how it chafed her husband.

"Papa finds it galling, but Copley insists it would be churlish to refuse, and perhaps might jeopardise poor Hetty's relationship with her husband if he was at outs over the business with his father-in-law."

Since Papa cordially disliked his new son-in-law, it was scarcely surprising that he had balked. But there could be no doubt the duke's bounty had done much to ease the financial strain upon the Latimers.

However, Silvestre was determined to pursue her course. Writing *Emmeline* had been such a different experience to penning the gothic tale. No dour and jaded literary spirit was going to put her off. She sneaked a surreptitious glance at the culprit and found him once more bent over his manuscript, divorced from everything else.

His words rankled. Passion? She had passion enough, she thanked him. She would positively welcome the task of checking proofs.

Before Silvestre could work herself up through the bubble of resentment, the page reappeared, followed closely by a young-looking fellow who beamed as he came energetically towards her, holding out a welcoming hand.

"Miss Latimer, how d'ye do? I do beg your pardon for keeping you waiting." He shook her hand with vigour and indicated the free table. "I am Christy, by the by. Will you sit?"

Cheered by his welcome, Silvestre took the chair he set for her, the thread of anxiety rising again. She watched him seat himself in the other chair. "You have seen my manuscript, sir?"

The beaming smile swept across his face. "Seen, read and thoroughly approved. Indeed, I was waiting only for Mr Beak's sanction to write to you, Miss Latimer."

Excitement leapt in Silvestre's breast. "Heavens, you liked it?"

He emitted a hearty laugh. "As to that, ma'am, it is not in my line. But I have great hopes of our customers. It is my task, you know, to ferret out what may be of coming interest and this manuscript of yours is unusual enough, we think, to intrigue a promising list of subscribers."

She heard this with mixed feelings. Hope rose at Mr Christy's encouraging words, but Silvestre was conscious too of disappointment. She had secretly hoped for praise of a different order, to know the story had touched him. But it appeared his interest was purely commercial. Was that not of more importance? "Well, that is excellent, sir." She added on impulse, "I was afraid you would dismiss it as you did my first submission."

Mr Christy frowned. "Your first?"

"I sent you *The Old Priory*. Or rather, my godmother Mrs Summerhayes sent it on my behalf." The frown was still in place. "You don't recall it? A story in the gothic mode?"

His brow cleared. "Ah, I see. We do receive a number of those. I fear the appetite for such stories is on the wane, Miss Latimer."

"But you publish Mrs Fossebridge." She wafted a hand towards the bookcases.

"Ah, but we have done so for an age. She has her followers, but the sad truth is the last we put out did not draw the customary number of subscribers." He pursed his lips. "Public taste changes, Miss Latimer. We must keep abreast if we can." He smiled again, rubbing his hands. "This is why your piece comes to us as a refreshing change." He put up a finger. "But Mr Beak is not happy with the title, and I believe he is in the right of it. How does this strike you? *Emmeline, or A Girl Most Ordinary?*"

The implication could not be denied. Silvestre's heart pumped hard and fast. "Do you mean you will publish it?"

His brows shot up. "Have I not said? It will mean a deal of preparatory work to pave the way and generate the necessary interest, but we mean to request Lady Whittlesford to read it ahead of publication. If she approves of it, the literary world will follow."

Feeling dazed, Silvestre struggled to follow it all, but the name was new to her. "Lady Whittlesford?"

"Ah, you are not acquainted with her ladyship? A stalwart supporter of the literati, Miss Latimer. Her approval counts for much. Where she leads, many will follow."

A hollow opened up in Silvestre's bosom. "What if she does not lead? If she dislikes *Emmeline?*"

Mr Christy gave one of his hearty laughs. "We are not wholly dependent upon her ladyship's approval. Dear me, no, Miss Latimer. We have our own lists. And you no doubt have acquaintances who will be delighted to support you. Did you not mention Mrs Summerhayes?"

"My godmother, but —"

"I believe she is one of our customers, Miss Latimer." He rose from his chair, glancing towards the counter. "Barty!"

The lad who had let Silvestre in was seated on a high stool behind the counter, writing in a ledger. He leapt off the stool and hurried to the table. "Mr Christy?"

"Check the ledger for the name of Mrs Summerhayes." He paid no further heed as the youth sped off, retaking his seat. "We will count it fortunate if I am right."

Silvestre drew a resolute breath. "Mr Christy, I do not mean to publish under my own name. I am sorry if that is —"

"Perfectly understandable, my dear Miss Latimer." He waved dismissive hands. "We would not advocate using a name at all at this juncture. We will merely ascribe it as being by *A Lady*."

She let her breath go again. Papa would be mortified if he knew. "Thank you. That is a considerable relief."

He put up a finger, the frown reappearing. "I must warn you, ma'am, that these things rarely remain secret for long. The anonymity is apt to intrigue, and I fear your sisterhood will not suffer to remain ignorant."

A little of her customary insouciance returned as Silvestre felt the stirrings of euphoria. "You mean my sex is apt to be gossipy and curious."

He laughed. "There speaks the author of *Emmeline*. Mr Beak was taken with certain morsels of dry wit he perceived to be dotted through your manuscript, Miss Latimer. He is convinced this is what raises the writing above the ordinary."

A strong desire to meet Mr Beak invaded Silvestre's breast. He liked it! He had spotted her wit and liked it. The euphoria was growing and she almost missed Mr Christy's next words.

"Now then, Miss Latimer, we come to the sordid part of the business. You will not object to it if we talk terms?"

A flurry disturbed her heartbeat and the excitement subsided a trifle. He must mean money. Her mouth went dry. "Terms, Mr Christy?"

His mien became serious all at once, his brows drawing together. "It will be in some sort an experiment, Miss Latimer. A risk. You perceive the difficulty, I am sure. We cannot therefore afford to be as generous as I might wish."

Silvestre's expectations were rapidly dropping, but before he could name any sort of sum, the lad Barty was at his elbow, a large ledger open in his hands.

"Sir?"

Mr Christy turned his head. "Ah, you've found the lady?"

"Yes, sir." He set the ledger on the table and Silvestre, looking at it upside-down, saw a list and a set of figures and ticks alongside each item. "There, Mr Christy, sir. Mrs Summerhayes, you said."

His superior tapped the book with a triumphant finger. "I thought so." He turned to Silvestre, beaming again, what time the boy picked up the book and retired. "There now, Miss Latimer. Your godmother, I think you said? If she will put her name down, we will have a satisfactory start. Do pray give us a list of anyone with whom you are acquainted in whom you might confide. Ladies in particular. If they are of superior rank, so much the better."

Hetty! She was a duchess now. She would support her twin without question. Perhaps persuade her mother-in-law too?

Even Theo's despised aunt was a possibility, for the dowager duchess ran in the best circles.

Before she could broach the matter, Mr Christy spoke again. "Let me see, Miss Latimer. What may we offer you?"

He set his fingers on the table, drumming as he lifted his chin and gazed at the ceiling, apparently in deep thought. Every consideration but one was swept from Silvestre's mind. She waited, her pulse behaving in an irregular fashion as unlikely sums dazzled in her head.

He lowered his chin at last, meeting her gaze. "I believe I may with confidence stretch to one hundred and fifty, Miss Latimer."

She swallowed. "Pounds, sir? One hundred and fifty pounds?" An enormous sum! She had hoped for fifty. One could do a great deal with fifty. But this? She opened her mouth to thank him, but the sound of a distant bell had Mr Christy leaping to his feet, much in the manner Barty had done at his earlier call.

"That is Mr Beak! If you will excuse me a moment, Miss Latimer? We will settle all upon my return." He hurried off, slipping behind the counter and disappearing through the door.

Silvestre sat in something of a daze, only half believing in the reality of what had occurred. Beardsley & Beak were going to publish her story! She would see her very own words printed in a proper book. The volumes would sit in the bookshelves across the way, like the others. She was going to be a real authoress.

A shadow crossed her vision and she looked up. The gentleman from the other table was standing over her, just like a vulture, the black eyes fierce under strong, dark eyebrows. He spoke in the same terse, staccato fashion, his voice low. "Don't buckle. Don't be fooled by Christy. He'll behave scaly if he can. Hold out for two hundred."

Silvestre blinked up at him. "Two hundred? But he won't pay that. I am just a beginner."

A finger came up, shaking in her face. "Beak likes the thing. Christy said so. Tell him two hundred. If he won't bite, threaten to take the thing elsewhere."

He sounded so fierce, she was hard put to it to respond. She wanted to ask why he should care. Instead, she said what was in her head. "I don't think I have the courage to do that."

He rapped the table. "Find some. Start out bold. He'll respect you for it." He thrust his head down towards her. "Use anything you have. A bargaining chip."

Close to, the vulture look vanished. Instead she saw a haggard face. Marked by suffering? She spoke without thinking, her attention catching on the evidence of a tortured mind. "What sort of bargaining chip?"

"Your people? Do you know anyone of note? Position? Rank?"

"My sister," she offered involuntarily, remembering her earlier thought.

He nodded. "Use it. Two hundred. Christy will cave if you hold out."

Then he was as suddenly gone. Bemused, and not a little apprehensive at the notion of bargaining with Mr Christy, Silvestre watched him exit the building, only now realising he had the batch of proofs upon which he had been working under his arm.

# CHAPTER TWO

The abstraction that had held Silvestre throughout the ride home in a hackney cab remained until she walked into the upstairs parlour in George Street. Her godmother's voice pierced through on the instant.

"Here she is at last! Where in the world have you been, Silve?"

"I've been out, Aunt Angelica. I am sorry to have gone without telling you, but —"

She broke off as she realised Mrs Summerhayes was not alone. For a moment she did not recognise the female perched on the sofa, fashionably attired in a round gown of leaf-green muslin bound round the neck with a yellow riband and inset with lace edging to the bosom, and a worked muslin cap tied round with a wreath of flowers over tumbling copper locks. These and the smile brought recognition.

"Gracious, is that you, Felicity?"

Lady Lynchmere rose and came at once towards her. "Indeed it is, Silve. I am so happy to see you again!"

In laughing astonishment, Silvestre embraced her as Aunt Angelica broke out. "She surprised me less than an hour ago, sly creature. No word of her coming from Raoul, the wretch, though he saw Hugh at Brooks's only last night."

The surprise of this encounter threw Silvestre's mind back to the spring, when she and her twin had briefly helped the then unknown schoolmistress, abruptly destitute, who was thrown upon Aunt Angelica's mercy only to end up married to Mrs Summerhayes' cousin Lynchmere in a whirlwind courtship. If one could call it that. But what a delight to see her here so unexpectedly.

"How is it you are in Town, Felicity? I know how much you dislike it." Silvestre urged her friend back to the sofa and dropped down beside her.

Felicity made a face. "Parliament is sitting and Raoul would by no means allow me to remain at Ruscoe Hall as I wished. I told him I would be better employed in preventing Lucille from careering all over the county in her gig, but he became autocratic on me and insisted."

"And you gave in? That is not like you," Silvestre teased.

Felicity laughed. "Oh, I made a bargain of my own, you may be sure. No political parties. If he wishes to attend them, he goes without me."

Silvestre seized on an unlooked-for opportunity. "How excellent. Would you settle instead for a literary party?"

"*Literary?*" Aunt Angelica fairly shrieked the word, suspicion in her face. "Silve, what have you been about?"

Felicity looked astonished. "Heavens, have you turned into a bluestocking?"

"Yes! At least, not quite that. But I know Aunt Angelica would much dislike that sort of gathering and I hope perhaps you may go with me in her stead."

Mrs Summerhayes was growing restive. "What gathering? What are you talking about? Silve, if you do not at once tell me what is going on, I shall scream!"

Silvestre drew a breath, turning to her godmother. "I've been to Beardsley & Beak."

Mrs Summerhayes' brows drew together. "The publishers? But they distinctly told me they had no interest in *The Old Priory*. Indeed, you read the letter, Silve."

"I know, but it was not on account of *The Old Priory* I went there."

Before she could begin upon the explanation which was likely to infuriate her godmother for being kept out of it, Felicity broke in. "What is this, Silve? Do you tell me you've penned a novel?"

"I have. Well, two, in fact." She threw a deprecating glance at Aunt Angelica, whose reaction was predictable.

"*Two!* What do you mean, two? You've finished the other? And you never told me? Silve!"

The hurt in her voice pricked at Silvestre's conscience. "Pray don't be upset. It's just… Well, the truth is I was not writing another gothic tale at all. *Emmeline* is quite different."

"*Emmeline?* How different?"

"But this is so exciting, Silve," chimed in Felicity. "I had no notion you were so talented."

"Well, as to that —"

"Silve, I will be answered! You sent this *Emmeline* to Beardsley & Beak without telling me? That's where you've been? You took the manuscript in person?"

"No, no, I sent it to them as soon as we got here. I went today in secret because I could not endure the suspense. I'm so glad I did."

"I don't understand. Why could you not tell me? Why be so secretive about it?"

Silvestre got up and went across to her godmother's chair, dropping down to clasp her hands. "Don't be cross with me, Aunt. The truth is I could not bear to tell anyone."

"But why not, Silve? After all, I have been instrumental in helping you with this writing scheme. I thought we were at one in this."

"I know, I know, and I can only beg you to forgive me. You see, it was not in the least like writing *The Old Priory*. That I wrote in a spirit of enjoyment, of... Oh, I don't know, I suppose I was not really serious about it. But this!"

"This what? This *Emmeline*? Why is it so different?"

"It is about a girl, an ordinary girl of no special means or ... or talent or looks. Just a girl like any other, but she loses everything."

Aunt Angelica's brows flew up. "How in the world have you made anything interesting out of that?"

Releasing her hands, Silvestre sat back on her heels. "If you must have it, the story fairly burned out of me after ... well, after Hetty was married and ... and I d-didn't have my s-sister with me any longer." Appalled at the unsteadiness of her own voice, Silvestre struggled to suppress the tears. She jumped up and turned her back, moving to the mantel and staring down into the flames.

She heard a rustle of skirts and Mrs Summerhayes' voice, gentle now, came from close behind. "My poor Silve, I'm so sorry. I had no notion how you felt." A hand on her shoulder tugged and she turned to find sympathy in her godmother's eyes. "Come, my dear, it's not like you to turn into a watering pot."

Silvestre gave a somewhat husky laugh. "No, that is more in Hetty's line." She sniffed back the last of the threatening tears. "I even missed her weeping, if you will believe me."

Felicity laughed at this. "Poor Hetty, she could not help it, could she? But she's happy, Silve?"

"Oh, ecstatic. I could not wish her back again, but it was hard at first."

Mrs Summerhayes was at the bell-pull. "That is the trouble with being a stoic. Not even your dear mama had an inkling you were unhappy."

Silvestre took the chair on one side of the fireplace. "I was not unhappy, precisely. Just lonely."

"That I fully understand." Felicity, who had risen during Silvestre's little loss of control, came to sit in the chair opposite. "I'm so lucky to have Raoul's young sister. Lucille is such a delight. Always so bright and enthusiastic."

True, but Felicity had also a loving husband and companion, just as her twin did with her precious Theo. But she must not say it. She was not jealous, after all. Merely bereft.

For no reason whatsoever, the image of the vulture-like gentleman at the publishers came into her head. A footman entering the room at that moment, she was able to indulge the memory while Mrs Summerhayes put in a request for coffee and cake.

Such a strange creature he had been. Yet she must be grateful to him. Without his intervention, she would not have dared to venture.

"Now, Silve, let me have a round tale, if you please."

She sighed out a difficult breath. Lord, why was it so hard to speak of this? "Well, it seems Mr Beak liked my story and Mr Christy thinks it may have a chance because readers are growing tired of gothic tales."

"Wait, who is Mr Christy?" Mrs Summerhayes brought a straight chair up close, setting it so that she might, disconcertingly to Silvestre, watch her god-daughter as she talked.

"He is the man who saw me. I believe he does all the negotiating. An ebullient type, but very shrewd. He says I must expect an invitation to Lady Whittlesford's salon."

"Good heavens, the bluestocking brigade indeed! That creature fancies herself a patron of the literary set. My dear, you will bored to tears."

Silvestre had to laugh. "But I don't think I shall be, Aunt Angelica. I shall be far too dazzled to be in the company of published authors. So intimidating. Which is why I need your support, Felicity."

The visitor raised her brows. "But you know I am perfectly useless at social chitchat."

"Exactly so, and it won't be like that at all, I am persuaded. You have been a schoolmistress and may be counted upon to speak of sensible things while I sit there mumchance and dazed."

Felicity fell into laughter. "I wish I may see you mumchance, Silve. I've never met such a pair of chatterers as you and Hetty."

"Yes, but it is no use my chattering of nothing in such company."

"Nonsense, my dear Silve," chided her godmother, entering the lists. "You are perfectly capable of holding your own. But I must say I should be glad of your going in my stead, Felicity. The thought of enduring such an evening with the ilk of Imogen Whittlesford makes me shudder. But have you indeed settled matters with the publishers?"

Silvestre's euphoria began to rise again. "Is it not wonderful? They will begin at once to engage subscribers and Mr Christy hoped you would be the first, Aunt."

"Naturally I will put my name down."

"You may count upon me, Silve," chimed in Felicity. "I cannot wait to read a story that came out of your head."

Silvestre's laugh felt a trifle hysterical. "It is to be hoped you will both like it. Oh, and I aim to beg Hetty to join the list, for I'm afraid I pledged her support."

Mrs Summerhayes threw up her hands. "I should think you might well. Some value must come out of her having become a duchess, even if she has not yet learned how to use the role."

"I don't know that she ever will, poor Hetty," said Silvestre, recalling her twin's wholly unlooked-for destiny. "She had rather Theo had been of a far less imposing rank."

"Well, I can sympathise with her there," Felicity offered. "I am still growing used to being the Marchioness of Lynchmere."

This took the conversation into other channels, rather to Silvestre's relief, and while refreshments were served, she was able to hug her triumph to herself. She had not yet disclosed the enormous sum Mr Christy had, with evident reluctance, agreed to pay for the privilege of publishing her novel. For which she had the vulture to thank. If, that was, she was ever to encounter him again. She did not even know his name, never mind his station in life. That he was a published author was no guarantee of his social standing. He did not look to be affluent, nor particularly well dressed.

She tried to recall his attire, but could only recapture the sculptured features, the untidy black hair and the hint of inner torment. An odd hollow opened up within her at the last. Somehow, he had commanded an intensity of attention, as if the passion he spoke of was etched in his face. An intriguing creature. It struck her she was actually anticipating a further meeting with some degree of eagerness. Was there a chance he attended such affairs as this literary salon?

# CHAPTER THREE

Lord Joscelin Diggory lounged in a corner of the crowded saloon and nursed the glass of claret he had barely touched. He surveyed the assembled company with a jaundiced eye. A curse on Christy for forcing him to show his face at this affair. He loathed reading his work aloud and would have refused point-blank to do it, if the rat Christy had not sold him out to the Whittlesford fright.

"I know how shy you are, my dear Degarre, but you need have no fears on this occasion. I will ask Pelham Ferneux to read for you. Such a mellifluous voice."

Mellifluous fiddlesticks! That posturing dilettante to be reading his work? He would go to the scaffold before he endured it. Moreover, Christy knew it. If it was not his Machiavellian hand behind the ruse, Joss might count himself a dunce. Such an air of bonhomie, of avuncular interest, just as he had shown to that unsuspecting female. She all eagerness and innocence, ready to scuttle into his trap like a hungry mouse. Offering one hundred and fifty, the nipcheese. Just as if he was conferring an honour, a favour, instead of naming the lowest possible figure.

It was none of his business. He should not have interfered. But it galled him to see the girl bilked. If Beak had approved the manuscript, it was worth a deal more than two hundred. Beak knew his business. He ought to, he'd been at it long enough. Shrewd as they come was Beak, with an eye for art. Unlike Christy. A shark, that's what he was. Useful to Beak, no doubt, with teeth ready to bite unwary authors and chew off their legs. Like the sewer rat Pinckney.

Joss watched with animosity in his breast as the critic passed across his vision, heading for their hostess, who was locked in animated discussion with the usual coterie of acolytes. If he loathed anyone more than Christy, it was Moreton Pinckney. The man had skewered his *Sunset of Atahualpa* last year and was no doubt only waiting for the next to stamp his muddy boots all over it. Critic? Assassin, more like. Using his rapier wit as a weapon. Lord help Miss Innocent if he got his dagger into this *Emmeline* of hers!

"Diggory! Thought I'd find you louring in the rear."

The man who had accosted him was large in both proportion and personality. He was one of the few of the bluestocking set whom Joss both liked and respected. But an admonishment was in order.

"Don't call me Diggory if you don't wish to undo me, Stanford."

His friend looked conscious. "Degarre, then. Keep forgetting. Mind, I don't believe this lot are unaware of your true identity."

"They don't care. But I refuse to trade on rank."

"Very well, very well," said the other with impatience, "but what possessed you to allow yourself to be dragged into reading when everyone knows how much you dislike it?"

"I had no choice, thanks to Christy's duplicitous machinations."

Stanford Wingley gave a hearty laugh. "Your trouble is your choice of medium, Joss. No one cares to hear my treatises read out. Should've stuck with history like me."

"And waste my time delving into ancient tomes and tombs? The only use I have for history is to furnish me with material I can use."

"Ha! Stealing a man's hardly earned facts for your damned epic poems, eh?"

Joss was betrayed into a rare smile. "Your treatise on Pizarro's expedition proved extremely fruitful, I thank you, Wingley. You have your uses, you historians."

He and Stanford Wingley had been up at the university together. Even as a student, Wingley's passion for history had manifested. He pored over books on the Middle Ages and the Renaissance while Joss devoured the artistic works of the ancient Greeks, Shakespeare and his contemporaries and every book of poetry he could lay his hands on. The rhythms of the language caught at his imagination and he became immersed in the battle to transform words into forms of beauty to convey the travails of the human condition. It was a constant struggle that drove him to the heights of elation and the depths of despair.

"It's no use your lurking here, old fellow, like a malcontented bat. You'd best mingle, or Whittlesford will winkle you out and park you with one of these wide-eyed newcomers she's touting about the place."

This intelligence sent Joss's glance streaking for his hostess. Lady Whittlesford had moved out of her circle and was seen to be ushering a pair of females into a group that included both Carleton Rode and Aspatria Glasson. Recognition hit. One of them was the girl who'd accosted him at the publisher's.

"I might have guessed it," he muttered aloud.

"So you might," returned his friend, clearly misunderstanding. "Our hostess will expect you to lionize."

"No, she won't. I never lionize and she knows it."

But his mind was once again jumping on Christy. Thrusting the innocent into this foul milieu without a qualm, ruthless manipulator that he was. Bound to have enlisted Whittlesford in hopes of puffing the girl into notice. What had the rat said to her? He'd been in the unfortunate position of eavesdropping without intent and recalled the spurious warning that the secret of her authorship was bound to leak out. Leak out? Yes, through Christy's tongue. Who was she? Or had she relatives of note? He would not be introducing her here unless he knew she had something he could use.

Stanford wandered away in search of more wine, leaving Joss riveted. He was bound to admit the girl did not look as if she resented being here. Nor was she gazing with reverence at Carleton Rode as most females did on finding themselves in the presence of one of England's premier essayists. Unless his renown had not reached her? She was young, despite the self-assurance she'd displayed. She looked to be more interested in Aspatria, who was no doubt discoursing upon her chief hobby horse.

"Aha, I've caught you, Degarre!"

With an inward curse, Joss turned to his hostess. Typical of Imogen Whittlesford to sneak up on him.

"Now, it is of no use to try and escape, my dear man, for I have your promise and I will insist upon keeping you to it."

Joss winced at the hearty note. Lady Whittlesford's strident voice jarred at the best of times. When it was directed at him personally, it fairly blared. It felt as if his brain hurt. "I wasn't trying to escape."

She wagged a finger in his face. "I know you, Gausselin Degarre. You are not above slipping away if the ordeal begins to seem too much for you. It is your own fault for refusing to allow Pelham to read in your stead."

"I never allow anyone to read my new work before it is published."

She gave her horsey laugh. "Such an idiosyncratic creature you are, Degarre. Most cannot wait to trumpet their wares, but you —! You are far too grudging, my dear, when you know we all yearn for a snippet to whet our appetites."

He all but groaned. "All who, ma'am? The majority of this company would much prefer to read their own work than listen to mine."

"You are an incurable cynic, dear man. Will you never acknowledge your own worth?"

"When the world so acknowledges, I might be induced to believe in it."

"Ah, the power of the puff. Christy does his best for you, Gausselin, but you do not make it easy for him. Now be a good boy and read with the passion inherent in your poems." With which, she sailed across the room, clapping her hands and calling out for silence. "Gausselin Degarre is going to read a piece from his upcoming book." She turned to Joss, who had followed her with reluctance and resignation. "This one is a collection rather than one of your epic narratives, am I right?"

He nodded, digging into his inner pocket for the folded sheets he had extracted from the proofs. After this he must return them to Beardsley & Beak, covered over with his pencil scratchings where the typesetter had made errors.

He took up the position into which Lady Whittlesford pushed him, central before the mantel as the assembled company began to shift into the accepted semi-circle around him. He unfolded the sheets and looked up, the inevitable heat rising in his face. His gaze passed across the familiar faces and caught on the one less familiar. The girl's eyes met his and a tentative little smile appeared at the corners of her mouth.

An odd flitter attacked his pulse and it speeded up. Joss quickly returned his gaze to the pages loosely held in his fingers. Nerves. He hated this. Why in Hades must *she* be here tonight of all nights?

The murmurings settled as he cleared his throat. Hardly conscious of the words, he began to read.

Listening with a degree of anxiety for which she could not account, Silvestre struggled to concentrate on the content of the poem rather than its creator. If she had before been exhilarated, she was now overwhelmed at the thought of her encounter with the vulture. How in the world was she to guess he would turn out to be Gausselin Degarre? The very poet Papa claimed might rival Shakespeare himself in his use of the language. She was ashamed she had not read his work, even at Papa's instigation. She had meant to, but somehow one thing or another had intervened to make her set the volume aside each time she took it up.

She tried to listen but the words jostled against her thoughts. He read badly. In that same staccato style she had noticed in his speech, fairly spitting out the words in a jerky fashion that did them no favours. He seemed to have no self-confidence at all. Not once did he look up at his audience, but kept his eyes firmly on the sheet which shook slightly in his fingers. Heavens, but he was nervous, poor man!

Silvestre's heart went out to him. She recalled his terse manner when they'd met. The way he leapt from his chair when she disturbed him, fiddled with his pencil and scraped the chair across the floorboards. She'd thought he was impatient, ill-mannered even. But, no. He'd been ill at ease, as awkward as he was now. He looked to be hating every minute.

Surely Lady Whittlesford must know he did not wish to read? Why had she forced him to it? She was certainly a forceful woman, seizing on Silvestre and Felicity the minute they came in and pushing them into ongoing conversations. It had embarrassed Silvestre. She could not but feel shy of being thrust at these established literary figures. But she had found her feet soon enough. To be actually listening to Aspatria Glasson! Mama would be thrilled. She so much admired her as a champion of the rights of women. Glancing at the woman, who was surprisingly young and dressed in a more fashionable way than one would have expected, she saw that Miss Glasson was listening to the reading with her eyes closed. Not so Mr Carleton Rode, to whom she had also been introduced. She'd heard the name on Papa's lips, but was obliged to admit to ignorance of his literary achievements. He was a spare man, a little grizzled at the temples, and he kept pursing his lips and shaking his head at the unfortunate poet, frowning through his spectacles.

Now who was that man with the curling lip, looking positively cynical? He was standing next to another tall creature, undeniably handsome, who was smiling in a patronising way, his eyes on the ceiling. Good heavens! Were none of them impressed? Why in the world did Mr Degarre agree to read his work to these people? Especially when it was obvious to the meanest intelligence that he did not wish to do so. How cruel of them to make him!

She was seized with a desire to soothe him and resolved to find a moment to speak to him when his reading was done. After all, she owed him her thanks. She had a very good excuse to accost him. At least she might show him someone appreciated his efforts. She would tell him how much Papa admired him, even if she could not, in all honesty, give her own heartfelt praise. She had hardly heard a word. Indeed, she was quite as bad as the rest and she ought to apologise.

Although it was hard to know how she might do so when she had spent the entire reading thinking of his shortcomings.

She was relieved when he at last ended the painful interlude, folding his sheets and shoving them into an inner pocket without even looking around at his audience, who began a desultory clapping. Gausselin Degarre barely acknowledged them with a nod before he headed out of the circle as Lady Whittlesford moved in.

"Wonderful, was it not? Degarre excels himself again. And now, we will have a little music while you refresh yourselves and mingle. A recital will follow later."

Silvestre paid scant heed, her gaze following Gausselin Degarre as he made for a deserted corner, pausing only to seize a glass from the tray of a passing waiter. Silvestre watched him knock back whatever it contained, dump the glass and proceed, head down, to his retreat.

"Well, that was a pretty poor showing," whispered Felicity in her ear, "though he looked to be nervous. He's a fine poet, but that reading —!"

Shocked to feel annoyance rising, Silvestre seized on the pertinent point. "You've read his poetry? I know Papa thinks well of it."

"Reading was my solace in my days at the academy. My one peaceful hour in bed at night, and my one extravagance."

"No, how could it be extravagant?"

"Wasting candles."

The dry note made Silvestre laugh. "Well, you may waste all the candles you wish now, I dare say."

"I might, if Raoul was inclined to leave me to read at night."

The implication could not but embarrass Silvestre. Her friend was ever outspoken. She hastened to return the conversation to her chief interest at this moment. "But Degarre's poetry?"

"Oh, it's beautifully phrased and you can almost feel an intensity thrumming under the rhythms. He must be a deeply feeling man, though his reading would not lead you to believe so."

An alien voice cut in. "You are correct, Lady Lynchmere."

Turning, Silvestre beheld a bosomy creature with a countenance interesting rather than handsome, with a mobile mouth, fleshy cheeks, a strong nose and bright, expressive eyes. She had her attention on Felicity, who looked taken aback.

"Ah, you wonder how I know you? I heard your name mentioned, ma'am, and thought I must make your acquaintance." She thrust out a hand. "Greta Fossebridge, ma'am, of a pen humbler than most in this assembly."

Startled, Silvestre jumped in as Felicity shook hands. "I have read your novels, Mrs Fossebridge. Or one of them, at least."

A gracious head was inclined towards her. "And you are?"

"Oh, I'm nobody, ma'am. A mere beginner. I am Silvestre Latimer."

There was graciousness in the smile as Mrs Fossebridge accepted her hand. "We must all begin somewhere, my dear."

"Well, to be truthful, I tried to emulate you in the gothic style and failed miserably, I'm afraid."

"Ah, it is not as easy as it looks, though I do not aspire to the heights of the likes of Carleton Rode or Gausselin Degarre."

Was it complacence in the authoress's eye? Silvestre instantly suspected her of false modesty. She could think of nothing to say in response and was glad when Felicity took it up.

"You are an admirer of Degarre, I take it?"

"Who could not be?" Mrs Fossebridge laid a hand to her ample bosom and rolled her eyes in a theatrical fashion. "Such passion! Such a wealth of meaning! One could peruse his poems over and over and still fail to penetrate the entirety of his intent."

"Well, that's no use," said Silvestre, unaccountably irritated. "Surely the point of poetry is to convey your intent with clarity, not to be obscure?"

The authoress fluttered her hands and tutted. "You misunderstand me, Miss — Latimer, was it?"

"Latimer, yes." How rude! Had she not been listening when Silvestre gave her name?

"You misunderstand me, Miss Latimer. The skill of Degarre lies in his layers of meaning. For me that is the chief charm of his work. Now, I am perfectly penetrable. It is in the nature of my style to allow the reader into the whole gamut of agonies experienced by my characters."

To some purpose, since they agonised throughout her stories. But Silvestre refrained from saying so. Indeed, she was not obliged to say anything, for Mrs Fossebridge appeared to be eminently capable of maintaining the entire burden of the conversation herself, once she was fairly launched upon discussion of her own writing.

"It is what my readers expect of me, you see. They wish to journey with my heroine through her trials and travails. I confess I do not spare her, poor girl, whichever of them it happens to be. Just at this present, if you will believe me, my poor Protasia is imprisoned in a dungeon by the terrible Mordecai. She weeps, she prays, she begs for mercy. But I must keep her there for a little longer, I fear, endangered for her life and virtue, before I will permit her to be rescued."

The recital was quite as theatrical as the outrageous plot, and Silvestre very nearly burst into a gale of laughter as she caught Felicity's eye. Fortunately, Aspatria Glasson came up, apparently having overheard the novelist.

"You don't aid my cause with these nonsensical romances of yours, my dear Greta."

Mrs Fossebridge did not appear to be at all affronted. "Adventures, Aspatria, if you please. Readers do not wish for reality, you know. It is precisely these poor women trapped in the cages of femininity who love to escape into the world I give them. I leave you to point out to them the dull inevitability of their lives. That is your forte. I do not pretend to your high-minded rationale. I write to entertain, my dear Aspatria, while you attempt to educate."

Silvestre's latent contempt for the woman began to dissipate. If she was sincere rather than merely complaisant, her frankness commanded respect. But Miss Glasson merely smiled and turned to Silvestre.

"How are you enjoying your foray into these distinguished circles, Miss Latimer?"

"I am enjoying it very much, ma'am, though I confess to feeling overawed. You are all so established, I feel a very tyro."

"We too were all beginners once, my dear." Miss Glasson turned to the gothic authoress. "Miss Latimer has penned a novel unusual enough to induce Mr Beak to take an interest, Greta."

"Indeed?" Mrs Fossebridge did not sound particularly interested, but Silvestre was caught by the words.

"How did you know? I did not think it was common knowledge as yet."

Miss Glasson's brows rose. "You will have to get used to that, my dear. Once our indefatigable hostess has hold of such a tidbit, the whole literary world will discover it in no time."

"I imagine you are something of a closed circle," Felicity remarked.

"Oh, I don't think so. There are avid followers here as well as writers. But news travels fast among us, it is true."

"Speaking of which, there is something I wish to ask of our hostess." Mrs Fossebridge smiled around the little group and fixed upon Silvestre. "I hope you will pay a call upon me, Miss Latimer. Christy will give you my direction. I do feel a duty to encourage fellow novelists."

With which, she swept off without giving Silvestre an opportunity to respond. She was not sure whether she wished to make Greta Fossebridge's further acquaintance, but at least she might obtain answers to a number of urgent questions about the publishing business.

Felicity was already asking Miss Glasson about some theory she had propounded in one of her books. Feeling scant interest in the ensuing discussion, apart from realising how well read her friend truly was, Silvestre glanced surreptitiously about in search of Gausselin Degarre. She spotted him sitting in a corner, evidently divorced from the company.

A pang smote her as she recalled his terrible unease. Without thought, she slipped away from the two women now deep in discussion and, evading another coterie who were plucking dainties from a waiter with a tray, moved to join the poet.

"Mr Degarre!"

He started out of his abstraction and sprang up as he saw her. "Ah … you again? What is it this time?"

# CHAPTER FOUR

It was scarcely encouraging. But Silvestre thought she had his measure now and refused to be put off. "Yes, I gather you would prefer to be left alone, sir, but at least allow me a moment of your time to thank you."

He stared at her, the vulture look pronounced. "Thank me?"

For some unaccountable reason, Silvestre's heart was behaving in a recalcitrant fashion, kicking in her bosom. She did her best to ignore it, producing a smile. "You told me to hold out for two hundred, and I did."

The horrid look cleared and his features lightened as his lips curved. "You found the courage, then."

The smile transformed him and it was a moment before Silvestre could find her voice. She was oddly breathless and had to chide herself for feeling stupidly nervous. "I did, sir." She gave a small self-conscious laugh. "Though I did not quite have the temerity to use your method."

One brow lifted, giving him a quizzical look which was oddly endearing. "Which method is that?"

"You advocated my saying I should take the manuscript elsewhere. I did not dare go so far, but I did use my sister."

"Your sister?"

"She has lately become a duchess."

The light of understanding entered his features and he became curt again. "Christy bit. Of course he did. I thought you must have some such handle to be thrust into this hell-hole."

Annoyance superseded her apprehensions. "It may be a hell-hole to you, Mr Degarre, but it is a godsend to me. I have met the most distinguished people. Yourself included, sir, though I dare say you don't care for that."

His brows drew together and the black eyes narrowed. "Not very much. You've read my work?"

Somehow Silvestre could not lie to him. "I'm afraid I have not. Nor was I listening closely as you read."

"You're not alone. I doubt any of them listened."

She ignored this. "But my father has spoken of your poetry with much admiration. He considers your talent akin to Shakespeare's, and that is saying something, I assure you. Papa thinks Shakespeare is next door to a god."

A laugh fluttered out of him. The change in his expression convinced her he was genuinely amused. "Divine inspiration? I hardly think I'm worthy of that accolade. It's deucedly hard work."

"Is it?" Interest burgeoned. "You see, I did not find it so. Not with *Emmeline*. But I believe I wrote out of ... well, out of a torment of loss." Why was she saying this? To Gausselin Degarre of all people. To her astonishment, he seemed to grasp the essentials at once.

"Your sister? You were close?"

"We are twins. I cannot remember a time before her recent marriage when we were not together every day. I miss her sorely."

"And you wrote it into your book." He nodded in a decisive way. "That's why Beak liked it. Shows through, I expect. The underlying passion."

It was suddenly easy to talk to him and Silvestre pursued it without even thinking. "Mr Christy said it was a smattering of dry wit that Mr Beak liked."

"Christy!" He snorted. "The man's a Philistine. Wouldn't recognise art if you shoved it in front of his face."

"Well, but it pleased me, I admit. I was delighted to think the humour in it had been noticed."

He gave another of those decisive nods. They appeared to be characteristic. "Leaven. Needed, and a sign of truth. Life is not uniformly grey, however burdensome it may be."

She was struck by the bitter note. "You find it burdensome? But you have your wish, do you not? Your work is respected and admired. You have a reputation. Why are you so bitter?"

He met her eyes, the black of his own seeming to darken the more. "Am I? You may be right."

Abruptly aware of having ventured too far, Silvestre backtracked. "I should not have said it. I beg your pardon. I apologise too for not listening to your reading. It was rude of me."

A harsh laugh escaped him. "Rude of me to subject the company to my appalling rendition. Hate it. Can't do it justice. But neither can I bear to hear it delivered by Pelham Ferneux, which was the threat hanging over me."

He spoke with more fluency at last, but with suppressed passion. Intrigued again, Silvestre did not hesitate to probe. "Who is Pelham Ferneux?"

"The pretty devil holding forth to those adoring females." He jerked his chin in the direction of the handsome man who had been contemplating the ceiling while Degarre read. He was now at the centre of a circle of women. "Posturing dilettante! Fancies himself a writer of note, but he's produced nothing. A couple of trumpery verses and an attempt at a parody."

"But why was he a threat?"

A look of contempt came into his face, his gaze remaining on the subject of his dislike. "Whittlesford would have had him read in my stead. Knew I couldn't stand that. Might as well cut my own throat."

Silvestre refrained from saying he had done so by reading himself. "Does he not read well?"

Degarre's gaze came back to her face. "He thinks he does. But he roars and postures like a play-actor. Loves the sound of his own voice." His brows drew together and an almost painful look of intensity was directed at Silvestre. "Poetry ought to be read plain. The words must speak for themselves. That's the point of it. It's not theatre. It is rhythm and sound curled around the meaning. If you overstate it, you lose it all."

"And if you understate it, nobody listens to you." He looked as if she had struck him and she burned with remorse. She put out an involuntary hand. "Forgive me! That was unkind. Cruel of me to say it! I'm so very sorry."

He drew a shuddering breath and the vulture look returned. "Truth is invariably cruel. None of us wish to hear it."

Distressed, Silvestre persisted. "I had no right to speak to you so freely. I don't know how it is I feel I can do so, but I ought not, Mr Degarre."

A faint smile appeared. "I never do what I ought. Why should you?"

"Oh, because I am merely a tyro and you have long proved your worth."

He frowned, pointing a finger at her. "Never belittle yourself. Others will do it soon enough. Stand by your efforts. Even Fossebridge knows to do that. I respect her for it, even if I can't admire her output."

Silvestre stared at him. "You are such a contradiction, Mr Degarre."

"Isn't everyone? No one is uniformly of one characteristic. People are made up of contradictions. They say one thing and think another. The civilised veneer is thin. Underneath, we are all savages. Or potentially so."

She was dismayed. "Is that how you see the world? Has it been so harsh towards you?" He made no reply, but his lips tightened and the dark eyes had a penetrating look that pierced her. She winced. "Well, I will not apologise again. You bade me do what I ought not."

"Did I? I have no recollection of it."

"You said you never do what you ought and why should I. It is the same thing." Aware her tone was both resentful and annoyed, she blew out an impatient breath. "There. I said what I thought and you didn't like it."

The vulture look vanished as he suddenly laughed. "No, I didn't, did I?"

"You see! Courtesy greases the wheels of social intercourse, Mr Degarre. Truth is painful. You said it yourself."

"I also said I prefer it."

"You didn't. You said it was cruel." She considered him. "But I suspect you, in your own way, Mr Degarre, are as much of a poseur as that poor man you despise so much."

His eyes flashed fire. "You cut up a character with flair, Miss Latimer. I must read your book when it comes out. I look forward to discovering your *wit*."

Silvestre smiled at him. "There now, sir, I have succeeded in breaking through your brooding reserve. I shall count it a triumph."

For a moment the issue hung in the balance. He lifted a hand and wagged a finger in her face, but he did not speak. Abruptly he grinned, dispelling the tension. "Go away, Tyro! Leave me to my brooding."

She laughed. "Must I?"

"Yes, I've had enough of you."

She raised her brows. "Oh! Well, if incivility is to be the order of the day —"

"It is."

"— then I shall not bid you good evening, nor tell you how much I've enjoyed our little chat."

His laughter followed her as she turned away, and Silvestre glowed with satisfaction at having indeed succeeded in drawing him out of his evidently habitual moodiness. A riffle disturbed her heartbeat at the thought. He really had the oddest effect on her. She was not even sure she liked him. She disliked his attitude to life, so opposite to her own. Yet she was drawn to his intensity. An intensity of passion, Mrs Fossebridge had called it. Silvestre was not so sure it derived from an underlying passion. Call it a deep dissatisfaction, rather. He seemed to feel deprived. Misunderstood? Cynical? No, not cynical. Bitter. An underlying bitterness.

She had asked him why, but he had refused to answer that. Yet he had spoken freely, treating her as an equal. There was nothing in him of that perfectly irritating male superiority. She had as well have been a man as far as Gausselin Degarre was concerned. Really, he was the strangest creature. He would have none of her thanks or apologies. He preferred plain speaking, and yet his reaction to it was as dismaying as you might expect. Yet he did not shy away from the hurt. Almost he embraced it. Did he enjoy wallowing in agony? It certainly seemed so. But she had made him laugh at the last. He could not be wholly irredeemable.

She tried to dismiss him from her mind as Felicity drew her back into the conversation she was still engaged in with Aspatria Glasson, but her interest in the rights of women proved spurious. Her attention kept dragging back to the brooding presence in the corner, and at length she could not resist looking back. In vain. He was not there.

A rapid scan of the room did not produce a sight of the black head and the vulture face. Gausselin Degarre had left the gathering. A horrid sensation of loss invaded Silvestre's breast. She had no reason to suppose she might meet him again. But oh, she wanted to!


He walked with rapid steps, wishing to get as far away from the literary crowd as he could. If he had his way, he would never go near these gatherings. They were nothing short of torture. If one was not dragged into the hideous cynosure of all eyes, one was subjected to the garrulity of so-called fellow authors determined on spouting on their penmanship. None of them cared one iota for the works of the rest. Self-obsessed, the whole race. Himself included.

A stray thought captured his attention. That girl. An exception? She had not talked at him of her wretched composition. Had her interest in his poetry been genuine? No, not his poetry. Her questions had pertained to himself. What had she asked? Why he was so bitter?

The word pierced him. Was he? Was it bitterness to be plagued by doubt and disbelief? He knew his worth, that was the trouble. Or he thought he did. Yet the accolades were few and far between. Even when he got them he refused to be satisfied. No, that was not it. They did not satisfy the yearning.

He had no notion if anything ever would, that was the truth of it.

Truth! She'd given it to him without compunction and seared him to the core. A sneaking admiration crept up on him. She had not buckled. She'd tried to retract and apologise. But she had not retracted her words, merely the saying of them. She stood by her conviction.

Which made him a contradiction. He laughed into the cold night air. Miss Latimer had gauged him exactly. He ought to be glad of his successes, yet they failed to please him.

*Ought to.* The little minx had picked up on that one fast enough. Teasing him. No one ever teased him. They were more inclined to nag or toady. Either one galled. To be teased was a new experience. Joss was not sure he either liked or approved it. Yet he found it refreshing.

"Diggory! Hold up there!"

Belatedly he heard the footsteps behind him and halted, turning to his friend. "You left early too?"

Stanford Wingley came up, puffing a trifle. "I've been chasing you all the way down the street. Care for a nightcap?"

Joss blinked up at his face. "Why? Do you want something?"

His friend threw up his eyes. "You're such a suspicious old rusty guts. Can't you do with company for an evening?"

Joss shrugged. "If you wish for it."

"Immaterial, is it?" Stanford shook his head at him. "Damned if I know why I bear with you. Come on, man. We're almost at my lodging."

They had turned in to Queen Street and the thought of Stanford's commodious bachelor apartment beckoned. His own, situated in a far less fashionable quarter of the town, was less comfortable by a considerable degree. "You chose the right medium for your talents," he observed, following his friend into the spacious hallway and waiting as Stanford lit one of the candles awaiting him, laid ready in their receptacles on a table near the door. Histories by Stanford Wingley likely sat on every other bookshelf in the country from here to John O'Groats. In school and university libraries too, no doubt. His work sold steadily and he made no secret of the fact it gave him a tidy living. Probably kept Beardsley & Beak in business, enabling them to support humbler poets and newcomers like Miss Latimer and her *Emmeline*.

He cursed himself for the thought, treading up the polished stairs behind the fortunate historian. This was bitterness indeed. Yet he could not refrain from contrasting his rather dingy skylight room with the welcome in Stanford's parlour, where his man was already busy lighting candles as they entered.

"Brandy, Notton. And then you can retire."

"Very good, sir. The decanter is on the tray. I will fetch another glass for his lordship."

He vanished into another room and Stanford threw himself down into a leather chair by the cheerful fire, reaching for the decanter. "Sit down, man. Night's young yet. We don't want you going off to brood in that garret of yours."

"I don't brood in it," Joss retorted, taking the other chair and setting his hands to warm at the fire. "I sleep in it. Occasionally write there too, if I am forced to it."

A rare penance, since he spent most of his days ensconced in a corner of the nearby coffee house, ignoring the smoke and chatter as best he could and nursing a neglected glass while he scribbled away. Armed invariably with inferior ink and stained parchments. The landlord knew him well enough to supply his needs with whatever he had available and leave him alone.

Stanford poured a measure of the golden liquor into the one glass and handed it to him. "Get that down you. Beats me why you don't ask the marquis to increase your allowance."

Joss made no answer as Notton returned with a second glass at this moment, instead sipping at the warming brandy. But when the valet had retired, he watched his friend pour for himself and could not keep in the protest. "It's all very well to say, but if you heard my sire expressing his opinion on my chosen profession, you'd know why I don't apply to him."

Stanford set his feet on a footstool, leaning back with a sigh of content. "He'll change his tune as your reputation grows."

Joss snorted. "My reputation? I've got one already, such as it is. Much my father cares. You should hear him say the word 'poet'. As if it chokes him. Still hopes I'll settle for the church in the end. Offered me a living again last time I ventured back to Aike Manor."

Stanford grinned. "Well, at least he's stopped threatening to buy you a commission."

"Only because he thinks I'm too much of a coward to go up against Napoleon if hostilities resume."

Wingley shook his head. "Wouldn't do for you at all. You'd be scribbling in a notebook in the corner of some tent and forget all about the battle."

The laugh they shared lightened Joss's mood. Why he was still crabby he could not fathom. He should be used to the bullying ways of that creature who had taken on the tiresome mantle of literary patroness.

"That Whittlesford fright is not unlike my sire, in manner if not temperament."

"Perfectly unlike in her penchant for the literati."

"Literati! Typical. I can't bear such pretension."

Stanford grinned. "Not much you can bear, old fellow. Anyone would suppose you loathe the whole business: the bluestocking set and writing itself as well as the purveyors of it."

"I think I do."

"Then stop doing it, you fool!"

"Sometimes I wish I could." He took an unwary gulp of his drink and coughed. "Damn it, I'm poor company."

Stanford laughed. "Of course you are. Always were. But I'm accustomed to the vagaries of the little runt."

"Any more, you big booby, and I'll fling the rest of my brandy in your face!"

"No, you won't. Too poor to go wasting good liquor," said his friend comfortably, grinning at him. "Tell me about the chit."

Thrown, Joss blinked. "What chit?" But even as he said it, the vision of Silvestre Latimer's animated features leapt into his head.

"You know who I'm talking about. Why did she waylay you? Praising you to the skies, was she?"

"On the contrary." Joss took a meditative sip and had to smile. "She took me to task for brooding and told me I'm a contradiction."

"Ha, there's for you, runt!"

He was obliged to join with his friend's hearty laughter. "Indeed. Ah, and not only did she not toady, she admitted she hasn't read my work and didn't hear it tonight either as she was too busy deciding how badly I read. As good as told me it's my fault nobody bothers to listen."

Wingley almost choked over his brandy. "She didn't say as much?"

"Something like. She apologised for saying it. Or no, was that for telling me I'm bitter? I don't recall. In any event, she left me chastened and thoroughly amused."

"If she succeeded in digging you out of your perpetual misery, she's a miracle worker. Who the deuce is she?"

"A tyro, in her own words. I ran into her at B and B. The rat Christy offered her a paltry sum and I told her to hold out for more. She did too. Good girl! He won't easily best her."

Sandford looked astonished. "D'you mean to say she isn't over the moon and dancing round the houses?"

Joss consulted his memories of Miss Latimer. "I think she is, yes. A trifle overawed by the Whittlesford set. But she's shrewd for all that. I think she'll do."

"Do for what?"

"I mean she'll cope with the vagaries of the publishing world. Got her head firmly on her shoulders."

Stanford thrust an accusing gesture at him, using the empty glass. "You like the wench!"

Conscious of an odd flitter in the region of his breast, Joss frowned. Did he? She'd made a refreshing change from the generality of females who followed the bluestocking crowd. He rather thought Wingley might be right, but he chose to prevaricate. "As much as one can on so short an acquaintance, I suppose."

His friend grunted. "Just as grudging as I might have expected." He set down his glass and wagged a finger. "I'll be watching you, my friend. High time you gave attention to a petticoat. So damned aloof with the sex, it's a wonder you remember what they look like. If you don't take care, Fossebridge will succeed with you and it'll be no more than you deserve."

A rude sound was all the answer Joss made to this sally. He was not so sunk in his own concerns as to be unaware of the lures thrown out by Greta Fossebridge. He had successfully ignored them for years. Little though Stanford knew it, he had his own method of dealing with the demands of his maleness. Ida was pretty and accommodating, understanding of his moods. Nor was she rapacious and she suited him, especially as her apartment was in the same building as his lodging. But as for Silvestre Latimer…

No, he must not couple her in the same thought with his mistress. Yet she'd had a disturbing effect upon him. She amused him besides. He would not be averse to seeing her again.

# CHAPTER FIVE

The house was not at all what Silvestre would have expected for an authoress of gothic novels. It was comfortable rather than elegant, almost every surface of the overstuffed parlour dotted with knick-knacks.

A china shepherdess fashioned into an inkstand stood upon the writing bureau at which Mrs Fossebridge said she worked. The mantel boasted a frivolous clock decorated with gilded curlicues, in addition to candlesticks of Chinese figures, a dome of floral shell work, a decorative silver cat and a pair of simpering lovers in porcelain.

Silvestre was pressed into one of a set of gilded and white-painted chairs cushioned in chintz, which was placed near the fire, and warned to be careful of the ormolu box sitting atop an embroidered cloth on the occasional table beside her.

"I cannot resist a pretty box and that is one I treasure. Are you a collector, Miss Latimer?"

"I must confess I am not, ma'am. My papa does not encourage what he calls wasteful expenditure on fripperies."

Mrs Fossebridge uttered a dismissive laugh. "He is mistaken in calling them fripperies. I derive a deal of pleasure from my little indulgence. Besides, I find it soothing to be able to refresh my mind by looking upon pretty things as I work." She moved to a bell-pull that matched the decorative flowered pattern on the wallpaper and tugged. "The worlds I create and dwell in are dark enough, you must know. I should not wish to live in one of them myself."

"No indeed." There did not seem to be anything else to say, but Mrs Fossebridge proved to have no need of a prompt as she sat her bulk down in a chair opposite.

"My dear, I am so glad you could come. I invited Aspatria too, but there is no saying if she can spare the time. I myself have little leisure from my labours, but I do feel it to be my duty to do what I may to help those starting out. Now feel free to ask me anything you wish, Miss Latimer, for I have no secrets. I am not one of these writers who hug my thoughts to my bosom."

Silvestre could barely hold back a laugh at this obvious truth, but she managed a polite response. "It is very good of you to offer to enlighten me, Mrs Fossebridge."

The authoress gave her a complacent smile. "As to that, I dare say you will learn as you go, the way we all must. But I maintain it does no harm to be forearmed. It can be a punishing business, after all. Those of us who are lucky enough to ride a wave of popularity must not be ungenerous in our sympathies towards those less fortunate."

"It is very good of you to think of others, ma'am." Silvestre drew a breath to ask one of the many questions she had, but she was given no opportunity.

"Take our poor Degarre. A genius, my dear, no less. Yet his standing in the public mind is far inferior to mine. I ask you, who is the more deserving? I do not flatter myself with the half of Gausselin's talent, despite the praise heaped upon my humble efforts by an adoring public. Why has he not acquired the accolades that are his by right? It is utterly distressing for the poor man and accounts in great measure, I believe, for his tendency to melancholy."

"Is he so melancholic?" Silvestre did not find it a penance to be deflected into talking of the poet, despite a sneaking feeling of disloyalty. Not that she owed him any particular faith.

"My dear, the poor man suffers so. He is the epitome of the struggling artist."

This would not do. "But he has been published for years. Much appreciated, indeed. My father speaks highly of his work. He is scarcely to be described as struggling."

Mrs Fossebridge threw out a hand. "Ah, you misunderstand me. I speak of the struggle in the mind. The torture of an artistic soul which marks the true creative individual."

Hard put to it not to laugh in her face, Silvestre was glad the entrance of a servant prevented her from making any reply. While her hostess put in an order for refreshments, she found the image of the vulture face again in her head. Tortured artistic soul? Well, she had thought of him as tortured herself, had she not? But she could not subscribe to this sort of romantic fancy. That he had his inner demons she did not doubt, but they were personal to himself and had nothing to do with artistic talent. She would wager a good many successful and exceptionally talented artists of all persuasions had no recourse to a tortured mind. Indeed, she was ready to believe Gausselin Degarre might be a deal more successful if he gave over being tortured and learned to get along better with his fellow man.

"Did you like him?"

The abrupt question pierced Silvestre's abstraction. The servant had retired and the gothic authoress was regarding her with an oddly unkind light in her eye. Her chest tightened a trifle. "Who, ma'am?"

"Degarre. I saw that you seized an opportunity to converse with him."

Was there an accusatory note? Silvestre hastened to deflect it. "Oh, that was because I wished to thank him."

Mrs Fossebridge's strange manner dropped. "Ah, you did recognise his huge talent, despite his difficulty in reading."

"No, I'm afraid I didn't," returned Silvestre before she could stop herself. "It was not for that reason I approached him."

"My dear, you must read his work yourself. It is a sad pity that he can do himself no favours. Pelham Ferneux would have read far better, and then you could not fail to appreciate the sheer beauty of his way with words."

Recalling the poet's round condemnation of that gentleman's manner of reading, Silvestre had to wonder at how Mrs Fossebridge misunderstood him. She made no attempt to correct the misapprehension. "I look forward to reading him further. But may I take this opportunity to ask you —?"

She was cut off without ceremony. "Do not attempt his epic works first, I charge you. One must ease into Degarre with the volumes of shorter poems. You will adore the rhythms at once, but he can be obscure and elusive. Layers of meaning, you must know, and the longer works demand a degree of concentration. It is not at all the same experience as reading one of my novels, where the story is laid out for you in all its patterns of feeling and conflict. You cannot mistake. But with Degarre, you must delve into the words again and again to extract the entirety of his intent. It is an exercise in persistence, I assure you, whereas my readers need only pick up the volume and they will find themselves immersed in a different world, racing along in quite a breathless fashion."

She paused for breath herself but Silvestre could not think of anything to say that would not sound horribly sycophantic and false. Had the creature not one iota of modesty? She could never speak of her own efforts with such candour. She began to suspect Greta Fossebridge had no real interest beyond her own novels. Her professed enthusiasm for Gausselin Degarre began to seem false. Could he truly be as difficult to fathom as she claimed? Papa had no problem with him, after all. Unless Mrs Fossebridge had difficulty with Shakespeare? "Well, I must put forth my best endeavours," she said. "I should certainly wish to become better acquainted with Degarre."

This brought back the odd accusatory look she had noticed before. Mrs Fossebridge appeared to study her. "You did like him, then?"

"Him? I was speaking of his poetry."

The intensity in the creature's eyes did not abate. "You find him mesmerising, perhaps? That passionate nature is attractive to you?"

Silvestre gave an embarrassed sort of laugh, feeling unaccountably oppressed by these questions. "I hardly know, ma'am. I — I really did not have much opportunity to notice."

"But you spoke with him for an age. I saw you."

What did she intend by this? "A few moments only, I believe. He was scarcely encouraging."

In a bang, Mrs Fossebridge changed, abruptly smiling as the oddity vanished. "Ah, he is more forthcoming with those he trusts. He is never dismissive with me. But then I believe he can see how I will not judge him as others do. Nor he me. Never once has he offered to despise my style as others have done." Here the creature's mobile features became suffused with disgust. "I regret you will find some of our fraternity inclined to patronise. It is the lot of women always to be subjected to the male sense of superiority. But of that I acquit Degarre."

So did Silvestre, remembering his attitude towards her. She began to suspect the gothic authoress of a regard for Gausselin Degarre that went beyond admiration of his work. Indeed, it might be that she preferred the man altogether. What else could account for the suspicious manner into which she fell when she supposed Silvestre to have an interest there herself?

She was relieved when a couple of servants entered, bearing trays loaded with the makings of tea and a platter of macaroons and pastries. A bell without sounded, taking her hostess's attention from directing the servants where and how to set out the refreshments.

"Ah, that will be Aspatria at last. Just in time for tea."

So it proved as the slim-figured woman Silvestre had met at the salon was announced within moments. She had evidently shed her outer garments and gloves, for she came in rubbing her hands together.

"Good day to you, Greta. This is very welcome. There is a sharp wind blowing this morning."

"Oh, my dear, I am so glad it did not induce you to remain indoors. You remember Miss Latimer, I hope? I thought you and I might join to support and welcome her into our ranks. There are so few of us poor females fortunate enough to rise above our allotted place in society."

"True enough," said the other, shaking hands with Silvestre, who had risen to greet her. "How did you fare in that milieu, Miss Latimer? Was it vastly overwhelming? I found it so myself at first."

Glad to be able to respond to a normal sort of question, Silvestre gave a little laugh. "I am glad to hear you say so, ma'am. I felt very much an outsider and could not think I had a right to be there at all."

Mrs Fossebridge, who was busy spooning tea leaves into the pot, looked up at this with an admonitory frown. "My dear, you must not take that attitude, as Aspatria will tell you at once."

But the champion of the rights of women smiled as she took a chair next to Silvestre. "Well, no, Greta, I do not feel it incumbent upon me to dictate to Miss Latimer. That would go against everything for which I stand, you know."

"How so, ma'am?"

The lady's brows lifted. "Do you not think the male sex sufficiently dictatorial without the sufferers themselves adding to it? That is the burden of my song, as it were."

Mrs Fossebridge, having poured boiling water from the kettle into the pot, took the spoon with which she was stirring the leaves and pointed it at Miss Glasson. "A song we should all be singing, my dear Aspatria. Had I not buried my poor Fossebridge, I should certainly have profited by your words and demanded my choice, my tastes, my wishes to be taken into account."

Miss Glasson gave a musical laugh. "Dear Greta, you stand in no need of my help, you never did. You will not pretend Mr Fossebridge ever prevented you from doing precisely what you wished, and since he left you very well provided for, you are at liberty to please yourself in everything. No, no, don't argue the matter, my dear, for you know I am right."

Surprisingly, the authoress gave a hearty laugh, evidently genuinely amused. But she addressed herself to Silvestre. "You see! Never attempt to get the better of Aspatria, my dear. She is frank to a fault and will give you your own again in a moment." She added, as she began to pour the tea, "Nevertheless, you must read her essays, which indeed ought to be read by every man in the country. The world would be a better place if only gentlemen might learn of Aspatria as well as we poor females."

"Gentlemen loathe my writings," confessed Miss Glasson, turning to Silvestre again. "Most would infinitely prefer their womenfolk to remain in the subjection to which the law of the land reduces the married female. But laws, you know, are made by men. It will take an enlightened select to create the needed change, and these are few and far between. Therefore women must stand up for themselves. Yet there, I fear I fight a losing battle."

"You think most women are contented with their lot?"

"Either content, or too fearful to attempt rebellion. That is why I find it most refreshing to meet a female as independently minded as your friend Lady Lynchmere."

Silvestre laughed. "Oh, Felicity is fiercely independent indeed. According to my godmother, that is precisely what attracted her husband. He is Mrs Summerhayes' cousin, you must know." She rose, moving to Mrs Fossebridge. "May I pass the cup to Miss Glasson, ma'am?"

"Very good of you, Miss Latimer, thank you." The authoress had been too busy with the tea to enter into the present discussion, but once Silvestre had served Miss Glasson with both tea and the platter of cakes and taken her own share back to her chair, Mrs Fossebridge was off again. "Now then, Aspatria, pray leave off your hobby horse and bend your mind to how we may guide Miss Latimer through the coming shoals. For you must know, my dear, it will not be all plain sailing."

"Yes, this is just what I wished to ask," Silvestre began on an eager note, "for I have no notion how —"

"Of course you have not, but we are in a position to advise and enlighten, are we not, Aspatria? Though I have been telling Miss Latimer how she must not judge Gausselin upon his performance the other evening and should read him for herself."

This again? Silvestre could not forbear a sigh. She took refuge in sipping her tea and looked over the rim at Miss Glasson to see how she took this. Amusement was plainly to be seen in that female's eyes as she nibbled at a pastry, and Silvestre could not but wonder at it.

Miss Glasson caught the look and gave a little smile. Was it of reassurance? She swallowed a sip or two of tea and then spoke directly to Silvestre. "I expect you wish to know what is likely to happen next."

"Indeed, yes," said Silvestre, turning gratefully to her. "I am ignorant of the whole proceeding."

"Nothing will happen until Christy has secured his list of subscribers," chimed in Mrs Fossebridge. "Beak will scarcely sanction the outlay on typesetting until they are secured."

"I disagree with you, Greta. From all I hear from Imogen Whittlesford, Christy is set to go to press within weeks. He is putting Miss Latimer's novel into the hands of his copyist at once and he hopes to bring it out in spring to take advantage of the coming Season."

Mrs Fossebridge was for once bereft of speech, staring open-mouthed. Silvestre was no less so, beset by a furious thump at her heart and a rising sense of excitement. She watched Miss Glasson take several sips of tea before she found her tongue.

"Is it so indeed, ma'am? I can scarcely believe it to be possible!"

Miss Glasson's eyes danced as she turned from the authoress's stunned features to smile at Silvestre. "It seems Beak has great hopes of your story catching the public desire for change. It is an unusual tale. Or so I hear?"

The interrogatory note flustered Silvestre. "I hardly know. I wrote it without any thought of how it might be received. It … well, it came from an intensely personal experience, you see, when my twin was married and I lost her daily company."

"Yes, and that fact is likely to be used to promote sales. I hope you are prepared for it to become public."

Horrified, Silvestre stared at her. "Oh, no! No, indeed, I should not wish for that at all. I particularly begged Mr Christy for my anonymity. Indeed, he said himself it would be better for the book to appear merely as by *A Lady*."

At this, the gothic authoress pounced. "Perfectly ridiculous. A ploy to generate interest, if only the book becomes popular. Which of course is only conjecture and not at all to be relied upon. You must not get your hopes up, Miss Latimer, I charge you. Why, I myself did not acquire my present popularity until my third novel appeared. You must also be prepared with a second as soon as may be, and it must be of the same quality or better. You cannot sit upon your laurels, my dear, I assure you."

"Nonsense, Greta. Let the girl have her triumph, if you please." Miss Glasson turned from her to Silvestre again. "Beak has an instinct for these things. I am confident he will succeed for you."

"But I thought it was Mr Christy who —"

"Christy!" Mrs Fossebridge snorted. "A mere cypher. Although it is he who manages the business side of things. Would you credit it, Aspatria? That mean little man will not budge upon the figure he means to pay me for my next, despite my saying I have a good mind to take it elsewhere."

For once Silvestre could not but be irritated at the authoress's tendency to monopolise the conversation and turn it again upon her own concerns. Miss Glasson made no attempt to stem the flow, but appeared to listen as she demolished two macaroons and disposed of a second cup of tea.

For herself, Silvestre found her appetite dissipated. The intelligence just conveyed had thrown her into a frenzy of apprehension and perfectly violent anticipation. On the one hand, she was ready to whoop with joy at the knowledge she was so soon to be published, and with every hope of success. On the other, she dreaded the notion of her authorship becoming public knowledge, especially if poor Hetty was to be dragged into the business. What in the world would Papa say to it all? She would be obliged to trust to Mama to smooth over the inevitable unpleasantness. Of all things, Papa detested deceit, and to hear she had done all this behind his back was likely to weigh on him even more than the fact she had done it at all.

Her ruminations were interrupted, Mrs Fossebridge again taking the floor. "Now then, Miss Latimer, there is much to be done. If you are wise, you will circulate the secret of your authorship amongst your acquaintance. Situated as you are, I dare say there are a great many females who, knowing you, will be intrigued merely at your having penned a novel at all. That will be enough to secure your list of subscribers. Of course, I had no such advantage and was obliged to rely for advancement purely upon my talent and the skills of my first publishers. Although I will admit Christy to know his business in that respect. Though it pains me to say it, I fear this notion of a change in public taste may play you false."

"Then don't say it, Greta!" For the first time Aspatria Glasson spoke sharply. "For heaven's sake, stop discouraging the poor girl. She is on the threshold of an exhilarating experience and it is quite unnecessary to enter warnings of the kind into the proceedings. For my part, I wish you every success, Miss Latimer. I would not for the world have you do other than enjoy the fruits of your labours. Take pleasure in it all, if you please."

"When she has acquired such an admiring following as mine will be soon enough to talk of enjoyment," put in the irrepressible Mrs Fossebridge.

Doing her best to ignore this pessimism, Silvestre fastened upon the salient point in her hostess's discourse. "But must I indeed attempt to generate potential subscribers amongst my acquaintance? My godmother and Lady Lynchmere will support me, I know, and I have promised my sister's patronage to Mr Christy. But I would blush to speak of it to others."

"Of what use is blushing, pray? You must not give way to false modesty, Miss Latimer."

But Miss Glasson, with a gesture, shushed her fellow author. "Enough, Greta. Do not be fidgeting the girl in this way. Miss Latimer, you will do only what is comfortable for you. It is the publisher's duty to procure subscribers and if the preservation of anonymity is your goal, you would do better, for my part, to leave it to Christy. By all means, encourage those close to you to participate, but do not feel obliged to do more."

"Aspatria, this advice is not sage. What, would you have Miss Latimer fail?"

"She will not fail, Greta. I have every confidence in Beak's judgement. Now there is a genius, if you will, Miss Latimer."

"Oh, piffle!" Mrs Fossebridge looked positively irritated by this encomium. "Will you set a mere publisher against even one of his accredited writers? Degarre is a genius. Carleton Rode is a genius, or so they tell me. Not that he is published by Beardsley & Beak, but nevertheless."

Miss Glasson let out one of her melodious laughs. "My dear, if we are to confine the accolade only to writers, we must count the rest of the world a poor place indeed. Excepting yourself, none of us would be where we are today if it was not for Beak's genius in descrying both talent and the public taste. I understand Beardsley was merely the business brain behind the company when they began."

This was at once of interest to Silvestre. "Was, ma'am? Is he no more?"

"Indeed. He died a dozen or so years ago, I believe, and Christy, who was apprenticed at the time, replaced him."

"Christy! You ought to hear Gausselin on the subject of Christy," said Mrs Fossebridge in a disgruntled tone.

This produced another laugh from Miss Glasson. "Or Gausselin on the subject of anything, Greta. A more discontented soul I believe I have never met."

A flutter disturbed Silvestre's pulse and she glanced with a trifle of apprehension at the gothic authoress, who indeed appeared upon the point of bursting out again.

The situation was saved by Miss Glasson setting down her empty plate and rising. "I must away, Greta. This was a pleasant interlude, but duty calls."

Seizing the opportunity, Silvestre rose also. "Indeed, I must go too, Mrs Fossebridge, for my godmother is expecting me. I must thank you for a most instructive morning."

At this, the authoress surged out of her chair. "My dear, I am so glad you found it so. You must come again. I like to encourage and guide our newcomers and I dare say Christy will feel indebted to me for taking the trouble. I shall speak to him about you, be sure, and do what I may to avert any cautionary measures he has in mind for your novel. You may be sure he will be seeking savings by any means within his power, and shoddy workmanship is one such he is apt to use. My last covers were positively dingy, and I am sure inferior leather was employed in the making of them."

Silvestre, taking advantage of following Aspatria Glasson from the room, managed to get away with only one more effusion of thanks towards her hostess, who at least refrained from seeing her visitors to the door.

Peg was awaiting her in the vestibule and a whoosh of relief escaped her as the footman who had seen them out closed the door behind them.

Aspatria Glasson took her arm in a friendly way. "Are you walking? Which is your direction?"

"My godmother's house is in George Street. I would be glad of your company, but I should not wish to take you out of your way, ma'am."

"Our ways lie together, for my lodging is in Mill Street. I am glad to have the opportunity of speaking to you alone. I must beg you will not take Greta's prognostications amiss. She is much more good-hearted than you would suppose from her tendency to be obsessed with her own concerns. I have reason to be grateful for her generosity, of both spirit and more material matters."

Was Silvestre to imagine from this that Greta Fossebridge had aided her in a pecuniary fashion? She did not like to ask, and instead took a chance on mentioning the poet. "I was afraid I might have offended her before you came."

"How so? It is not like Greta to be cherishing a grudge." Silvestre walked on a few paces, thinking how best to phrase her concern. Miss Glasson looked round with a smile. "You need not fear to speak plainly, Miss Latimer. I am always discreet."

She let her breath go. "Thank you. It is a trifle difficult to say, but I think she misconstrued my approaching Mr Degarre. I tried to mention that he had helped me with a pertinent piece of advice, but I —"

"Could not get a word in?" Miss Glasson laughed in her merry way. "Greta is nothing if not garrulous, poor love. She has no understanding of the value of sharing conversation, I'm afraid."

Silvestre might have put it differently, but it was plain Miss Glasson had a kindness for the gothic authoress and she did not wish to offend. "Well, I can only hope she accepted my interest was purely coincidental."

"Hope it no longer, my dear. Poor Greta has long cherished a *tendre* for Gausselin and becomes as jealous as sin if he takes the slightest interest in any other female. A hopeless passion, of course, for nothing could be more unsuitable. She is years older than he is, for one thing. For another, Gausselin is probably as self-obsessed as she and the clash of personalities would be loud enough to be heard all over London."

This intelligence could hardly please Silvestre, and the rider made an unwarranted streak of indignation rise up. As self-absorbed as the Fossebridge woman? That he was not and never could be. He was undeniably inclined to a brooding intensity, but he had enough observation to notice others. Otherwise he would not have eavesdropped and troubled himself to give her the benefit of his advice, however tersely couched. Nor would he have listened to her with patience. And some amusement, she recalled with a little flurry of pleasure. But she must acknowledge Miss Glasson's words. "I am glad to know it, ma'am, and thank you for confiding in me."

"Oh, it's no confidence, my dear. The entire literary community is well aware of it. Indeed, I should suppose the only person who remains ignorant is Degarre himself."

"But what does she hope for from him?" The question was out before Silvestre could think of the wisdom of asking it.

"Not marriage, you may be sure. Even Greta is not so foolish as to suppose the youngest son of a marquis would ally himself with a woman whose origins are firmly entrenched in trade. Into which she married, in addition. Even a man as rebellious and dismissive of his rank as Degarre would not stoop so low."

Silvestre hardly heard the rider, her attention fixed, her astonishment total. "Youngest son of a marquis? Gausselin Degarre?"

"Did you not know?" Aspatria Glasson sounded perfectly unconcerned. "It is a pseudonym. Derived from an early version of his true name, which he refuses to use. He becomes infuriated if anyone dares to address him as Lord Joscelin Diggory."

"Is that his true name?"

"Yes, and spelt the usual way. Gausselin, though it sounds the same, originates from the Middle Ages. Degarre is an old French form of Diggory. Clever, but a trifle pretentious, though it has served him well. Outside our circles, his identity is not generally known."

Astounded and, if truth be known, a trifle shocked, Silvestre spoke out without thinking. "But this is mad! If he is so well connected, why in the world does he not use it? Indeed, it is by his advice I mentioned my sister to Mr Christy, so it is not as if he has any objection to making full use of any possible patronage."

"What is the virtue of your sister, if I may ask?"

"Oh, she has lately become a duchess. Most unexpectedly, I assure you. It was quite a love match and her road was proverbially rough, I'm afraid, but she is wildly happy." Realising her confusion of mind was causing her to be indiscreet, she hastily added, "But I must beg you not to speak of that, ma'am. I should not be bandying my twin's affairs."

Miss Glasson laughed. "You need not fear me. I am delighted to hear that the privileges of rank have been broken through on account of a romantic attachment. I am an advocate for a female's following her inclination in matrimony, if she can."

"Well, it was touch and go for a time, I can tell you. But we were speaking of Mr Degarre. Or rather Lord Joscelin."

"For the Lord's sake, do not call him that to his face, if you should meet him again. The wretched man is perfectly capable of blasting you where you stand. He cares not a whit for what anyone may think of his manner or temperament."

Yes, that much she had deduced. "But why is he so sensitive upon the subject?"

The trilling laughter came. "Cannot you guess? His father does not approve of his profession."

A sliver of fellow feeling snaked through Silvestre, convinced as she was that Papa was scarcely likely to approve of her new career. Yet she could rely upon Mama to smooth it all over when it came to the point. "Is his family uniformly against him? Has he no champion to persuade his father to his wishes?"

"My dear, I have no notion. All I have told you comprises my full knowledge of the matter. You may imagine Degarre himself is not forthcoming. He will never speak of private matters and he regards any such question as an impertinence.

But he had no hope of his true identity remaining secret amongst the bluestocking set once published by Beardsley & Beak."

"Mr Christy?"

"Indeed. Christy uses Imogen's patronage unashamedly and he will reveal any little tidbit that may intrigue or amuse her into taking up one of his authors. We all owe our introduction to the circle as protégés of Lady Whittlesford. Except Greta, of course."

"Why not Mrs Fossebridge?"

"She was published by Taylors first. Christy poached her and benefited from her renown. She was already very much a fixture in Lady Whittlesford's salon."

But the gothic novelist could not hold Silvestre's attention, taken up as it was by the revelation of Gausselin Degarre turning out to be Lord Joscelin Diggory. She was on fire to know more. Did Hugh Summerhayes keep a Peerage in George Street?

She was distracted by Aspatria Glasson halting her with a tug on her arm. "My way lies across the road." The warm smile came. "I am so glad to have had this little opportunity to converse with you."

"And I. It is good of you to —"

"Oh, nonsense. I am always delighted to meet a female who has broken out of the mould." She put up a finger. "Loath as I am to give advice, I will say one thing. If Imogen Whittlesford invites you to one of her dinners, do not fail to attend. They are not at all like the salons and you will undoubtedly have an opportunity to converse with one or other of some of the most distinguished literary individuals. Her dinners are highly prized and invitations are therefore infrequent."

Silvestre thanked her. "Though I cannot suppose I may be singled out."

"Oh, she will sprinkle newcomers in now and then. She is adept at generating interest and it will certainly pay dividends if you are chosen."

Intrigued, and a little intimidated, Silvestre again thanked her before they parted and she continued on to George Street. Her recalcitrant mind, however, did not for long dwell on the possibility of a distinguished invitation, returning instead to the extraordinary turn in her understanding of Gausselin Degarre.

# CHAPTER SIX

A hunt through the small library Hugh Summerhayes kept in Town failed to turn up a Peerage. Frustrated, Silvestre contemplated the wisdom of asking her godmother if she knew of the Diggory family. But Aunt Angelica was nothing if not shrewd. She would infallibly enquire as to her interest, and Silvestre had no wish to fall into the indiscretion of revealing Gausselin Degarre's true identity.

Or was that the reason? If she was honest, she was loath to give any hint of her interest in the poet. Aunt Angelica would see through her in an instant. Nothing could be more embarrassing than for her to suspect she cherished any sort of admiration for any man, let alone a creature as divorced from the norm as the vulture. Aunt Angelica would unhesitatingly condemn any sort of intimacy with so unsuitable a *parti*. As if there was the faintest chance of him being one! But there was no reasoning with her godmother on the subject of potential suitors. Any mention of a man was enough for her mind to jump to matrimony, determined as she was to get Silvestre off, as she put it.

"Now that Hetty is so well established, you will find them beating a path to your door, my dear Silve. To be allied so closely to Charlton is almost as good an inducement as a portion."

In vain had Silvestre tried to quash the notion. "But I don't wish to be married, Aunt Angelica. I have not come to London for that purpose, as well you know."

"My dear child, you cannot be supposing you may support yourself by your writing? That would be foolish indeed."

"No, but at least I need not be such a charge on Papa. I can contribute. It's why Hetty and I formed our Plan, you must recall. She with her dried flower pictures and me with my novels."

Mrs Summerhayes dismissed this with a wave of her hand. "Of course I know all that, but now that things have turned out otherwise, we may hope for a far better future for you."

Silvestre had given up the argument, acquiescing in her determined godmother's scheme to relaunch her in Society only because there were so few engagements at this time of year. But it would not do to alert Aunt Angelica to her interest in Gausselin Degarre.

This, to her chagrin, was threatening to become all consuming. Really, she was as foolish as Mrs Fossebridge. It was not as if the man was prepossessing. Nor was he encouraging. She was persuaded he would run a mile if he had an inkling of the strange attraction he held for her. Indeed, she could not understand it herself. But the tidbit Aspatria Glasson had let fall had undoubtedly added piquancy to the spark. Who were the Diggorys?

His father must be a proud man to be despising a literary career. Especially when his son was a poet of renown. Although was that perhaps the bone of contention? If she feared Papa's reaction, it was not unreasonable to suppose this marquis might cherish a dislike of having his name associated with the business. Yet his son had carefully avoided any such possibility.

Gausselin for Joscelin. Degarre for Diggory. Yes, it was indeed clever. Could she take a leaf out of his book? Her own name was unusual in itself. There was nothing she might do with Latimer, was there? Madame Latimere? No, too close. Reverse it? Remital? Or Merilat? Oh, ridiculous. Time enough to be thinking of all that when it became necessary to do so. There was no saying after all that Mr Beak's confidence would prove sound.

The flutter in her stomach arose again. It was becoming all too familiar, whenever she thought ahead to next year's Season and the possibilities inherent in the direction her life had taken. She dared not believe in the dazzling future that danced in her imagination. She ought to take a lesson from Mr Degarre. Success did not necessarily breed happiness. Far from it, in his case.

*Oh, stop thinking of the wretched man, Silve!*

She did her best, instead sitting down to the bureau in the Yellow Parlour to write an overdue letter to her sister. Remembrance of her twin proved efficacious in diverting her thoughts. Hetty would be delighted by her news, and only too willing to do everything in her power to help.

*My dearest Hetty*, she began, and the words flowed readily from her pen as she became absorbed in relating as much of the adventure as she knew her twin would enjoy. If there was a trifle of reticence in her mentions of Gausselin Degarre, she did not regard it, concentrating on those details Hetty would be eager to hear.

She had almost finished when the door opened to admit Maunder, who announced the Lynchmeres. Realising Felicity's husband had accompanied her, Silvestre at once set aside her pen and rose.

"Gracious, are you already writing another story, Silve?"

She greeted Lord Lynchmere before responding. "Nothing so exciting, Felicity. I am writing to apprise Hetty of all that has passed. I'm afraid Aunt Angelica is out visiting."

"So Maunder informed us," said Lynchmere in his deep voice. "But you are here, Miss Latimer, and I understand congratulations are in order."

The relation of her triumph took a little time, interspersed as it was with Felicity's comments upon the persons they had met at Lady Whittlesford's salon. This brought out Lord Lynchmere's cynical side.

"I must beg you will not drag my wife to these events again, Miss Latimer. I have been subjected to far too much impertinence since she met this wretched Glasson woman. Felicity has imbibed some very improper notions, I'll have you know. She has become decidedly obstreperous."

His target snorted. "As if you did not know I was impertinent and obstreperous when you married me, Raoul."

He nodded in a mock glum fashion. "True. I should have taken note of it at the time. I live under the cat's foot, Miss Latimer. It is too bad."

"Any more and I shall write a treatise myself — upon the recalcitrance and pig-headedness of marquises."

Silvestre was obliged to laugh at their banter, but an idea leapt to her mind and she gave it instant voice, forgetting discretion. "Speaking of marquises, do you happen to know which one bears the family name of Diggory?"

Lord Lynchmere's brows rose. "Rotherhythe? What do you want with that old martinet?"

"Is that who he is? Lord Rotherhythe? Do you know anything of him? Why do you call him a martinet? Where is his seat?"

The eager questions fell from her lips, drawing Felicity's attention. "Silve, what in the world has brought this on?"

Recollecting herself, she uttered a frustrated mewl. "Oh, my wretched tongue! Felicity, if you give me away to Aunt Angelica, I shall never speak to you again!"

Amusement lightened Lord Lynchmere's rather saturnine features. "Are we to understand my cousin is importuning you to matrimony? I should not advocate your venturing into Rotherhythe's family, though if memory serves me, his heir is already burdened with a wife and several offspring."

Silvestre became agitated. "Nothing of the kind. I wish you will not jump to conclusions."

But Felicity was studying her with deepening interest. "Silve, what is this? Of course I shall say nothing to Angelica. Nor will Raoul, will you?"

Her spouse ran a finger across his lips. "I am dumb."

"He never tells Angelica anything if he can avoid it, in any event. She complains of it all the time. But you don't speak, Silve!"

"You don't give her a chance, my love. However, I begin to feel *de trop*. Shall I retire?"

"No, you don't, Raoul. You promised to drive me to Hatchards." Felicity turned back to Silvestre. "I want to find Degarre's latest volume. I have been telling Lynchmere how well worth reading he is, though one would never suppose it from his own rendition."

This intelligence had the unfortunate effect of increasing Silvestre's agitation. She found her breath short and had great difficulty in speaking at all, never mind saying anything sensible. "Oh! Yes … that was why — I mean, I should also like to… Oh, heavens, what am I saying?"

Felicity stared at her. "Silve, I have never seen you so discomposed. What is the matter?"

To her relief and astonishment, Lord Lynchmere answered her. "I apprehend, my love, that Miss Latimer has somehow contrived to discover that this poet of yours is related to Rotherhythe. One of his many sons, I believe."

Silvestre found her tongue, cutting across Felicity's startled exclamation. "How did you know that, sir? Are you acquainted with the family?"

"Barely. But Rotherhythe is active in politics and one sees him about at Westminster. I've heard him grumble about his poet son upon more than one occasion. He is apt to pronounce the name of Gausselin Degarre with the utmost contempt and disgust."

"Good heavens, Raoul, why didn't you say so when I mentioned him?"

"Why should I? Especially when I was thrown into apprehension by your intemperate speeches on the subject of the rights of women."

Silvestre interrupted his wife's heated rejoinder without compunction. "Pray don't bicker, but tell me instead if this Lord Rotherhythe is in Town, sir."

Lynchmere gave over teasing his infuriated spouse and turned to answer. "If memory serves me, I spotted him in the House the other day, though I don't recall seeing him earlier." He rose. "If you wish to visit Hatchards, Felicity, we should go."

"Indeed," she agreed, getting up and coming over to hug Silvestre. "We only came for a moment in case there was any more news of your novel."

"No, I have heard nothing further from Mr Christy, but Miss Glasson thinks Mr Beak means for the book to come out during the spring Season."

"Miss Glasson? You've seen her?"

"I met her yesterday at Greta Fossebridge's house." Silvestre smiled at the marquis. "You need not fear her influence, sir. I found her quite charming and a good deal less forthright than that gothic authoress."

He grimaced. "Worse and worse. Snakes have been known to charm, you know."

"Raoul, you are perfectly provoking! Pay no heed to him, Silve. I shall come back another time without him and you may tell me all about your talk with Aspatria Glasson."

"That she will not! You are henceforth forbidden to leave the house, wicked female. I am taking no chances."

Felicity threw up her eyes. "This is what I am obliged to endure, Silve. If you value my advice, have nothing to do with any noblemen. They are arrogant beyond belief and think they may order others about at will."

"If that is to my address —"

"It is!"

"— I take issue with the charge. Noblemen have nothing on schoolmistresses when it comes to ordering others about."

Felicity burst out laughing. "*Touché*! Why must you always have the last word, you wretch?" She gave Silvestre another quick hug, whispering close to her ear. "I hope to see you again soon. I am agog to hear more."

Silvestre watched her slip out of the parlour in the wake of her husband, feeling perfectly filleted. She did not for an instant suppose Felicity wanted to know more of Aspatria Glasson. She had given herself away. Or had her friend suspected her even at the salon? She had said nothing then, and Silvestre had thought Felicity too engaged to notice her talking to the poet. However it was, she had undoubtedly taken note of her interest now. Not that it mattered. She had no occasion to hope she might meet him again. A thought she found depressing. But she was cheered by the reflection that at least she now knew where to look when she was able to get hold of a Peerage.

# CHAPTER SEVEN

An urgent knocking fought its way into Joss's foggy mind, dragging him out of the heavy sleep engendered by an unaccustomed night of revelry.

"Joss! Joss, wake up, you lazy dog! I know you're in there!"

He pulled himself up on one elbow, cursing as pain caught him across the brow. "Aubrey? That you?"

His brother's voice came again, loud and too brash for one who ought to be similarly incapacitated. "Get up and open this damn door! Quick, man, or there'll be the devil to pay!"

Joss was already tumbling out of bed. He staggered to the door and turned the key in the lock. It opened and he had to leap back to avoid having it shoved in his face.

Captain Lord Aubrey Diggory thrust into the room and slammed the door to behind him. "Get dressed!"

Joss stumbled back to the bed and sat down. "Go to the devil! I'm not fit for anything and it's your fault."

His brother, disgustingly alert for one who had imbibed at least twice as much as Joss last night, cast an exasperated eye over him and went across to the washstand.

"If you dare throw water over me, Aubrey, I'll kill you!"

"Not a chance, little brother." The captain seized the jug on the floor and poured water into the basin. "If you'd joined me in the regiment, you'd at least have half a hope. And you'd be able to hold your liquor. Here!" He threw a wet towel at Joss, who caught it and wrapped it about his aching head.

"Damn it, this is like ice!"

"It'll sober you up."

"I'm sober, I thank you, but my brain is coming apart at the seams."

His brother ignored this, casting about the attic room and picking up the scattered items of clothing Joss had thrown off the night before. "Put these on! Why you must needs live like a pig is beyond me."

Joss cursed. "I live like a pauper. It's tidy enough as a rule. I don't usually get hauled out by redcoats on furlough who have nothing better to do than lead their little brothers into evil ways."

Aubrey cracked a laugh and threw the clothes at him. "Well, I'm making up for it now. I came to warn you. Father's on his way over."

Horror leapt in Joss's breast. "He's coming here? Damn him to hell!" One of the reasons he had drunk so much last night was the intelligence, imparted by the captain who was staying in the family's London house, that Lord Rotherhythe was in Town and had been raving again about the vagaries of his youngest son. "For God's sake, Aubrey! If this is a joke…"

"Would I drag you through a nightmare if it was? The moment I heard his intention, I cut out and came here to warn you. He was still at breakfast when I left, but he'll be here all too soon."

"You're a godsend, Aub!" But Joss cursed freely as he threw off the towel and forced himself up, galvanised by the ghastly prospect of his sire's imminent arrival. Dipping his head, he threw water over his face, stripped off his nightshirt, and washed, the cold water jerking him into full wakefulness.

His brother grabbed the nightshirt and hid it under the pillow, throwing the covers over the cot bed and making it swiftly tidy. "A good thing I've got military training, little brother. Speed is of the essence. Our respected sire won't care for your living arrangements. At least let's make the place look respectable."

He glanced around the room and Joss heard him shifting things as he dried off and pulled on his clothes as quickly as an aching head would allow. Why his father must needs chase him down to his lodging was a mystery. His direction was known in the family, but hitherto only his brothers or Stanford Wingley ever came here. What maggot had got into his sire's head to come in person instead of sending the usual peremptory summons?

He moved to the small bureau under the skylight which served for a dresser as well as a desk and grabbed up his hairbrush. "Hold up that mirror for me, Aub!"

His brother obligingly picked up the small mirror he kept on the end of the desk and held it in a convenient position for Joss to drag the brush through his tangled raven locks. Aubrey, who had the same dark hair worn in a military queue, eyed him in a critical fashion. "Pity you wear it so long. He'll hate that."

"Makes no odds. He hates everything about me. Damn it, I need a shave!"

"No time. Ten to one he won't notice in the general shambles of your living arrangements."

Joss laid down the brush and rubbed at his chin as if he might erase the growth of stubble by that means. "What's eating him now to bring him here, I wonder?"

Aubrey threw up his eyes. "What isn't? You haven't waited on him, for a start."

"How the deuce am I supposed to wait on him when I don't even know he's in Town?"

"That won't fadge, little brother. If you lived at home, you'd know."

"I'd rather live in a rat-infested hell-hole!"

"And this isn't one?" Aubrey snorted. "Couldn't you find anything better than a garret?"

"I can't afford anything better." Joss groaned as his headache intensified. "Hell and the devil, I need coffee!"

"It's coming. I dropped into Catterlen's and told him to send some up. With luck it'll be here before Father."

No sooner were the words out of his mouth than a knock on the door produced one of the lads who served in Joss's favoured coffee shop a few doors along the street. He was bearing a tray containing a steaming pot, cups and a bowl of sugar lumps.

Joss leapt upon the tray while his brother slipped a coin into the lad's hand. He dumped the tray on the bureau and lifted the pot only to discover his hand was too unsteady to pour with any degree of accuracy.

"You'll have to do the honours, brother. My blasted hand is shaking."

Aubrey laughed at him, but shut the door and came across. He shoved Joss into the one chair. "Sit down before you fall down."

A moment later, a cup was in his hands and Joss sipped the black brew, its welcome aroma in his nostrils. Warmth began to permeate his body and even his headache receded. "That's better." His mind began to work again and he looked up at his brother, who was lounging against a wooden support, sipping his own drink. "He can't just be coming to ring a peal over me for not visiting him. What does he want?"

His brother shrugged. "Beats me. But you're probably right. He mumbled something more, but I wasn't attending. Knew what state you were likely to be in and I was too exercised by the need to make you presentable before he got here."

"My thanks, Aub. If he'd found me still abed, he'd probably have hauled me out bodily and thrashed me there and then."

Aubrey grunted. "Doubt he'd actually go that far. Unless he was riding and had his crop to hand. He isn't. He ordered the carriage. In any event, he hasn't thrashed any of us since we came of age."

Joss wouldn't put it past his honoured sire to resume such punishment if he was driven into one of his rages. He sighed. "I just wish he'd leave me be. I don't bother him. I don't wish to. The less I see of him the better. Why has he got to get after me all the time?"

"You're a disappointment, Joss," said his brother with brutal frankness. "Not just on account of your plaguy versifying."

"If you read it, you'd know it isn't plaguy," Joss said, aggrieved.

"Whatever it is, little brother, Diggory tradition it is not. But that's not it. Five sons and you're the only one who won't knuckle under. That's what drives Father crazy. Not that the rest of us don't admire you for it. At least Peregrine, Rupert and I do."

Joss grimaced. "Not Tristan. He's in the same mould as Father." He had little love for the heir. Lord Aike was a good many years his senior and Joss avoided him as assiduously as he did their sire.

"And you're in the same mould as Mama." Aubrey chuckled. "The one person he can't browbeat."

"He wouldn't try. She says he cares for her and that's why."

"Balderdash! She's too elusive, like you. She agrees with everything he says and then goes her own way."

Joss sucked up a draught of coffee. "I may be elusive, but I've never agreed with what he says."

"But you don't argue, little brother."

"What would be the point?"

"He'd think you have backbone, at least."

"I don't care what he thinks. I really don't care what anyone thinks."

There was time for no more. His ears caught the sound of a heavy tread ascending the staircase. Aubrey, dumping down his cup, had heard it too. "Damn it, here he is! I meant to escape before he got here."

Joss set down his cup and rose, crossing to the door and opening it. "Slip along the landing, Aub. He won't see you there. Then you can make yourself scarce as soon he's in."

The captain needed no further urging. Joss clapped him on the shoulder with a word of thanks and he vanished into a convenient recess at the end of a short passage. Joss closed the door with care and retired to the bureau, bracing for the coming clash.

In a moment, Lord Rotherhythe's gruff tones hailed him from the other side of the door, accompanied by a thump on the wood. "You had better be in there, Joscelin Diggory!"

Joss's pulse pumped uncomfortably, but he moved towards the door as the handle rattled and it opened, revealing his sire's rangy figure and fierce eyes, black like his own. He was swathed in a great-coat against the cold, a beaver hat atop his neat black locks, silvered at the temples.

"Ha! You discourteous young hound," he growled by way of greeting, "why haven't you had the decency to wait on me?"

Joss stepped back as his sire swept into the room, seeming to dwarf the place with his height and breadth of shoulder. "I did not know until last night that you were in Town, sir."

His father ignored this, the long nose sniffing as his mouth curled with distaste. "Had a whore in here, have you? If you desired to live in a stink-hole, you had as well have followed your brothers into the military."

There did not seem to be anything profitable to say in answer to this. Joss stood well back and waited as Lord Rotherhythe prowled his quarters. He glared up at the skylight. "An attic! My idiot son insists on living in an attic!" He turned his gaze upon Joss, the high-boned cheeks giving him the look of some bird of prey. "You're fifty kinds of a fool, boy, but you're my son and I won't have this any longer."

Joss concealed a sigh. "Won't have what, sir? If you are bent upon offering me a commission again —"

"Pshaw! Commission? Wouldn't be able to tell one end of a damned musket from the other!" His eye lighted on the tray. "If that's coffee, you may give me a cup."

Mystified, Joss moved to the tray and filled his brother's neglected cup. He knew his father's tastes and dropped one lump of sugar into it, stirring it well before putting it into Lord Rotherhythe's ready hand. Feeling in need of a restorative, he refilled his own cup and offered his father the only chair.

"Take it yourself. I've no wish to risk a flea infestation."

Though he still felt a trifle shaky, Joss did not avail himself of the offer. He resembled his sire in looks, but he had his mother's form. To sit in the presence of the towering figure would give him too great a disadvantage. He used the meek approach that invariably got him cursed, but which successfully evaded the roaring bad temper. "What brings you here so urgently, sir? I would have come to you at a word."

"Think I'm willing to hang about at your convenience? I'm a busy man. Wasted enough time and patience on you already."

This time Joss could not forbear the sigh. "Not by any wish of mine, sir. I am content to be left to my own devices."

"Content, are you? I'll warrant you are! Content to squander your days writing trumpery verse and lazing the hours away."

Joss held up a hand, the inevitable indignation rising. "One moment, sir. My verse, as you choose to call it, may be a waste of time in your eyes, but it is not trumpery. My publishers would scarcely waste their blunt on me if it were."

Lord Rotherhythe blew out a scornful breath. "Publishers! And what do they publish? A worthless lot of idle wastrels!"

With an effort, Joss controlled his rising temper. "You may despise the literary world, sir, but you will scarcely deny the value of literature. Your own library is extensive."

"So it may be, but it's not filled with volumes of poetry. Poetry! If you had chosen history like your friend Wingley, I should have been the better pleased."

Taking refuge in his coffee, which was lukewarm by now, Joss managed to refrain from retort. He ought to be used to these discussions, but his sire's dismissive attitude still rankled.

A sour smile indicated Lord Rotherhythe's satisfaction at routing his son. He took a gulp from the cup in his hand and made a disgusted face. "This is damned revolting! What do you mean by serving it to me if you knew it had gone cold?"

Joss took the cup and set it down. "Accept my apologies."

"I don't want your damned apologies, boy! For once in your life, I want you to attend to me. This time, I won't brook your defiance, so be warned."

Joss gave an inward groan. Oh, dear Lord, what now? Not another scheme to thrust him into an occupation he was bound to detest? "What is it this time, sir?"

"Don't dare throw my words back at me, impudent dog!"

"I beg your pardon, sir. I had no intention —"

"Yes, yes, very well," snapped his father in a testy fashion. "Just listen, will you?"

Joss held his tongue, unwilling to draw any more fire. It was clear his sire was labouring under suppressed annoyance. Was he expecting rebellion to whatever he was about to propose? He ought to. So far Joss had rejected every occupation proffered, from the armed services to the church and politics. He waited in silence.

Lord Rotherhythe took a couple of paces about the room and then halted, fixing his son with a glare. "This is not what I intended for you, and it is scarcely my idea of a proper sphere for any son of mine. However, your mother thinks it may answer. She says it's in your line. Not that it gives me any satisfaction, but I should be glad to have you settled at *something*."

Worse and worse. Joss's heart sank. If his sire was willing to allow his mother's intervention, he was determined indeed. He did not speak, judging that any words of his would serve only to exacerbate his father's distempered mood.

The hawk look speared him where he stood. "You'll not defy your mother, I hope, Joscelin?"

Damnation! Must he use that against him? Were it not for Mama, he would have run away from home when he was barely a cub. She alone understood the sensibility he could not help, the demons that were his constant companions. His father considered it a weakness and held him up to contempt against his more robust brothers. But Mama had ever protected him from the worst excesses of retribution when he could not enter into the rough and tumble pursuits his sire considered appropriate to boys. His studiousness, his preoccupation with books and learning was little short of an insult to Lord Rotherhythe. But his mother fostered and encouraged his interests, which had bound him to her in love and gratitude. Was he now to be coerced by that? He prevaricated. "How can I answer you, sir, when I don't know what you intend?"

His father champed a moment, and then jerked his head in a nod. "Very well, then. Your mother has gone to some trouble on your behalf. She has secured you a post as a librarian."

"Librarian?" Startled, Joss frowned. "Librarian to whom?"

His father chose not to answer this. "Ought to suit you, your mother says. You can prowl these damned books you care so much about and receive a stipend for doing so."

"But why would anyone wish for my services as librarian? Don't most men rely upon their secretaries for such work?"

"No use asking me. All I know is, your mother and her sister put their heads together and your aunt arranged it. With your cousin taking the title last year, Isobel's influence bore fruit. You'll live at his expense and do whatever it is he needs you to do. You'll take up the post when your aunt sends to you."

Bemused, Joss eyed him. He did not look to be enamoured of the scheme. He must be at the end of his rope to be allowing it. A librarian to his cousin? Who had likely been jockeyed into it. Joss was not even well acquainted with him, for his cousin had spent much of his life abroad before inheriting and the two families met rarely.

His sire, it appeared, was not yet done. Lord Rotherhythe fixed him with a piercing eye. "Until then, you'll reside in Berkeley Square. Understood?"

He reacted without thought. "I thank you, sir, but I am suited here."

The storm broke. "Suited? You damned young jackanapes, how dare you? Suited to be living in this hovel when you've a mansion at your disposal and servants to keep you halfway decently clean and clad? Pshaw! You look like a scarecrow, boy! If you've had a proper meal in a se'ennight it's more than I'd bargain for. My son to be living in little better than a pigsty!" A wild gesture encompassed the attic room. "I won't have it, Joscelin. By God, it's a damned insult!" He came up close, wagging a finger in Joss's face. "I want an end to this, you hear? Enough! Enough, damn you!"

Custom failed to keep the sick sensation from his stomach, but Joss stood his ground. He would not hit back as both Peregrine and Rupert were apt to do, though he knew their father liked them for it.

The tirade ended as he had known it would, with Lord Rotherhythe glaring at him for a moment. Then the fire died out of his eyes and a long sigh escaped him as he rocked back on his heels. He looked spent. When he again spoke, he sounded defeated. "What the devil am I to do with you, boy?"

Joss drew a breath. "Nothing, sir. Just let me go my own way." He essayed a faint smile. "I'm astonished you have not washed your hands of me long since."

A bark of a laugh came, mirthless. "Wish I might, but I can't." He set a hand on Joss's shoulder and squeezed. "You're breaking your mother's heart, Joss."

A shaft went through him. "That was below the belt, sir."

"It's the truth." The hand shook him, quite gently. "Come home, Joscelin! Take this post. To please your mother, if nothing else." He let go, a spasm crossing his face. "Promised Amelia I'd not thunder at you and I've broken that already.

Don't oblige me to go back to her with a mouthful of apologies."

He was returning to his customary manner, but the effect of the brief change was total. Joss felt all the force of his words, for the first time recognising his sire's latent affection. Was it at the root of the bullying? He had thought it came from pride, the arrogance of his class. Impossible to resist an appeal couched in such terms. Damnation! Why could he not have kept to bluster?

"Very well, sir, I will give it a try."

# CHAPTER EIGHT

Aspatria Glasson was right. The guest list for Lady Whittlesford's dinner looked to be exclusive in the extreme. There were half a dozen other guests, amongst whom Silvestre recognised the spare and grizzled Carleton Rode, the florid good looks of Pelham Ferneux whose manner of reading the vulture despised, and Gausselin Degarre himself.

Thoroughly conscious of her unwarranted investigations into his antecedents, her pulse went awry the moment she spied the poet. She had not expected him to be present, though the thought he might be there had kept her nerves a-flutter as she prepared for the evening, with Peg's help. Flattered to be invited, she dressed with care, choosing in hopes of blending in a modest gown of white India muslin spotted with silver and trimmed with lace at the neck and hem, wearing only her pearl necklace and earrings. In the event, only one other female besides the hostess was present, and an elderly one at that, which made her feel all too conspicuous.

"I think you know everyone," said her hostess erroneously. "Mingle as you wish before we dine, Miss Latimer. We stand upon no ceremony here."

She gave Silvestre no time to respond but sailed off towards the essayist Carleton Rode, who had just been announced. In fact at that point the only other person she knew was Mr Ferneux, whom she was loath to approach. She gravitated to the elderly female seated on a sofa and surveying the company with a detached air.

"May I join you, ma'am?"

The creature was gaunt, with iron-grey curls and a pointed face, considerably withered, attired in an old-fashioned gown of dove-coloured silk. She held up a lorgnette and surveyed Silvestre through the glass in a manner as unnerving as it was rude. "You're Imogen's latest protégée. Sit, sit, sit!"

Amusement rose up and Silvestre took a seat beside her, giving her name.

"Latimer? Have to change that. Won't do. Nothing fancy, mind. Choose well, my dear, for you'll be stuck with it for life."

"A pseudonym, you mean?"

The old dame tapped her on the knee with the closed eye-glasses. "Mary. That's an easy one to remember. But not Smith or Jones or Brown. Don't fall for that little temptation."

Her manner could not but raise a laugh. "Thank you, ma'am, but I believe Mr Christy intends for me to use an anonymous designation."

The creature tutted in a disapproving fashion. "Won't do. Typical of him, I believe. Likes to make a mystery. Should have gone to Rivington. He took me on at the start, advised an appropriate name for me and I've not looked back."

Intrigued, Silvestre eyed her. "What do you write, ma'am? Ought I to know?"

She emitted a snort. "You'd know if I told you. Most young gels are force-fed my books at school, poor things. Feel sorry for 'em. Never taken my own advice in my life, but it's kept me afloat telling others what to do."

A vague memory surfaced. Hetty and she had indeed been obliged to read a series of cautionary tales meant to scare young girls into behaving with modesty and decorum. She let out a disbelieving laugh. "You are not Madam Prudence, are you?"

"The very same. Prudence! Suits the purpose, though."

Silvestre fell into laughter. "Oh, dear, how we loathed you, my sister and I!"

A mischievous look flitted across Madame Prudence's face. "Don't blame you. Couldn't stand it myself if I had to listen to such drivel."

"Why in the world did you write it, then?"

"It sold, my dear. Whereas my novels didn't. Still wrote 'em, but Rivington wouldn't take 'em. Don't do it now. Given up both. Don't have the energy. But Imogen," she said, indicating Lady Whittlesford, "likes to trot me out every now and then. I'm likely the longest in the tooth of the lot, and those wretched tales still sell. Survival is everything, you'll find. Take a lesson from that gloom-ridden boy over there."

She nodded across the room and Silvestre looked round to find Gausselin Degarre had entered. Shock ripped through her veins. Oh, no. She was wholly unprepared. What in the world could she say to him?

Then she realised Madam Prudence was still speaking. And about Degarre. Her attention snapped back.

"Ought to be thankful he's been able to bring out one volume a year, but not a bit of it. Spends too much energy fretting, that one. He'll learn. No profit in it. Buckle to and do the business and be thankful for the bank drafts. If there's one piece of advice I'd not object to giving, it's that."

"Sage advice it is too, ma'am. I shall bear it in mind."

A snorting laugh greeted this. "You won't. Nor should you. Find your own way. And don't you go listening to that Glasson woman either. Get a husband, my dear, and that right speedily. The world works the way the world works. I've buried two of 'em and sent four children into the world and I'm thankful for it. Most gels haven't the gumption to do other, but any woman of sense knows it's the best protection from a life of loneliness and poverty."

Silvestre could not let this pass. "That may be so, ma'am, but don't you think it ought to change?"

"Not in the years I've got left to me, it won't. Nor in yours neither. Men won't readily relinquish their power. Why should they? Would women, if our positions were reversed?"

"You make a valid point, ma'am, but if no one stands up to speak of the unfairness of it all, change will never happen."

The lorgnette patted a tattoo on her knee again. "It never does, my dear. People are people the world over. They don't change. You'll learn that by the time you get to my age. Waste of time trying to make 'em."

"Yet you did your best to do just that with your cautionary tales, Madam Prudence."

The old lady laughed in a hearty fashion. "Told you already. Did 'em for money. No warnings will stop a young gel who's fallen for a handsome feller, however rascally he may be."

Really, she was as cynical as Gausselin Degarre, though in a different style. Remembrance of the poet sent her gaze hunting for him, and she found him in conversation with a man Silvestre did not know. Well, at least he was not hugging a morose corner like last time.

"You don't want to go sighing after a feller like him, my dear."

Startled, and considerably ruffled, Silvestre brought her gaze to bear on Madam Prudence again. Had she given herself away? Almost unconsciously, she sat up straighter. "I am not sighing over anyone, ma'am."

The lorgnette was up and the old lady tittered as she eyed her through it. "Blushing as you say it, gel." The eyeglass came away and tapped at Silvestre's breast. "In there already, is he?

Wish you joy of him, but you won't get a scrap if you pursue it, and so I warn you."

So far from being full of Gausselin Degarre, her bosom heaved with indignation. "Heavens above, ma'am, you presume too much!" Unthinkingly, she lowered her voice to a savage murmur. "I should like to know why everyone is so set against the poor man. It is unkind to be forever condemning him for what he cannot help."

To her intense mortification, the old lady raised her voice and called across the room. "Degarre! Get over here at once!"

"What in the world are you doing?" A frantic whisper as she saw the poet's head turn. "Madam Prudence, I beg of you!"

The creature paid no heed, beckoning to Degarre. Silvestre's breath became suspended as she watched him respond to the summons, his gaze flicking over her as he approached. Dear heaven, what must he think? What was the wretched woman up to? Surely she would not say…

"Miss Latimer." He gave a brief bow which encompassed her companion, who was peering at him through her lorgnette. "You wanted me, ma'am?"

"Not I, young feller. This gel wants you, only too shy to say so."

"Madam Prudence, please!"

The black gaze shifted to Silvestre's face. She threw him an apologetic glance but could not meet his eyes, her cheeks burning.

"Blushing, you see," said the old witch beside her. "Won't say it to your face, but she thinks you need a champion."

"I do not! I never said — I wish you would stop, ma'am!" As she turned to glare at the creature, she caught the amused look on the vulture's face.

"You have it wrong, Madam Prudence. Miss Latimer is all too ready with her tongue. I don't find her shy at all. Last time we met she gave me pepper."

Madam Prudence let out a crack of laughter. "Did she so? Good gel! But she defended you nevertheless."

Incensed, Silvestre made haste to defend herself instead. "No such thing! I wish you will say no more, ma'am. She is making something out of nothing, Mr Degarre."

His lips twitched. "Is she? You don't mean to champion me, then?"

"Certainly not. I mean — there is no question of — I didn't say — Oh, this is absurd!" She unfurled her fan and fluttered it before her heated face just as a distant gong sounded.

"Ah, food at last," said Madam Prudence with satisfaction. "About time too. I'm famished."

A measure of relief entered Silvestre's breast, but it was short-lived. The old lady rose and tapped the poet on the chest with her weapon of a lorgnette. "Take the gel into dinner, young feller. More she sees of you, the more she'll know you ain't worth her time."

With a nod, she swept off, leaving Silvestre torn between embarrassment and fury. The latter won. "What a terrible woman! How dare she behave in this fashion?"

The poet, apparently unmoved by these machinations, let out a dry laugh. "The privilege of old age."

"Poppycock! She is just plain rude." She was staring after the creature but she turned back, still fuming. "To think Hetty and I were obliged to read her ghastly stories and were expected to profit by them! Now she tells me she wrote them for money and does not agree with her own advice."

"Did you profit by them?"

"Of course not. We hated the wretched things and groaned whenever Mama brought out the book." Belatedly she recalled the fruits of Madam Prudence's intervention. She infused apology into her tone. "I wish you won't pay any heed to what she said, Mr Degarre. It was a perfectly unwarranted assumption and … and I really don't know what to say to you." She could barely endure his gaze as he eyed her in a ruminative fashion. It struck her he looked a little less vulturish than when she'd last seen him. More than a week ago now, and he had filled out a trifle. Her tongue betrayed her. "You look less frazzled tonight, Mr Degarre. More rested. Better fed, if you'll forgive me for saying so."

His brows snapped together. "Does it show?"

"Yes, it does. Has something changed?"

He blew out a breath. "A deal, in fact." He did not elaborate, instead offering his arm. "We should go in. We're tardy."

A glance showed her the room had emptied, all but a footman waiting just beyond the open doorway. At once conscious again, she set her fingers on his proffered arm and allowed him to lead her out. The footman led the way to a well-lit dining-room where the other guests were already taking their places around a table set for eight.

Degarre led her to the last free seat on one side and set the chair for her. It was, she was glad to see, enough removed for safety from Madam Prudence, who was on the other side of the table between the unknown gentleman opposite and Pelham Ferneux. *Let him suffer instead*, she thought with venom, only half-consciously looking for where Degarre would be obliged to sit.

The only other chair available was two places along from hers, on the hostess's left. Lady Whittlesford called out as he moved in her direction. "Take the foot, Degarre. You may entertain Miss Latimer. Carleton, change places with him, if you please. I need you by me. I cannot think what you are about to be sitting so far away."

The essayist did not appear best pleased, but he obeyed, rising and moving down the table.

Gausselin Degarre took the vacated seat, grimacing at Silvestre. "Stuck with me after all, ma'am?" He leaned a little towards her and lowered his voice. "Frankly, I prefer you to my hostess, despite your tendency to criticise me to my face."

"I did not!"

"Don't trouble to deny it. Can't remember the half of the insults you threw at my head."

Her consciousness dissipating rapidly, Silvestre hit back as she picked up her napkin and shook it out. "I did not insult you. At least, I never meant it so. You are the one who insisted on truth and plain speaking."

"For my sins. I must have been mad. Or drunk."

"You were neither. You were skulking in a corner feeling sorry for yourself."

He flicked his own napkin towards her before setting it in his lap. "There you go again!"

A giggle escaped her. "Oh, dear, must I beg your pardon?"

"No, since you clearly feel no remorse."

Contrite, she smiled at him. "Well, I will. I'm sorry. There." He eyed her in silence and she raised her brows. "Measuring my words, Mr Degarre?"

"Judging your sincerity."

Mischief possessed her all at once. "Oh, of that you must remain ignorant. Come, you are a poet, sir. Is it not the part of women to maintain the allure of mystery?"

His lips twitched. "I am not that kind of poet, Miss Latimer."

She was obliged to attend to the footman who was offering to spoon soup into her bowl. When he had done, she turned back to Mr Degarre. "Have you penned no romantic poetry at all, sir?"

He was being served in his turn but he threw a frowning glance in her direction. "Is that a serious question?"

"Yes, since I have not yet had an opportunity to read your work."

"The answer is no." Flat and repressive.

A tiny flutter disturbed her stomach. She picked up her spoon, taking refuge in beginning upon the soup. How prickly he was! Just when she was beginning to find pleasure in his conversation. She was tempted to ask about his true identity, but she shrank from his potential reaction. Aspatria Glasson had said he became infuriated if one called him Lord Joscelin. She did not want to alienate him. The reverse, if she was honest.

A wave of dismay flooded her. Heavens, what was she about? That wretched Madam Prudence! Had she divined her interest? But she was not *sighing*. Indeed, she did not even think she liked the man. Especially if he meant to be as touchy as this.

"Have you any idea how your face mirrors your thoughts?"

She dropped her spoon. It splashed into the remains in her bowl, splattering green goo above the edge and onto her fingers. Silvestre cast a frantic glance about. Her immediate neighbour had his nose almost buried in his own bowl, but to her embarrassment, the elderly gentleman across the table was looking directly at her.

She wiped her fingers on her napkin, hissing at the culprit. "See what you've done? What did you say that for?"

"I speak as I find, Miss Latimer. Just as you did."

She kept her voice low. "Well, you didn't *find*. How dare you suppose you may read my thoughts?"

His hair had fallen about his face and as he tossed it back, Silvestre saw that faint smile of his that signalled amusement. "I can't. Not precisely. But you've not mastered the perfect mask, have you? One can see changes as your mind flicks from one thing to another."

The implication he'd been watching her threw warmth into her bosom and her breathing became erratic. Heavens, why must he have this effect on her? She tried for a neutral note. "I did not know I was so transparent."

"For pity's sake, don't try to be anything else!" His vehemence brought the vulture look back. "Can't bear the duplicity of the *Ton*. Wearing a public face, saying the right thing while thinking the opposite. That's why I like old Prudence. Says just what she thinks and to the devil with the rest."

Silvestre was recovering fast. "Yes, I think you have made your preferences obvious to the world, Mr Degarre."

He gave a laugh. "Ought to have known you'd take a swipe at me for that."

"I'll take another, sir. There is a difference between polite candour and outright rudeness. You appear to despise every social grace."

"Which is as much as to say I am guilty of outright rudeness."

"If skulking in corners and refusing to speak to anybody at a social gathering is not rude, I don't know what is."

"Why should I speak to them if I don't like them?"

"Because you're there! You're here, I mean. I must suppose you found it impossible to go and scowl in your corner tonight because the gathering is so small."

"I found it impossible because a mischievous old lady summoned me to tell me I had a champion. Clearly she knew nothing of your tendency to berate me at every opportunity."

Guilt swamped her. She had to shift back as a servant whipped her bowl away, but she leaned in and met his now smouldering gaze. "Forgive me! I seem to be forever having to apologise to you."

A spasm crossed his face. "Don't. I hate apologies. You don't mean it either."

She sighed. "I can't think why you bring out the scold in me, but you do."

His lips twitched and the fire died out of his eyes. "You're not alone. I have that effect on my father too."

She could not withstand a giggle. "Lord, what an appalling comparison!"

He grinned. "It is. He's a bully. But how did you know?"

Consternation enveloped her. "Oh! It was — I heard it from… Oh, heavens, I am undone!"

His brows snapped together, but she was saved by the entrance of the next course. A footman set down a dish of sliced veal cake, another of omelette and a plate of meat patties onto the empty spaces on the table. A filled platter appeared at her elbow and another footman stood ready to serve her with a ragout.

"A little, if you please. Thank you."

She stared at the slivers of lamb on her plate as the man went on to Degarre, her mind far from food even as her neighbour began to ply her with viands from the dishes on the table. She chose at random, seeking this way and that for a way out of her dilemma.

How in the world was she to account for her knowledge of Lord Rotherhythe's reputed character? Without revealing that she knew Degarre's real identity? It could not be done. He was too astute to be fooled. Whatever excuse she offered, he would judge at once she had been inquisitive enough to make enquiries about him. Would it infuriate him the more? She dared not suppose he would be flattered, as prickly as he was. Aspatria Glasson had warned her he was likely to go off into a tantrum if anyone addressed him by his proper name. What would he say if she dared to use it?

"You are doing it again."

Her gaze flew to his and found the black eyes intent. "Doing what?"

"Thinking rapid thoughts. I would enquire of them if I supposed you might oblige me with an explanation. But you won't."

"Won't I? How do you know?"

"You'll prevaricate. You'd have answered me directly if you intended to speak the truth."

His insight was intriguing. She picked up her knife and fork. "You are building my interest in reading your poetry, Mr Degarre."

He had a forkful of meat halfway to his mouth and paused. "There you go. I said you would prevaricate."

She could not prevent the smile forming. "And now I'm going to chew my food in a marked manner and ignore you for several minutes. Had you anticipated that?"

To her mingled dismay and delight, he burst into laughter, almost choking over the food. Silvestre picked up his glass of wine and put it into his hand. He drank, eyeing her over the rim in a baleful fashion that almost overset her. Controlling the burgeoning mirth, she addressed herself to her meal in a pointed fashion, casting a glance about the room as she chewed.

A vicious whisper reached her. "You need not suppose yourself safe, Miss Latimer. Revenge will follow in due course."

She flashed him a mischievous look and turned to her neighbour on the other side, who was shovelling beef into his mouth. "It is very well roasted, do you not think, sir?"

The gentleman, who was of middle years, turned a florid countenance towards her, his mouth too full for speech, and nodded.

The poet spoke across her. "You must entertain Miss Latimer with an account of your satirical pamphlets, Swavesey. She will likely prefer them to poetry."

The unfortunate Mr Swavesey, still struggling to be rid of his mouthful of beef, looked to be horrified, his eyes popping at Degarre and then equally blinking at Silvestre.

"I should be very happy, sir, but I would by no means interrupt your enjoyment of the meal. Later will do." With which, she turned away and leaned a little towards the poet. "That, sir, is how it is done."

His brow lifted. "A lesson in courtesy?"

"Just so." Forgetting caution, she added, "Though I should have supposed your upbringing to have taught you everything you could possibly need for the purpose."

His gaze narrowed, a glint entering in that caused an uncomfortable flutter in her breast. His tone took on the flat, hard note she had noticed before when his personal life was touched. "You have that, have you? Who told you? Whittlesford, I suppose."

She tried to dismiss a wave of guilt, but confession leapt to her tongue. "No, it was Aspatria Glasson. But she only gave me your name and mentioned your father was a marquis. I found out the rest from Lord Lynchmere."

His features were tight, his black gaze seeming to darken the more. "The rest?"

"Not much. J-just that your father does not approve of your p-profession and that he is presently in Town." To her chagrin, her voice shook under the inimical gaze. "I won't apologise for prying. I was — I was intrigued." She paused. Still he said nothing and a sliver of defiance rose up. "Well, if you don't wish people to become interested in you, you shouldn't be so infuriatingly mysterious, my lord."

His eyes flashed fire and he pointed his fork at her. "Never call me by that appellation!"

"Very well, *Mister* Degarre, if you insist. But if you are minded to behave in this disagreeable fashion, I shall not be calling you anything at all for the future." Her breath ragged, she seized up her glass and gulped wine, aware of the tremor in her fingers. She set her eyes on her plate and her stomach revolted. "I can't eat that."

Aware of muttering, she sipped more wine, throwing her glance across the table. Anywhere but at the horrid vulture at the foot.

Her eye alighted on Pelham Ferneux, who happened at that moment to look her way. He gave a smile Silvestre found both unctuous and patronising and inclined his head towards her. Heavens, did he suppose she was admiring him? She disliked such flashy good looks. Though not as much as she disliked the horrid creature who looked too much like a bird of prey for any girl in her right mind to be sighing over. Sighing? Oh, that wretched Madam Prudence! The creature was dividing her attention between her meal and the man of similar age, serenely unaware of what she'd begun.

"Miss Latimer?"

Her throat ached. Why must he speak in that soft manner? It was nothing like him and he did not mean it. She would not look at him.

The voice came again, a very murmur. Not harsh at all, but insidiously gentle. "I rarely feel remorse for my behaviour, Miss Latimer. Now, however…"

Afraid of showing how near to tears she was, Silvestre kept her eyes on the silver gravy boat ahead of her. "It makes no matter, sir. You owe me no extraordinary civility."

Aware her voice was unnaturally husky, she took refuge in her wine again. No more words came and her depression increased. She was glad of the respite when the servants began the remove. Laughter and chatter around the table rang in her ears but found no echo in her breast. She regretted the necessity to sit through another course as fresh dishes began to make an appearance.

"Are you not going to look at me?"

Without will, she turned her gaze and found Gausselin Degarre rueful, as hurried and staccato as the first day they'd met at the publishers.

"Don't heed me. I could wish you would ignore my moods. Ingrained, I fear. If I hurt you, I'm sorry. Unkind of me. Discourteous. I know I am. Not your fault. It's my blame entirely."

No longer plagued by the urge to weep, she felt all the force of this unprecedented apology. Yet the hopelessness of an unacknowledged wish pricked deeply. "I have no power to change you, sir. It is no business of mine what you are."

# CHAPTER NINE

The words hit Joss unexpectedly hard. He had hurt her indeed, and the outcome redounded upon him in a way he had never before experienced. Why this girl should have the effect of making him feel a perfect monster he had no notion. He was not in the habit of considering others. A bad fault. Mama had taken him to task for it more than once.

"It is very well to go your own way in this care-for-nobody fashion, my dearest, but it is quite as brutal as your papa's forthright manner."

He remembered protesting. "Forthright? That's what you call it?"

"I said brutal, dearest. Little though you think it, you have inherited Papa's strength of mind. None of the other boys withstand him as you do."

"Much good may it do me!"

"Oh, you think him implacable, cruel even. He is sometimes. But have a care, Joss. Indifference to the feelings of others can be just as cruel."

He had ignored the warning. Thinking himself hard done by, he took licence to punish the world. Not that the bluestocking set gave a tinker's damn. Indeed, he was perfectly aware Whittlesford continued to patronise him because his attitude lent a cachet to her gatherings. She made it a point to use him as a curiosity. Convenient, since it permitted him to do as he pleased and skulk in corners, just as the tyro had accused.

But she was an innocent. Unpretentious and brave enough to pierce his self-obsession. And he had crushed her. He had no notion how to undo it. Unpractised in the art of gallantry, he could not think of anything he might say to bring back the teasing warmth with which she addressed him. He was astonished to realise he liked it.

She had not, as he would have done, taken to sulking with her attention on her plate. Instead, she had struck up a conversation with Swavesey. Asking about his pamphlets? Her voice sounded normal again, without the husky note that had taunted his usually dormant conscience.

"Are your subjects uniformly political, sir?"

Swavesey appeared flattered by her interest, becoming expansive as he explained how he wrote both of Tories and Whigs, depending upon their current activities. "Impartial, d'you see? My task is to poke at their foibles."

"You are a satirist, then?"

"Upon occasion. Been given to rant, don't y'know, when it suits. Depends on who's paying, ma'am. Cut my coat to suit the piper."

That little smile of hers appeared, together with a mischievous twinkle. Damn it, he missed that already!

"Ah, yes, Mr Swavesey, I understand. You must look to how your bread is buttered, and who shall blame you?"

The fellow gave his hearty guffaw. "That's it, ma'am. Old Johnson set the way. It's a fool who writes for other than money."

That ancient saw? Irritation claimed Joss. Yet Samuel Johnson had plugged away at that dictionary of his for years on end. He could not have earned the half of what that work deserved. Too many writers were apt to use his dictum, likely thrown out to impress, as an excuse to indulge in hack work merely to keep the wolf from the door. Joss was not of their number. He had rather starve than turn out anything less than the very best he could achieve.

Yet he need not despise his fellows, need he? Had he not just made his own compromise, falling in with his father's demands? Or rather, his mother's arrangements. Would he have acquiesced if it had not been Mama's hand in the making?

Her voice in his head came again. *Indifference to the feelings of others can be just as cruel.*

He eyed Miss Latimer's profile. He ought to mend it. Somehow. He wanted to. How? She had already refused his olive branch of an apology, bowing out as it were because she could not change him. But she already had. At least, she had touched something in him that no one other than Mama had managed before. She had been studiously ignoring him, dividing her attention between Swavesey and her plate. But the latter was empty now and she refused a dish proffered by the pamphleteer.

"Thank you, but I have eaten sufficient."

Joss watched her sip wine, her free hand coming up to rub her neck on his side. Was she conscious of his regard? He racked his brains for something innocuous to say that might bring her back to him, but his mind refused to oblige him. Then his hostess was rising. Too late.

Automatically, he got to his feet like the rest of the gentlemen as the ladies rose to retire. Joss almost went to pull back Miss Latimer's chair, but Swavesey beat him to it. She managed her exit without once catching his eye, though she was obliged to turn in his direction to leave the table, her gaze lowered. Deliberately, no doubt.

*Look at me!*

But his silent plea had no effect. In a moment she was gone, and he was condemned to the port decanter and the company of his fellow males who immediately relaxed in the absence of their formidable hostess, Carleton Rode taking her vacated seat at the head of the table.

Swavesey waved his glass towards the door. "Nice girl, that. Forgot to ask her what she's done to merit being invited."

Joss found himself responding, his tone crisp. "She's written an unusual novel. Beak likes it."

The pamphleteer nodded sagely. "Then it's good. Or don't you think so?"

"I have no notion. I've not read the manuscript."

Swavesey's pudgy features creased. "You surprise me, Degarre. Seemed to be thick as inkleweavers with the wench, d'you see. Not like you at all."

"She thinks I need reforming." Aware he sounded sour, he was relieved when Swavesey took it as a joke, letting out a belly laugh that drew the attention of Pelham Ferneux.

"Good God, man, is it Degarre exercising his wit? I wish we might all benefit by so rare a treat."

He was in no mood to put up with the fellow's patronising remarks. "I frankly doubt you would find it funny, Ferneux."

"Nor anyone else," put in Swavesey. "Have to be acquainted with the lady."

Oh, Lord! Must he bring Miss Latimer into it? Predictably, this piqued Ferneux's interest.

"The latest protégée? The epitome of wide-eyed innocence, I gather. Aspatria says she is refreshingly modest and feels privileged to be drawn into our set."

The decanter had just reached Joss's elbow and he grabbed it up, plagued by the usual irritation the wretched man invariably provoked. "More a penance than a privilege. She'll learn that soon enough."

Pelham Ferneux tittered. "Back to your growling self, Degarre? I should have known the chit's happy influence could not last."

Willing himself to ignore the man, Joss poured port into the clean glass supplied by a footman and passed the decanter to Gransmoor, seated between him and Ferneux. The elderly biographer, who had so far taken no part in the conversation, nodded his thanks. He poured ruby liquid into his own glass and held the decanter towards Ferneux.

"Take this. Drink. Leave the boy alone." He handed the decanter over to the dilettante, now smiling in his superior fashion, and then leaned towards Joss. "Don't heed him. Pompous windbag!"

His victim turned swiftly. "I heard that, Gransmoor!"

The old man gave him a look. "You were meant to. When you can boast as admirable an output as this young fellow here, you may earn the right to sneer. Until then, learn to keep your tongue between your teeth."

Reddening, Ferneux threw a dagger look at Joss and turned away with an air of deliberation. A glance showed Swavesey to have retired from the encounter; he was now talking to Carleton Rode.

Joss lowered his voice. "Thank you, sir." It was heartfelt. He was not well acquainted with Gransmoor, who was in general inclined to melt into the background among the stronger personalities in the set, and this was unprecedented.

The scholarly old fellow likewise kept his voice low. "No need. Heard you conversing with that young lady. If you won't object to an old man's opinion, I suggest you cultivate her acquaintance."

A sliver of something very like distress passed through Joss. "I fear I've lost any chance of that, sir."

"Nonsense, my boy. She likes you. Any fool can see that. Do the pretty for a change. It won't hurt you to pander to a petticoat's whims. They like to be wooed, you know."

Startled, Joss stared at him. "Wooed?"

Gransmoor tutted. "No need to take fright. I don't mean in the way of marriage. But soft words will go a long way. You can rescue the situation. Go to it, I say." With which, he drew back and addressed himself to his port, once more disinterested.

Joss listened with half an ear to a lively discussion going forward among the rest concerning the nipcheese ways of publishers. A perennial complaint. It held scant interest for Joss tonight, his imagination winging to the moment when the gentlemen joined the ladies. He must seek out the tyro. And say what? Apologise for taking umbrage? Ask her to smile again, berate him if that was what it took to bring that look into her eyes?

An odd jolt attacked him. He could see her expressive countenance in his mind's eye, redolent with question, with interest, with — damnation, yes! — with warmth.

No one looked at him like that. They were more inclined to eye him with contempt, or resignation, or outright fury and frustration like his father. Even Greta Fossebridge showed him a predatory gleam despite her avowed partiality. But the tyro's interest was genuine. Or had been. Until he'd stamped all over it with his hobnailed and petty megrims. If she had indeed liked him…

Who the devil else, besides Mama, *liked* him? He took pains to ensure no one did. Yet Miss Latimer had, in spite of his disgraceful manner. No longer. He had seen to that. More fool he, and he had come by his deserts.

"Shall we, gentlemen? Our hostess will be fretting."

Carleton Rode had risen, taking the lead. Ferneux tossed off his wine and rose too, the others following suit.

Joss got up, at once eager and reluctant. He was no nearer thinking of a way to bring the warmth back into the tyro's eyes and he was repulsed at the thought of seeing again the look that closed her against him at the last.

He entered the drawing room behind the rest. A swift glance showed the Whittlesford was already occupied with the tea kettle while Miss Latimer was settled in a nearby chair. Madam Prudence, comfortable on a sofa by the fire, had nodded off. Safe to assume the tyro had borne the brunt of their hostess's conversation.

To Joss's chagrin, her attention had already been claimed by the ubiquitous Ferneux, plonking himself in the next chair as if of right. Rode and Swavesey were both crowding the tea table, while Gransmoor gravitated to the fire to join Madam Prudence.

Inwardly cursing, Joss hovered. He was stymied. Unless these wretched men shifted themselves. He could scarcely oust Ferneux, who looked to be setting out to charm the only young woman in the room. She could not admire the man, could she? Or was it a deliberate ploy to frustrate him? What had Ferneux said? Something about Miss Latimer's influence on him. Drat the man!

Swavesey had begun handing out tea at Whittlesford's instigation. Which meant the party would break up before long. His chance of placating the tyro was vanishing.

He took the tea the pamphleteer handed him, rejecting the offers of cream or sugar. He preferred coffee, but at this present anything would do. He watched Pelham Ferneux supply Miss Latimer's wants with that disgusting air of gallantry he invariably used towards women, handsome brute that he was, damn his eyes.

Swavesey moved off towards the fire, armed with cups for the older pair ensconced there, but Rode remained by their hostess, drinking as he talked.

A step or two to one side enabled Joss to get a clear view of the tyro's face as she drank. Was she avoiding his gaze? She did not look to be enamoured of her companion's efforts to entertain, giving him an absent smile. She lifted her cup to her lips and her lashes flickered as she looked over its rim. Joss tried to catch her eye, but signally failed. Hopeless, the whole thing.

Dispirited, he drifted away, only half conscious of stealing towards an unoccupied corner. Realisation made him halt before he reached it, and he could not withstand turning to look back at the tyro who had accused him more than once of skulking. She was watching him!

He caught it just as she dropped her gaze to her cup. He regarded her intently as she lifted it to her lips and drank. He would swear she was colouring up. A riot of confused emotions invaded his breast, not least a violent rise of yearning. Different to the one that usually plagued him, but quite as painful.

He watched her for several moments, hoping for an opening. She did not once look in his direction, yet there was no animation in her face as she listened to Ferneux. Or appeared to. Why could not the wretched fellow shift himself? If he could only think of an excuse to interrupt! What, and draw Ferneux's mockery? Yet he must attempt something.

His tea drunk, he moved across to the table and set it down. Feeling awkward, he stood over Miss Latimer. "Have you finished? May I take your cup?"

"Thank you." A low murmur. She cast a fleeting look up at him as she passed him the saucer. The same dread look that had seared him earlier.

He turned to set down the cup, feeling numb. His maladroitness was not forgotten. Nor forgiven. He had forfeited any chance of furthering their acquaintance. Her warmth was lost to him.

# CHAPTER TEN

A week later, Silvestre was back at home with her parents in Berkshire. It was a relief. The strain of keeping up pretence for Aunt Angelica's benefit had given way to genuine pleasure in relating all that had happened to Mama, with some reservations. Silvestre was loath to say as much before Papa, though he had not reacted as badly as she'd feared to her confession.

"This is an achievement indeed! My child, why did you not tell me you were writing a novel?"

Astonished, she had blurted the truth. "I thought you would heartily disapprove. I did not dare!"

A distressed look came over Papa's countenance. "My dear Silve, have I been so severe upon you that you fear me? I could never wish such a thing upon my daughters."

To Silvestre's relief, Mama intervened. "It is nothing of the kind, Henry. Of course Silve is not afraid of you. She knows you've had much to bear lately, however, and she did not wish to add to your burdens."

Silvestre seized on the excuse. "No, indeed. Besides, I could not even bring myself to tell Mama or Aunt Angelica when it came to my *Emmeline* story. I kept it to myself, for I hardly dared suppose it might be accepted. But the publisher likes it, sir! He thinks it is unusual and there is an appetite for change from the gothic."

This at once piqued Mr Latimer's intellectual side as Silvestre had known it must, and a lively discussion on the merits of different types of writing persisted for some time and was continued at the dinner table. She ventured to mention the names of the authors she had met, touching only lightly on the name that had contributed so much to her discomfort.

"I am persuaded I have heard you speak of Carleton Rode, have I not, Papa?"

His brows rose as he looked at her, his spoon poised over the soup bowl. "Rode? Gracious, my dear, you met him? A most erudite man from his essays. Did you find him so?"

She was obliged to disclaim. "I'm afraid I did not have speech with him, Papa. He did not deign to notice a mere beginner."

She went on to describe his appearance and manner, and moved on to Mr Swavesey's talk of his pamphleteering, which amused Papa. A mention and dismissal of Pelham Ferneux left her with no alternative but to bring up the one name she had managed to avoid so far. She drew a breath against the rise of distress.

"B-but there is one writer you will know with whom I did have speech, sir." She swallowed painfully before she could say his name. "Gausselin Degarre."

"Degarre? The poet? Gracious me!"

Aware of Mama's narrow regard, she tried to make light of it. "I seized the opportunity to tell him what you said of his poetry. Comparing him to Shakespeare?"

Her father set down his spoon and wiped his mouth with his napkin. "Ah, now I trust you did not give him the impression that I think him Shakespeare's equal. None can claim that honour."

Remembrance of exactly what she had said and how Gausselin Degarre had answered flitted through her mind, causing an upsurge of the regret that had plagued her since that dreadful night. She beat it down again. Useless to repine. She had chosen a path and she must live with it. But Papa was still engaged with his theme.

"If I did make such comparison, it is fair to say Degarre shares the great man's ability to delineate the human condition. In a very different style, but his work has a resonance one must admire."

"Not when he reads it himself." It slipped out, and Silvestre cursed her unruly tongue. "I mean, he — he does not read well. He seems — he seems to be somewhat reserved."

"Shy, perhaps?"

"Aloof. He does not mix. I found him … difficult." To say the least. Heavens, but it was torture to speak about him in this indifferent fashion. She cast about for a change of subject and recalled the champion of women's rights. "But, Mama, I met one lady of whom I know you will wish to hear."

Mama smiled through her spectacles, unsuspecting. "Oh? Who was that, my love?"

Silvestre brought it out with a ring. "Aspatria Glasson."

Mama's jaw dropped. "No!"

"Indeed, yes. She is not at all what you might expect either. She is quite young and perfectly fashionable."

"Heavens above! Not a bluestocking, then?"

"Oh, yes, very much so, though she does not have that appearance. She was amusing and interested, and most friendly towards me."

Mama's eyes were shining through her spectacles as she resumed her neglected soup. "Aspatria Glasson! Fancy!"

Silvestre's heart lifted. Here she might speak with more freedom, but she reserved the relation of the morning visit to Greta Fossebridge until they were alone. She need not hold back with Mama, but she was still reluctant to say anything of her dealings with Gausselin Degarre.

The morning after her return home, Mama sought her out in the old nursery, now Silvestre's sole domain, and drew her to sit on the worn sofa.

"Now, my love, tell me it all. I am agog, you know, and eager to hear your adventure."

The little core of distress receded. "Well, I didn't feel quite comfortable saying too much before Papa. Did you prime him, Mama? I expected a severe scold."

Her mother patted her hand. "Nothing of the kind. I don't say he would have been as forgiving of that gothic effusion —"

"*The Old Priory*? Heavens, no!"

"— but when he knew you had written quite an ordinary sort of story, Papa became intrigued. Besides, Angelica explained it was to be anonymously ascribed."

"Then you did speak to him about it before I came home. I have to thank you, Mama, for I quite dreaded what he might say. Though I'm afraid Miss Glasson thinks my identity will leak out."

Mama's eyes shone through her spectacles. "Aspatria Glasson! You must tell me more about her, Silve. How did you meet her?"

The question opened the way and the resulting conversation gave her an agreeable respite from the pangs that had rendered the remainder of her time in London more pain than pleasure. Useless to be wishing she had taken the opportunity to revive her growing friendship with the poet. She dared to believe he wished for it, though he had not approached her while tea was drunk. Though she was aware he watched her. At the time she had been too upset, too proud even, to accept his retraction. Now it was too late. There had been no more salons, no further invitations to dinner, nor to visit any of the bluestocking set. Mr Christy, once she had provided him with the names of her acquaintance, had no further need of her until the new year.

"We will send you the proofs, Miss Latimer. You need not make the journey. But you must send them back with your annotations as swiftly as you can."

Mr and Mrs Summerhayes were wishful of returning home to see how their children did and to prepare for Christmas. Silvestre saw Felicity once more, too briefly to allow for any confidences, and then the Lynchmeres were off as well.

There was nothing to stay in London for. No reason to linger in hopes of a chance to see him, to redeem herself in his eyes, to tell him she would indeed wish to ignore his moodiness if only she might be at ease with him once more. He could not help being a vulture, and if she could not change him, she might at least tease him into laughter.

Useless to repine. Stupid to imagine her life blighted when she had everything in the world to be happy about and to hope for. Really, she was being as idiotic as Hetty had been in the summer, so wholly under the spell of her Theo she was utterly cast down.

Silvestre had no right to be miserable. Her book was to be published. She had hobnobbed with some of the brightest and best of the literary world. She was promised a future, if not glittering, at least far more inviting than hitherto. Really, what did it matter if one perfectly sulky poet chose a brooding resentment over a potentially romantic entanglement?

Here she caught herself up. Romantic? What was she thinking? Merely because the wretched creature intrigued her? Ridiculous. As for entanglements — heavens above! Could one even wish to be enamoured of such a difficult man? Touchy. Quick to take offence. Unpredictable — except to know he was bound to fall into brooding melancholy. That was predictable enough. Wretched, horrid, unspeakably discourteous *vulture!*

Yet in relating her doings to Mama, she could not mention his name. It stuck at the back of her throat every time he loomed into her story and she had to change tack and eliminate all mention of him. Mama enjoyed the tale of Madam Prudence, but it very nearly undid Silvestre in the telling as she struggled to avoid saying anything of the creature's deliberate coupling of her with Gausselin Degarre.

She took refuge in her cup of coffee, which the maid brought in a few minutes after Mama came into the nursery.

"Ah, there you are, Dinah, thank you. Now we have nothing to wish for, Silve. Yes, yes, leave the tray, Dinah. I will pour. Now, what were you saying, my love?"

But at last there was no more to tell, setting aside her encounters with the vulture, and Silvestre ground to a halt. Mama did not appear to notice her hesitations, acute though she was as a rule. Was she merely being tactful?

But in a moment the reason became clear. Mrs Latimer set down her cup and saucer and turned to Silvestre, picking up one of her hands and holding it fast between both her own. "My love, I have something to tell you."

She looked so serious, the breath at once caught in Silvestre's chest. "Oh, what is it?"

Her mother squeezed her hand. "Nothing to alarm you, Silve. The reverse, rather." A deprecating smile came. "But I would not mention it to Papa until I had spoken with you. You know how he feels about Hetty's new situation."

Silvestre's alarm, so far from subsiding, increased. "Hetty? Is something wrong? Is she ill? Have they quarrelled?"

Mama tutted, releasing her hand. "Do strive for a little patience, my love. Nothing so terrible. Did I not say it was good news?"

Drawing a breath, Silvestre tried to smile. "Forgive me, Mama. I am being bird-witted."

"Not bird-witted. Distrait. I noticed it at once." She peered through her spectacles, a tiny frown between her brows. "You've said nothing of it and I don't mean to pry. But I am not blind, Silve. Something has happened, has it not?"

Silvestre struggled with herself. The urge to unburden her heart was strong. But to talk of it must give it a substance it did not deserve. Besides, whatever it was, or might have been, it was over. She summoned a tenuous smile. "Tell me about Hetty, if you please, Mama."

A shade of disappointment crossed her mother's face, but she accepted the rebuff. "Hetty wants you to go to Devenal for Christmas."

This was so unexpected, Silvestre blinked at her. "Me? Go to Devenal Castle?"

Mama clicked her tongue. "Yes, you. She misses you, Silve."

"I miss her! That's what made me write *Emmeline*."

"Yes, I know, my love. Angelica wrote as much to me. Which is why I am eager for you to go."

The thought of seeing her twin again could not but revive an echo of her loss and her eyes pricked. "Hetty said nothing of this when she wrote to me in London."

"Our poor Henrietta is afraid Papa will not permit you to go. Such nonsense. As if he would prevent you from visiting your sister, despite his reservations."

"But you said you didn't mention it to him. He won't like it, Mama. You know how much he dislikes Theo."

Mama tutted again. "He does not dislike him."

"Well, disapproves of him, then. But for my part, I agree with Hetty. Papa is particularly blind where Theo is concerned. He's a good man, Mama. And he loves Hetty." Why she should be so vehement about it, she really did not know. It was not as if the duke needed her to champion him. Unlike a certain other person who had no one to fight his corner. She thrust the stray thought from her.

"Papa knows that, Silve. He would not otherwise have consented to Hetty marrying the duke. He is growing accustomed. In any event, I know he will put no bar in your way. But there was no point in distressing him until I knew if you would wish to go."

Unaccustomed tears spilled over. "I should like it of all things!"

Mama patted her, laughing. "There is no occasion for all this misery, Silve. I should expect it from Henrietta, but not from you."

Sniffing back the tears, she managed a laugh. "I have become a perfect watering pot. I beg your pardon."

"Dry your eyes, dearest, for all is well now, though it has been uncertain until a few days ago, and I did not wish to trouble Papa unnecessarily."

Silvestre made use of her pocket handkerchief. "Why was it uncertain?"

"Because Hetty knew not how to arrange for your travelling to Devenal in safety. It is a long way to Northamptonshire and you must spend at least one night on the road, and Hetty had no solution. Fortuitously, however, the dowager duchess is sending her steward to the capital to purchase particular gifts for the children. He will escort you, picking you up on the way back. Hetty has arranged for him to take one of the maids from Whisley Park here to accompany you, so you may travel in perfect propriety."

Silvestre had to laugh. "I imagine that is a sop to Papa's notions. Surely I cannot need a maid?"

"To my notions too, Silvestre. It would scarcely be seemly for you to travel alone with her grace's steward. Besides, I understand the dowager insisted upon it."

Silvestre's spirits began to lift. This was just what she needed to turn her mind from dismal thoughts of what she had left behind. "Oh, it will be so good to see Hetty again! When am I to go?"

# CHAPTER ELEVEN

The journey promised to be both tedious and a good deal more comfortable than Joss had expected. The summons came with his aunt Isobel's letter, addressed to himself rather than Lord Rotherhythe, to his surprise. But there was matter for astonishment.

*A great deal of fuss and bother has been going forward, my dear Joscelin, you can have no notion. Not, I may say, upon your account alone. Although your mother's conviction you would take the common stage if left to yourself has operated powerfully upon those wracking their brains for solutions.*

Knowing his aunt's tendency to witty exaggeration, Joss did not take this in any very serious spirit.

*Sanity has prevailed through the madness, you will be glad to hear, and various birds are to be slaughtered with the same stone.*

Amusement lightened his enwrapping gloom, though it could not hope to lift the core of discontent. He yearned for his attic retreat and could wish he had never agreed to be incarcerated in his cousin's library. Now that he was to be denied the company of the fellow scribblers he had uniformly avoided or despised, Joss was inclined to recalcitrance. Not regret. That was reserved for an instance of stupidity and cowardice upon which he preferred not to dwell despite its tendency to sneak disturbing memories into his mind. He read on.

*A coach, you see, is to be put at the disposal of all. It will find you out in the metropolis and you may travel in the warmth of hot bricks, furs and all manner of such coddling as will satisfy my dear sister's notions of securing you for the hazardous journey. Do not, I charge you, distress her by rejecting these vital accessories, or I shall be subjected to several more pages of distressful concern about you on Amelia's part. She worries far more about your fate, my dear boy, than she does that of her three sons in the military, despite your being in no danger whatsoever from cannon or camp fever. But we mothers, you know, are forever convinced our boys are incapable of looking after themselves without mama to cosset and fuss over them.*

Torn between laughter and a prick to his conscience, Joss regretfully accepted there was no going back. He had agreed to try and the penance must be endured.

His father left the capital before he did and Joss bid him farewell, trying not to resent the inevitable admonitions.

"A fair trial, boy. Remember your promise. I hope you won't disappoint your mother."

"I won't, sir."

Lord Rotherhythe had eyed him with, Joss thought, a degree of uncertainty. "Don't neglect to write. Amelia will wish to know how you are managing."

He sighed. "I have given my word. I can't do more, sir."

His father became testy. "You can, but you won't. Lord knows how I came to sire such a stubborn cub!"

"If you don't know that, sir, you cannot know yourself."

A bark of laughter, rarely heard by Joss, greeted this impertinence. His sire gave him a hearty buffet, told him to eat properly and stop looking like a scarecrow, and departed.

In the event, Joss had time only for one last visit to Beardsley & Beak, an evening of carousals with his friend Stanford

Wingley, and had barely wrestled with his latest idea for a new work when he was collected and whisked off upon the road to his despised appointment. A somewhat harassed fellow of middle years, in charge of what he termed "the expedition", proved to be a disappointing companion. Swarland was neither well read nor sufficiently interested in books to provide Joss with any information concerning the extent of his employer's library.

"It is large, my lord, and that is all I can tell you since it does not lie within my province."

After two attempts to get the man to drop the use of the appellation he disliked, Joss gave up. Swarland's entire conversation was larded with references to "graces", of whom there were three, and their various requirements, likes and dislikes. Not to mention ladies both young and old. It was plain he would brook no downgrade of Lord Joscelin Diggory to a mere mister, and his deferent manner could not but grate.

"We will break the journey early, my lord, that I may fulfil the rest of my commission. It is only half a day's travel to our first destination."

It made little difference to Joss. "I am in your hands, sir. Remember I am as much an employee as yourself."

Swarland looked pained. "I should doubt of your relationship permitting your lordship to be treated as such."

Useless to argue the point. Joss retired into his own thoughts, trying to set them rather upon the idea with which he had begun to toy. Triggered by the tyro's reference to Shakespeare. The plays, but in relation to the sonnets. He must revisit them, discover if his notion of the poet's suffering there depicted extended to his art as well as his life.

But his mind refused to oblige him, insistently returning to the tyro herself and that last meeting, memorable more for the abrupt curtailment of its pleasure than the pleasure itself. He had wished the result of his ill-considered words undone a hundred times. Futile. There was naught he could do to change it. Especially now, when he was being spirited away to the north with scant hope of a return to the metropolis at an early date.

He cursed. If his thoughts were this unruly, he would do better talking with the steward. A series of blunt questions at least provided him with some notion of the extent of his cousin's domain, the inmates of his establishment and the daily habits of the various members of the family. The interrogation beguiled most of the first leg of the journey and armed Joss at least with some foreknowledge of his coming situation.

He found himself treated with just as much deference at his cousin's summer retreat, where the travellers passed the first night. Upon resuming the journey the following day, however, he found the company augmented by a maid, who took the forward seat.

"This is Martha, my lord, who is to travel with us. For this present, we must make a brief detour to Moss House to collect the duchess's sister."

Joss barely withheld a groan. They were to be burdened with a petticoat? Dear Lord, was he expected to do the pretty? Was this why the wretched Swarland had insisted upon maintaining formality? As a member of the duke's family, he was of similar station to the duchess's female relative, his position in the household notwithstanding. Damnation! Was it to fall to him to entertain her?

Fervently did he wish he had not yielded. Never had his abandoned attic room seemed more attractive. What, had he sold his soul only to be thrust into precisely the milieu he had successfully avoided for years?

His mood worsened as the coach made its ponderous way towards Sinsham village, as Swarland unnecessarily informed him. He cared not what village it was. He wished himself a world away. Or at least back in the capital. The duchess's sister forsooth! He was supposed to be the librarian. Now he would be forced to adopt the trappings of his rank.

By the time the coach came to a standstill, he was so deeply back in the brooding resentment that habitually plagued him, he could not even bring himself to exit the coach for the sake of politeness.

Fortunately Swarland did not seem to expect it, himself making ready to jump down as the groom came to open the door. "I believe Miss Latimer will be ready. I came last evening to inform her of our time."

With which, he exited the coach, leaving Joss blank with shock and disbelief.

Miss Latimer? *Silvestre* Latimer? She was the duchess's sister? Impossible coincidence. No, it could not be.

But a sneaking memory slipped into his mind from those early meetings. He had urged her to use anything she had against the rat Christy's parsimony, had he not? She had thanked him for it after. He remembered her words now. Her sister had lately become a duchess.

His brain whirled. She was Charlton's sister-in-law! And she was about to enter this very coach to accompany the party to Devenal. Joss knew not what to think nor how to act. The fateful memory of their last meeting swept into his head and lodged there like a malevolent beast.

Within far too few minutes, giving him next to no respite in which to formulate any kind of plan, the sound of anxious voices mingled with Swarland's instructions to the groom.

"Write at once upon your safe arrival, my love."

"Secure this in the boot, Skipsea. There should be room enough."

"I trust it won't come on to snow, my dear. I don't like the look of the sky."

"I am persuaded it won't, Papa."

"Wrap up warm, my love. I don't doubt her grace's steward will have thought to provide a hot brick and blankets."

"Will you enter, Miss Latimer?"

This last jerked Joss into full awareness. Lord in heaven, she was about to get in! He strove for calm, but his nerves were jumping as badly as they ever did when he was called upon to read his work.

Footsteps approached the coach. Many of them. Accompanied by words of farewell he scarcely registered. The door opened again. Then a familiar figure was stepping up into the coach, swathed in a thick cloak, a bonnet partially concealing her face at first. She slipped into the vacant seat beside him in a flurry of petticoats, turning her head at once towards the open door where a bespectacled female and a severe-looking man were anxiously watching. Swarland followed her in and settled beside the maid in the forward seat. The door closed and Miss Latimer leaned to the window, calling out.

"I will write at once, Mama. Pray don't fret. Goodbye, Papa!"

Then the coach was moving and she waved through the window. At last she sat back, taking time to re-arrange her skirts and cloak.

Dreading the inevitable moment of discovery, Joss shrank back into his corner. His pulse was in shocking disarray and his tongue felt thick in his mouth.

For a moment, she was occupied with making herself comfortable and he began to hope she might not look around, although his gaze was riveted upon her profile. She did not at first. He caught the corner of her smile as she glanced towards the steward.

"Thank you, Mr Swarland. It's good of you to break the journey to accommodate me."

"Not at all, ma'am. Their graces were particularly concerned for your comfort. Pray make use of the hot brick."

He bent to pull the blanketed object into a suitable position and Miss Latimer snuggled her feet upon it. Her gaze, as she settled again, travelled to the maid and Joss saw with discomfort how her face grew animated as she presented him with a better view of it.

"Is it you, Martha? How kind of you to consent to come on my behalf."

The girl looked gratified. "I'm very happy to, miss. Mrs Oughtibridge says her grace wishes me to wait upon you at Devenal too."

"Well, I am delighted to have your help, Martha, especially since you were so very kind to my sister back in the summer."

The girl blushed, though she bridled with obvious pleasure and a memory shot into Joss's mind. *That is how it is done.* A lesson in courtesy? Yet the tyro was so practised in the art she did it without thought or premeditation.

Then his mind shut down on him as Miss Latimer turned in his direction. He saw recognition hit. Consternation? Confusion? Shock? Horror in her gasp?

"Mr Degarre!"

The vulture, here? Silvestre's heart felt as if it jumped out of her bosom. For a wild instant she supposed her imagination to be playing her false. It could not be he!

"What in the world are you doing here? You cannot be going to Devenal! Is it you? I have not run mad, have I?"

At that, an odd sort of laugh escaped him. It sounded strangled. "Not out of your mind. It is I."

Yes, it was. He looked as thoroughly self-conscious as he had that very first day. The horrid memory of the dinner at Lady Whittlesford's rushed into her head and embarrassment rendered her momentarily tongue-tied. There was an awkward silence, and then Gausselin Degarre cleared his throat.

"I am quite as much astonished to see you, Miss Latimer."

To her immense relief, Swarland took the matter up. "I was about to perform the introductions, my lord, but I perceive you are acquainted with Miss Latimer."

"Yes. Yes, I am."

My lord? He was become my lord? Indignation burned through Silvestre's discomfort, rendering her dumber still as all the force of the reason for the division revived. It had begun with the wretched appellation. Hampered by the presence of Swarland and Martha, she turned her eyes upon the passing greenery at the side of the road, fearing she might otherwise say aloud the words teeming through her head. None of them complimentary.

His voice came again, sounding quite as embarrassed as she was herself. "I did not know Miss Latimer was the duchess's sister. Not until you mentioned her name just before we stopped."

Was that for her benefit? He was speaking to Swarland. She turned back to the steward. "Mr Degarre, as he prefers one to call him, professes disinterest in any circle beyond the literary,

Mr Swarland. Personal accoutrements, by way of stray duchesses or his own aristocratic connections are of no account. Is that not so, Mr Degarre?" She threw a venomous look at him as she spoke and caught both hurt and fury in his eyes. Torn between guilt and defiance, she turned to the window again, not missing the reactions of the two on the forward seat. Mr Swarland looked perplexed, Martha agog. She ought to be ashamed of herself, but there was a curious satisfaction in having discharged a little of her own hurt.

A low-voiced murmur reached her. "Uncalled for, ma'am."

"Possibly." She turned to confront him. "And possibly not."

He met her gaze and she read reproach in his eyes. He hesitated, the vulture look pronounced, his skin taut. "A discussion for another time, ma'am." He flicked a glance towards the forward seat.

Silvestre felt heat rising into her face. She could not but acknowledge the justice of the admonition. Apology hovered on her tongue, but a core of discontent would not permit its utterance. She gave a nod and turned away again, her unseeing gaze trained upon the shifting colours beyond the window.

Guilt swamped her at remembrance of the spilt words. They had been waspish. It was unworthy conduct and would have grieved her parents.

Yet a rebellious demon persisted its dance in her bosom. *He* had no qualms before this. Was he become censorious of her manners only because he was wearing his rank? When his own left much to be desired. It was not to be borne. What, was she to be censured by a creature known for his outright rudeness in despising his company and refusing to participate in social discussion? One, moreover, who had not scrupled to blast her where she sat for daring to address him as 'my lord'.

Here her conscience intervened. He did apologise. An apology she had refused to accept. And had thus spent the remainder of the evening plagued by doubt and yearning.

Oh, impossible! To be imprisoned in a coach for the Lord knew how many hours, unable to speak freely for the presence of others who ought not to be made party to her dissatisfaction. There was no bearing it. She had to speak, say something to break the horrible silence. She seized the first thought out of the air, turning to address the steward.

"My sister wrote that we must spend a night on the road, sir. Is it so?"

Mr Swarland looked visibly relieved at the change of subject. "Indeed, ma'am. I have secured rooms at Brackley and arranged for Martha to be accommodated with you. Her grace was most anxious you should not be alone in a common inn."

Hetty cared for that? It did not sound at all like her wholly unsophisticated twin. Silvestre regarded him with some degree of puzzlement. "My sister requested it?"

Swarland coughed. "Her grace the dowager, I should have said. Her grace is most particular about such matters."

Did not Silvestre know it! She wondered for the first time whether Hetty had succeeded in placating the duchess she had supplanted. Theo's aunt was notoriously conventional and her disapproval of Henrietta Latimer as a bride for the duke had been patent. She was obliged to accept his choice, but it must have stuck in her craw. Though how could anyone fail to succumb to Hetty, so lovable as she was?

A sliver of the anticipatory delight returned at the notion of being with her twin again, superseding the present discomforts. She spoke without thought. "I'm so pleased to be visiting my sister, sir. I've missed her sorely. But you've seen her very lately. Is she well? Is she happy in her new life?"

The steward looked taken aback. "I hardly know, Miss Latimer. It is not for me to judge her grace's condition."

"But you would know if she was ill, or — or if there was anything…" She faded out. No, she could not expect the steward to satisfy her concerns.

"As far as I am aware, ma'am, her grace is in perfect health."

Silvestre smiled, feeling a trifle tremulous. "Thank you. That at least is good to know."

At this point, Martha piped up. "Ooh, don't you worrit yourself none, miss. There ain't been no horrid accidents like there was in summer or we'd have heard of it right enough. Nor his grace wouldn't let nothing bad happen to her, sure as eggs is eggs. I know that much."

The steward frowned her down. "That will do, Martha."

Recalling how the now abashed maid had looked after her twin, Silvestre gave her a warm smile. "Thank you, Martha. That is a comfort."

The girl threw her a grateful look, rolled expressive eyes towards Swarland, and subsided into her corner. Silvestre was suddenly glad she was to have the maid's company. It was plain the servants must be in regular contact between the houses, and Martha would have no hesitation in responding to her queries.

Silence fell again. Silvestre became aware once more of the still figure at her side and constraint returned. She racked her brains for an innocuous turn of subject, without result.

# CHAPTER TWELVE

Several miles rolled by without a word uttered in the coach. Silvestre's unquiet thoughts lulled at last into tedium to the accompaniment of the unceasing clopping of the horses' hooves, the jingle of harness and the clatter of the wheels on the packed dirt road.

Her limbs began to feel numb. It was growing chill and the warmth from the hot brick had dissipated. Or was that merely her fancy? She wriggled her toes in her boots, feeling for the heat, and hugged into her cloak, rubbing her gloved fingers together.

"Are you cold, Miss Latimer?"

Startled out of her abstraction by the softly uttered query, she looked round. Mr Degarre was watching her, his brows drawn together. Her throat became constricted, but she answered in a low tone. "A little. Nothing to signify."

"I believe there are rugs to be had. Shall I wake him?" He nodded across to Swarland, who was lying back in his corner with closed eyes. A glance showed the maid to have similarly dozed off.

She shook her head. "I dare say we may stop for a change soon enough. I will get down and walk about for a bit."

"Sitting still does make for a trifle of numbness in this type of weather."

Silvestre thought she detected a cautious note in his voice. Tentative? To hear Degarre speak about inconsequential things was novel. Was he trying for a neutral topic? An olive branch again? It felt perfectly unnatural, but she matched the attempt. "My father feared there might be snow in the offing."

"Ah. We must hope to be spared that."

"Yes. It would be decidedly inconvenient."

And this conversation was decidedly mundane. Dismayingly so indeed. Hardly better than the preceding silence, so thick as it was with the unspoken words that lay between them.

She urged the due apology onto her tongue but it would not be said. Later perhaps, when they were alone. A flutter disturbed her pulse at the notion. Unlikely they would be alone on the journey. Or perhaps at Devenal…

Heavens, she had not learned his business there! On the thought, hesitation vanished.

"You did not say why you are also visiting the Charltons, sir. I had no notion there was a connection." She heard a tiny sound in his throat and all at once felt the nervousness she had seen in him before. Affected, she eyed him with a diminution of her erstwhile resentment.

"Charlton is my cousin. But I am no visitor. I am to be his librarian."

"His librarian!"

He grimaced. "A whim of my mother's, arranged by my aunt."

"Lady Lionel Devenal is your aunt?"

He gave a sign of assent. "I understand the sisters put their heads together, as my revered sire had it, and my aunt Isobel applied to Charlton, who agreed to the scheme. For reasons that presently escape me. I can't imagine he actually needs a librarian."

The sceptical note overlaid a deeper one of dissatisfaction Silvestre had heard before. "If you did not wish for the position, why take it?"

His mouth curled and the black eyes took on a look of resignation. "You may well ask." He hesitated, his gloved fingers moving restlessly in his lap. She thought he was going to clam up as he usually did if one touched on his personal affairs. He glanced at Swarland. Checking if the man was still safely slumbering? His tone lowered the more and he leaned slightly in her direction. "It was in some sort forced upon me."

"I see." Silvestre would have liked to know more, but he was so sensitive she was reluctant to ask. It was not precisely a resumption of their former ease, but at least the constraint had dropped somewhat and she was loath to revive it.

"I agreed to a trial, and have been bemoaning the fact since this journey began."

What was she to say to that? From the little she knew of him, she would expect no less, but she dared not say so. A feeling of frustration crept over her. She had never been this reticent with Gausselin Degarre. Yet was this the poet? He was different. As if Lord Joscelin Diggory had emerged from some dormant chrysalis, ousting the literary lion. She fell back upon convention. "I am going for the Christmas festivities."

"Yes."

"I have not seen my sister since her marriage, you must know, and it is in truth the first time we have been separated."

A frowning look came her way. "I recall now that you told me she is your twin and that you are close. You are fond, I take it?"

"Very."

"Are you alike?"

Silvestre was conscious of a degree of relaxation as the subject seemed innocuous enough. Family was easy to talk of, for her at least. "In looks we are much alike, though not identical. We are rarely mistaken for one another, if that is what you mean. But in temperament and character we are wholly dissimilar."

A little to her surprise, Mr Degarre — or Lord Joscelin as he now was? — appeared interested. "How so?"

"Oh, Hetty is all sensibility while I am the practical twin."

He smiled. "You do not strike me as lacking in sensibility, Miss Latimer. Or perhaps I mean empathy? You could not write well without it."

She was gratified but felt obliged to disclaim. "I am nowhere near as tender-hearted as Hetty. She is a volatile creature, you must know. She weeps at the drop of a hat, but is just as likely to lose her temper and fly out at you. But no one could fail to adore Hetty. Yes, we are extraordinarily fond, to use your word. We have no other sibling, you see. Whereas I understand you have several brothers, do you not?"

The closed-in look instantly overspread his features and Silvestre felt at once alienated. How could she have slipped again? Talking of Hetty loosened her tongue so readily she did not think. Now he would retire into his shell.

For several moments he did not speak and Silvestre felt wracked all over again. Then a grimace crossed his face.

"I have four brothers and three sisters."

She was so surprised, her guard dropped. "Eight of you? Heavens, your poor mama!"

An odd sort of laugh escaped him. "Worse than you know. She bore my father twelve children, but the others did not survive infancy."

"Are they all grown?"

"My brothers are. I am the youngest of the boys. Two of my sisters are married. Louise is not yet out."

"But the girls are all younger than you?"

"Two of them. Selina comes after Tristan, who is the heir."

"Well, I am astonished. Imagine what Aspatria Glasson would say of your mother's martyrdom in this cause."

This time he appeared genuinely amused. "I trust she won't discover it."

"No, for I dare say she would harangue you on the subject and it's scarcely your fault, Mr Degarre."

His features became taut again and he eyed her in a fashion she was unable to fathom. The ease she had recovered in talking of family slid away and Silvestre was again conscious of constraint. Why had he pokered up again? Was he recalling that awkwardness of the dinner? Before she could think further upon it, a change in the pace of the coach impinged upon her senses.

"I believe we are slowing. We are likely due for a change of horses."

The break in the rhythm had apparently woken Mr Swarland, who sat up abruptly and looked out of the window. "We must be at Deddington." Then he uttered a startled exclamation. "Oh, the deuce! It is snowing!"

His unaccustomed language passed Silvestre by as she saw there was indeed a fluttering of white flakes. Anxiety threw her into speech. "Will we be delayed? Or, no — it looks to be a light shower. A flurry only, perhaps?" She turned on the words, hopeful of reassurance, and found Swarland regarding the phenomenon with frowning intensity.

Mr Degarre, leaning to look out of the other window, was first to respond. "It does not look to be settling. We may be in luck."

Martha had woken and was sitting bolt upright, staring about. "Ooh, what is it?"

"Snow, Martha," Silvestre said. "We hope it is but a flurry."

As the coach swung through an archway, Swarland made ready to alight. "I will ascertain the likely conditions, ma'am, while the team is changed. It will be well to press on, if possible, but there will be time to stretch your legs if you so wish."

Silvestre took this in the spirit it was intended and determined to seize the opportunity to take advantage of the facilities of the house. She had no wish to use a bordaloo behind a bush in this weather. Mr Swarland clearly did not intend the travellers to take refreshment at this halt.

The business of getting down, accompanied by Martha, who discovered the whereabouts of the privy, meant she lost track of the poet until the party reconvened by the coach, now harnessed with a fresh team. Swarland was conferring with the coachman, but the groom hurried up to let down the steps.

"It appears we are to continue now the snow has stopped," said the poet, suddenly appearing beside her. He held out a hand. "Allow me to help you in, ma'am."

Such courtesy from him was unprecedented. She threw him an astonished look. "Oh. Thank you." Awareness of his statement penetrated and she looked up at the grey skies. "It does not look promising."

"Get in, Miss Latimer."

The curt instruction was much more in his usual style and irritation flickered for an instant. But she climbed into the coach and settled into her place as the poet came in behind her and crossed to his corner, followed by Martha and the steward, who immediately reported his findings as the coach moved off.

"Tumby is confident of getting us to Brackley, where our rooms are already bespoken at the Crown."

"Even if it comes on to snow again?"

"Indeed, Miss Latimer. Skipsea made enquiry of the landlord and it seems the stage coachmen, who generally have knowledge of the likely weather, exhibited no qualms and were confident of being able to keep to the waybill."

He then distributed fur rugs he had caused to be unearthed from the boot and Silvestre snuggled into the additional warmth.

For a while she was preoccupied with the question of getting through to Devenal despite the snow and wondering if they might indeed be delayed. But her thoughts presently turned again upon the man at her side and his odd assumption of the common courtesy of his rank. It had not lasted, of course. Or was he merely in a hurry so as not to delay the steward? Was it because he considered himself an employee? Ridiculous in the circumstances. The whole situation was peculiar. But was that not just what one might expect from the vulture? Was it this strangeness of manner that had intrigued her from the outset? Or, no. Rather had she been caught by the intensity within, a sense of held-in depth of feeling. Both threat and challenge? She wanted to probe within. She wanted…

A rush of heat swept through her as an image of what she truly wanted from the poet crept into her head. His lips on hers? Oh, heavens, had she lost her mind? No, no, no. Impossible. Wrong. Utterly, completely wrong. Degarre was not at all the kind of man to inspire her with that sort of feminine fancy. She was not like Hetty, to be losing her heart in a bang. Not that hearts were in question. If anything, this peculiar physical manifestation betokened an odd sort of … of…

*Of what, Silvestre Latimer?*

Well, she had no notion, had she? The whole thing was ridiculous in the extreme. There was nothing remotely romantic about Gausselin Degarre. He had even denied it to his poetry. He was not that sort of poet, had he not said so? Which meant he was not that sort of man.

But not in a spirit of romance, for heaven's sake! Annoyed with herself, she tried to recapture her earlier frustration with the man and found it dissipated. Instead, a sneaking thread of anticipation was roving her veins for the potential in their both being at Devenal. She might at least repair the silly division that had arisen at Lady Whittlesford's dinner. Or had she already done so? They had conversed. Not with ease, it was true. But they were overheard. One could not say what one wished to say before the servants.

"What is going on in that head of yours, I wonder, Miss Latimer?"

A flutter of shock went through her at the low-voiced utterance and warmth rose to her face. She turned to find the poet watching her, wearing an expression of faint amusement. "Why do you ask?" It slipped out before she could think of a suitably innocuous response.

"Did I not before mention how your face mirrors the changing adventures in your mind?"

"Adventures! I should hardly describe them in such exciting terms."

"No? They looked to be entertaining at least."

How in the world was she to answer that? Consciousness compelled her to check the other two occupants of the coach. Swarland had his gaze upon the window, a frown between his brows. He did not appear to be paying attention. Martha's eyes were closed, but whether she slept or merely rested was a question.

Silvestre drew a breath, determined to be bold as she faced him. "I was wondering how I might contrive to overcome that unfortunate contretemps when we last met." She thought he stiffened and the half-smile faded. Without thought, she put out a hand, speaking low. "You were more generous than I, sir. I was ungracious."

His brows drew together. "This was the substance of your cogitations?"

An uncomfortable little laugh escaped her. "Not entirely."

He nodded. "We will speak of it again, ma'am."

With which, he retired into his corner, turning his gaze upon the window. Silvestre felt it as rejection and was obliged to damp down a rise of distress. She need not take it amiss. He meant only to defer discussion to a more private moment. Only could he not have been a trifle more amicable?

Dissatisfaction with him revived. Really, he was a perfectly irritating creature. Why must he come the vulture just when she was warming to him again? Well, she would not give him the satisfaction of brooding. That was his province. Let him stew in it, wretched man!

With deliberation, she turned to the steward, seizing upon a question that had crossed her mind earlier. "You have had a deal to contend with upon this trip, Mr Swarland, have you not? What with myself and his lordship added to your burdens."

The steward inclined his head. "It is kind of you to think of me, ma'am, but I am happy to serve their graces in any way they require."

"Yet I understood from my sister that you had business in London to bring you south?"

He cracked a smile at last. "Christmas gifts, ma'am. Her grace the dowager wished for particular items to be procured for their ladyships."

Come, this was a promising subject to beguile the time. "You mean Lady Ella and her little sister, I suppose. Ah, then you have been obliged to go hunting for toys?"

"Indeed, ma'am. Lady Prudence being an infant, her needs were easy enough to be met. Lady Ella's requirements presented more of a challenge."

The former name could not but recall the indiscretion of the elderly Madam Prudence to Silvestre's mind and her consciousness of the silent man at her side increased. But she managed a laugh. "Yes, I have met Lady Ella. Mere dolls are to be despised, I take it?"

Swarland laughed, relaxing a little of his punctilious manner. "Just so, ma'am. His grace, well acquainted as he is with Lady Ella's preferences, recommended me to search rather amongst the sort of toys suitable to young gentlemen."

Silvestre laughed. "Did he so? I am agog to know what you settled upon."

"In the end I procured a set of toy soldiers. However, her grace the dowager is anxious for her ladyship to acquire a suitable feminine outlook and requested me nevertheless to find a doll that might interest her ladyship."

"A tall order. And did you?"

"Yes, a mechanical one."

"In hopes that might prove more in her line, I take it? Ingenious, Mr Swarland."

He appeared gratified. "I must hope it will answer. Although I may say that her grace the duchess has a way with Lady Ella, and it may be she will choose to ape her conduct."

"If you ask me," piped up Martha, "that little madam won't do nothing she don't wish to. Ooh, a naughty piece she is, that Lady Ella!"

"Nobody asked you, Martha," said the steward, reverting to his usual manner. "I must request you not to speak of her ladyship in that unbecoming fashion."

The maid subsided into muttering sulks. Silvestre felt sorry for the girl, but she could scarcely gainsay Swarland and undermine his authority. She was more than ever glad to think she would have Martha's company and might make up for the steward's strictures with a little kindness.

But Swarland seemed inclined to unbend and responded more freely as Silvestre questioned him about Devenal's proportions and learned something of the original ruined castle. The time passed quicker at least, although Silvestre could not avoid an increasing feeling of annoyance that the poet made no effort whatsoever to participate in the conversation.

The light had begun to fade by the time the travellers at last reached Brackley. Feeling both tired and jaded, Joss could not but admire the tyro's resilience. She had not once closed her eyes in sleep, as far as he could tell, closely watching her whenever there was a lull in the conversation. Although she retired into her own thoughts, even in profile her features remained animated.

Joss found the phenomenon fascinating. Also immensely pleasurable. Although he was obliged to be careful of her glance. She was capable of asking him why he stared in so rude a fashion, a question he could not answer since he did not know himself. All he knew was an unprecedented and confusing mix of frustration and anticipation at the notion of her sojourning in the very establishment in which he must perform his penance of employment.

He did not wish to be plagued with yet another complication. Bad enough to be obliged to interrupt his creative labours with whatever his cousin required him to do, if anything. The distraction of a female who possessed an undeniable ability to draw his interest he could well do without. The last thing he needed was a petticoat on his mind.

Swarland's attitude had made it clear he was not going to be allowed to sink into the background in the reclusive fashion he preferred. He was not well enough acquainted with his cousin Charlton to judge his likely expectations, though he knew the fellow to be something of a wanderer who had spent an inordinate amount of time abroad. But he would scarcely be paying down his dust for a librarian for nothing. With luck, Joss could avoid social mingling for the most part. Yet he could not contemplate the notion of Miss Latimer's presence in the place, as an honoured guest, while he laboured in a lowly capacity. It put him at a disadvantage. He could not meet her on equal terms. Moreover, she was not a female who feared to cross the line. He felt compelled to keep her at arm's length. Yet the temptation to succumb to her warmth threatened to undermine his resolve.

It nearly collapsed when he found she was indeed near exhausted as the party crowded into the Crown. Joss stood back to allow her to enter and was at once dismayed to see her set a hand to the balled baluster at the bottom of the staircase in the hall and lean against it. He moved to her side.

"Are you all right, Miss Latimer?"

She straightened, although she kept hold of her prop, but her features under the bonnet looked strained. "I am more tired than I realised."

"You look wholly done up. Wait! Stay there."

Joss moved to Swarland, who was conversing with a burly individual, and interrupted without ceremony. "Did you procure a private parlour? Miss Latimer needs to sit down at once."

The steward's consternation was patent. "Oh, dear, does she? Yes, indeed I arranged for it." He turned back to the man. "Show us to the parlour immediately, Postwick. We will look to the rest afterwards."

The fellow addressed bobbed his head. "Certainly, sir. It is upstairs, if you will follow me."

He made for the stairs and Joss slipped back to Miss Latimer. "Take my arm. This fellow is going to lead us to the parlour."

She looked surprised, but said nothing as she set her hand in his crooked elbow and supported herself on the other side with the bannister. Joss was conscious of feeling uncommonly protective towards her as he helped her mount the stairs. Stupid, of course. A female less in need of protection he had rarely encountered. She was decidedly independent. Rather like the rest of the bluestocking coterie. The literary life seemed to attract such females.

Within moments, he was able to settle Miss Latimer in an upholstered chair near a flickering fire in the small but tolerably comfortable parlour allotted to the party. A square table was situated in the centre, set with several wooden chairs with caned seats, and a long settle against one wall gave access to the latticed windows which overlooked the busy yard.

"I have requested tea to be brought up," Swarland informed them. "We will dine in here in about an hour. I must see to the luggage and have it conveyed to the rooms, so you may wash off the stains of travel before dinner, if you wish. Martha will come to show you the way, Miss Latimer."

Upon the words, he departed in the landlord's wake, leaving Joss alone with the tyro. He eyed her with growing concern. She was leaning an elbow on the arm of the chair, resting her head in her hand in an attitude that looked to be dejected. Instinct sent him to her side.

"Are you warm enough? Don't you want to get out of that heavy cloak?"

She glanced up with a wan smile. "But then I shall have to stand up again, and I don't think I can."

"Then stay there." Joss perched on the chair opposite, regarding her in a good deal of dismay. The words came without premeditation. "I've never seen you like this, Tyro. Usually you're all bright animation. Travel has this effect always?"

She regarded him without shifting her pose. "Not in general."

He found her oddly vulnerable, head on one side like that. "Tea will revive you."

She gave him a strange look he could not interpret and turned her gaze upon the fire. "A luxury. We usually take coffee at home."

"I prefer it."

Her eyes came back to his, a tiny cleft between her brows. "Why did you not ask for it instead?"

"I'm not a guest, Miss Latimer."

A faint smile came. "I think I prefer Tyro."

A laugh escaped him. "If it comes to that, I prefer Joss to Mr Degarre." He amended this on impulse. "From you, at least."

To his consternation, her eyes rimmed with moisture, though the smile grew. Her voice became husky. "You would not care for my secret name for you."

He was intrigued, if a little apprehensive. "You have one? To do with skulking or brooding, I dare guess, of which you have more than once accused me."

The shine at her eyes receded as she laughed, pushing herself upright. "Nothing half as complimentary."

"You alarm me."

"With reason. But I shan't tell you, however much you plague me to do so."

He cocked an eyebrow. "What, and invite the insult? I won't ask — Tyro."

She raised her brows at him. "You can't suppose I should fall into so obvious a trap?"

"*Touché!*" He looked her over and was relieved to see the colour had come back into her cheeks. "You look a little less peaked. Let me take your cloak." He rose and held out a hand. "Come, I'll help you up."

Was it surprise in her face? Did she suppose him incapable of any sort of courtesy or service? She allowed him to pull her up and turned slightly, shrugging out of the cloak as he grasped it. She sat down at once, undoing the strings of her bonnet. He took it from her as she removed it and stood watching as she ran fingers through her crushed hair, forcing it to spring up a trifle untidily. A flicker of desire went through him, shocking him out of his contemplation.

At the same instant she looked up and met his eyes, her fingers going still within the strands of hair. A flush mounted to her cheeks. Joss willed himself to look away, but the rising heat held him captive.

A rat-a-tat knocking at the door broke the moment. Joss turned, calling to whoever was without to come in, and went blindly across to the long settle at the far side of the room. Confused, unable to think, he dumped the cloak and bonnet. His breath was short, and a curse rumbled up into his mind.

Hell and the devil and damnation too! What was he thinking? What must she think? No hope of her mistaking what had passed. She was too acute. Lord help him, but this was a disaster! Only one thing to be done. He must act as if it had never happened.

He heard the clink of crockery and turned to find a waiter had set down a tray upon the table and was setting out cups and the accoutrements for tea.

When he retired, Miss Latimer was already moving to the table. She looked and sounded perfectly normal. "They have sent a pot up ready-made. Would you care for a cup, Mr Degarre?"

The resumption of formality both chilled and irritated. That little interlude of intimacy might never have been. Joss felt bereft. He crossed to the table. "I'll take a cup." Aware he sounded gruff, he struggled for a lighter note. "As it comes, if you please."

She was pouring, her hand a little unsteady. Joss was conscious of a curious sort of satisfaction to know she was affected. Stupid. He did not wish her to be affected. He wished she might forget it. Erase it.

She lifted the cup in its saucer and set it down nearer to where he stood. Then she poured another, added a dash of cream and a lump of sugar, and set the whole near the edge of the table. She pulled out a chair and sat down, not looking at him as she took up her cup and sipped.

Joss followed suit, drawing his saucer towards him. He drank. The brew was pleasant to his palate. He tried to think of some innocuous subject and could not.

She looked up at last. "We seem to have escaped the snow."

"Yes." Snow? Must they talk of snow? Too mundane now. But, no. Mundane was good. Safer. "If it holds, we ought to reach Devenal by this time tomorrow."

She was sipping her tea, eyeing him over the rim. "Will you be glad?"

What did she mean by that? Glad of arriving? Glad to be done with this embarrassing journey? "Will you?"

She set down her cup, looking into the brown liquid within. "Yes and no." She drew a visible breath and looked him straight in the eye. "We have a moment now, Mr Degarre. There may not be another. Allow me to say that I should have accepted your apology on the instant — that night, I mean. It was not for me to interfere with your preferences."

This was unbearable. "Miss Latimer —"

She threw up a hand. "No, let me finish."

"Don't! I prefer your bite, if anything."

A little grimace came. "But I didn't bite, sir. I sulked. That was selfish and unworthy. Papa did not bring me up to behave in such a churlish fashion and I have been ashamed of it."

He felt a perfect fool. "I cannot let this pass, ma'am. What shall I say of my conduct? I know it leaves a deal to be desired."

A look of mischief crept over her features and Joss rejoiced to see it. "But if you change, sir, I shall have nothing for which to berate you. That would never do."

He burst out laughing and had to set down his cup. "You … you *tyro!*"

A giggle escaped her and she twinkled at him, her cup poised. "There now, Sir Poet, we are even."

He grimaced. "Joss will do. Really. I cannot tolerate Sir Poet."

"Indeed?" Her brows rose. "You do realise you have just handed me ammunition?"

"Silvestre Latimer, you are a wicked female."

"My friends call me Silve."

The smile that accompanied the words shot a flitter of heat down his veins. This was becoming dangerously intimate again. He dared not avail himself of the invitation.

To his relief, the door opened to admit the girl Martha, come to show her temporary mistress the way to her chamber. Thank the lord! There would be no further time alone. Swarland at least would make a restraining third at dinner. There must be no more of these intimate moments. It was not fitting. Besides, he could not endure the stress.

# CHAPTER THIRTEEN

Waking to eerie quiet, Silvestre listened in the dimness of the curtained bed. Stealthy movement indicated the maid was up and dressing.

"Martha?"

The sounds stopped. A hushed voice answered. "Yes, miss?"

"What is the time?"

A flurry at the bed-curtains produced a chink of light and Martha's plump young features appeared in the aperture. "Early yet, miss. I thought you was sound asleep."

Silvestre dragged herself up on one elbow. "Something woke me." She saw consternation appear on the girl's face and flapped a hand. "Oh, not you. The quiet, I think. Why is it so quiet? It must be seven at least."

"Nearer eight, miss." Martha pulled the curtains back, introducing more light. "Nor it ain't nowise as quiet as you think. The place is buzzing already."

As she dealt with the curtains on the window side, brightness flooded the room from the open shutters.

Silvestre sat up. "Gracious! It looks a deal sunnier than yesterday."

Martha crossed to the window, looking grim. "That ain't sunshine, miss. Snowed in the night, it did."

"Snow? Oh, no!"

"Yes, miss. Everything is blanketed, the trees and all. If you ask me, we ain't going nowhere today."

She nodded in a decisive fashion, but Silvestre was already scrambling out from between the sheets. The maid began scolding as she got out of the bed.

"You'll catch your death you will, miss!"

But Silvestre was at the window in a trice, a well of dismay rising as she looked out over the transformed inn yard and the rooves across the way, thick with a covering of white. The gallery balusters were encrusted, the bannisters plastered with it. Below, ostlers were busy sweeping with birch brooms which showed the snow to be inches deep. The roads would be impassable.

"Do you get back in bed, miss, and I'll bring you up a cup of chocolate before I fetch your hot water. You've no call to be getting up quite yet."

Silvestre allowed herself to be ushered back to the bed and tucked in, but her mind was running upon the difficulties ahead. "I must find out if Mr Swarland thinks to attempt to continue the journey. If it doesn't come on to snow again…"

"Don't you fret none, miss," said Martha, producing a shawl and setting it about Silvestre's shoulders. "I'll ask Tumby, or more likely Walter. He's the groom, miss. He'll know."

She bustled out and Silvestre sat contemplating the overbright cast of the sky, her mind running over last night's dinner. No suspicion of a snowfall had been prognosticated then. Swarland's talk was all of his expectations of reaching Devenal today, and before they lost the daylight. No hope of that now. Even if the travellers took the early start he had anticipated after breakfast, the snow must slow them down considerably. Indeed, she could not but believe a man as cautious as Swarland would consider it foolhardy to set out at all in such conditions. In which case, she was marooned in the company of the vulture.

An anticipatory flutter in her stomach greeted this thought. She had not dared to hope for another chance to talk to him alone. Not that the brief exchange in the parlour had served to settle her mind. The reverse, if anything.

The poet had been as remote and reserved as ever throughout dinner, leaving the burden of the conversation to herself and Swarland. Such remarks as had been drawn from him were both grudging and brief. Indeed, she had become so out of charity with the wretched brute, she had determined to ignore him for the remainder of the journey. A resolve to which it would now be impossible to adhere.

Not, if she was honest, that she wanted to. Why she found him so intriguing, so engaging to her senses, was a mystery. Yet he had shown her a very different side to that which he exhibited to the world at large. His thought for her when they'd arrived had touched her, though it had surprised her too.

Remembrance of the little moment of intimacy crept into her head. He had let her in, if briefly. She could no longer be certain she had indeed caught a gleam in his eyes of … of a different sort of interest. As if he too envisioned the notion of a kiss.

Even the memory of her idiotic idea had the power to make heat rise to her face. To imagine he felt it too was wishful thinking, was it not? Besides, it was wholly out of the question. A gentleman — and he was one, whether or not he wished to acknowledge his rank — would not steal a kiss from a lady. Nor would any lady with the smallest pretension to gentility be imagining herself in a gentleman's arms. Especially those belonging to a man as unprepossessing as the vulture.

Heavens above! If she must dream, could she not at least find a handsome creature to swoon over? Some suave flatterer like Pelham Ferneux, perhaps.

A giggle escaped her. Please God, no. How Joss would hate it if she did!

She was brought up short. Where did that come from? She was not to be calling him Joss, despite his invitation. He had reverted to Miss Latimer at the first instant. Why should she adopt the less formal appellation?

Oh, ridiculous! Chances were he would take the opportunity to write poetry while they were held here. She ought to be thinking of her own writing. She had no notion of any sort of story she might write to follow *Emmeline*. Nor did it seem possible she could do it again. Not with that same passionate intensity.

Martha's arrival with her chocolate put an end to her cogitations. "Seems as Mr Swarland is waiting to see if the snow starts to melt, miss. He's anxious as everyone should be ready to leave in any event."

Within the hour, washed and dressed for travel, Silvestre entered the private parlour to find Swarland and the poet already at the table. Both rose at her entrance, the steward moving to set a chair for her.

"Good morning, Miss Latimer. You've seen our difficulty, no doubt?"

"Indeed, yes. But I am perfectly ready to set out at need. Martha found out your intentions for me." She took the chair and glanced at the poet, who had not spoken. "Good morning, sir."

He murmured an indistinguishable reply, but waved a hand across the silver-covered dishes, pots, jugs and baskets of bread crowding the table. "Coffee? There is no tea. Ale?"

Silvestre let out a laugh. "Ale! I thank you, no, Mr Degarre. I will take coffee."

He upended a cup and began to pour, what time Swarland enumerated the viands on offer, lifting covers to display the contents of the dishes beneath.

"Scrambled eggs, ma'am? Ham? Or there is bacon if you should prefer it. Cold beef?"

She opted for scrambled eggs with bacon, and selected a warm roll from a proffered basket. The poet put the coffee before her and set cream, sugar and butter within her reach. Her needs met, the gentlemen re-seated themselves and continued their own meals.

Silvestre could not avoid noticing how sparingly Joss partook of the ham and beef upon his plate, in contrast to the steward, who addressed his full one with a hearty appetite. She was tempted to urge the poet to eat more, but his attitude was scarcely encouraging. Instead, she pressed the steward on the problems confronting them. "Have you any real hope of our setting forth, Mr Swarland?"

He swallowed his mouthful before answering. "I am doubtful, ma'am. I propose to inspect the road again after breakfast and confer with the coachman. In my view, if we cannot start within the hour it would be foolish to set off at all."

"You think we may find ourselves marooned elsewhere?"

"Just so, ma'am, and there is no guarantee I can secure rooms, even supposing we were to reach a suitable inn. His grace would, I am sure, counsel me to caution."

From what Silvestre knew of the duke, this seemed unlikely. Her brother-in-law was not noted either for caution or for doing what others expected of him. But the steward had charge of the journey and it was not for her to cavil. "Well, I must confess, though I shall be sorry to be delayed, I had rather not be obliged to tramp through the snow for miles should we founder."

Swarland took this in a more serious spirit than was intended. "Under no circumstances would I expect that of you, Miss Latimer. Your safety and comfort is paramount. I could not wish her grace the duchess to be distressed by your being so severely inconvenienced."

She could barely contain her amusement. As if Hetty would be in the least discomposed by her twin being obliged to walk in the snow. Really, the fellow was too punctilious for words. She cast a glance at Joss and found him regarding the steward with one of his enigmatic looks. Impossible to tell what he thought. On impulse, she rallied him. "Ought you not to eat as if we are to make the journey, Mr Degarre? A sparrow could not survive on what you have consumed."

His gaze came around to hers. "I don't travel well on a full stomach."

"Oh. Does the motion make you nauseous?"

"Only if I've eaten too much." He continued to survey her, an odd light in his eye. "Sparrows, incidentally, like all birds, are obliged to eat several times their own weight in order to survive. A prospect that leaves me shuddering."

Silvestre's laughter nearly choked her and she had to swallow down the food in her mouth before she could berate him. "Wretch! How could you? Just when I had taken a mouthful too!"

That faint smile was on his lips. "Tit for tat. I believe I owed you that one, ma'am."

She recalled the occasion when she had made him laugh when he was eating. She shook her knife at him. "True, Mr Degarre, but disgracefully mean to take your revenge."

His smile grew. "I warned you at the time. You will heed me for the future, no doubt."

"Yes, and pigs may fly! Heed you? I had as well take my lessons from the man in the moon!" As she spoke she caught the look on the steward's face and had much ado not to burst into laughter. Instead, she nodded in his direction. "You do not know this poet of ours, I fear, Mr Swarland. He is either morose and silent or witty beyond endurance. I must say I am glad I borrowed my father's copy of one of your volumes, sir, for I am more than ever eager to discover how you see the world."

To her surprise, he flushed, reverting to the staccato nervousness she'd encountered at the first. "You have it? With you here? Don't read it. At least, you may. But not now. Not in my presence. You might loathe it. Don't say so. If you do hate it, I mean."

Stirred to her depths, Silvestre softened into pity without will. "I could not if I wanted to. It is stowed in my trunk, and that is no doubt strapped onto the boot, is it not, Mr Swarland?"

Swarland nodded, his mouth again full. Silvestre turned back to the poet, who had taken refuge in pouring out a second cup of coffee for himself and hidden his face in the cup. His lush hair had fallen forward and she was irresistibly reminded of her first sight of him. Warmth slid through her veins. She wanted to put her arms about him and hug him tight. She wanted to show him he was not alone, that someone cared. That she cared.

Then he set the cup down and the vulture look was back. That alienating, distant look of internal hunger. She had to look away, beset by a cruel sense of hopelessness. She picked up her own cup and found it empty.

"Would you give me more coffee, if you please, Mr Degarre?" Aware her tone was cool, she seized another roll and began to butter it as he rose and poured coffee for her, his hand distressfully unsteady. Silvestre tried for a warmer note. "Can you see any preserve on the table?"

His glance matched hers, searching. But Swarland intervened, reaching for the hand bell.

"I can ring for some, ma'am."

"No matter. Don't trouble."

But the poet's fingers set a pot down by her plate. "Honey, I think."

He sounded more normal and she dared to glance up with a tiny smile. "Thank you, that will be perfect." She did not really want anything, but she made a play of buttering the roll and filling the halves with the thick spread of honey.

Swarland rose. "If you will excuse me, ma'am, I will go and check the conditions. Pray remain here until I am able to advise you, if you will be so good."

Silvestre agreed to it and bit into the roll. The sweetness was cloying but satisfying and she ate with relish, hardly daring to look at Joss. He had pushed his plate away and was applying himself assiduously to his coffee. Silvestre cleared her throat. "This is delicious. You should try some."

"I don't eat sweet things as a rule."

A wave of irritation threw her into speech. "Well, you ought to. It might help to sweeten your disposition." The instant the words were out of her mouth, she could have bitten off her tongue. At once, she retracted. "I didn't mean that. Forgive me."

He looked as if she had slapped him. "You did mean it. Why not? You read me aright."

She drew an unsteady breath and set down the half-bitten piece of roll. "You keep saying you prefer my bite, but you flinch when I say horrid things of you. And it's not true. You can be perfectly amiable when you choose."

"I don't choose often. As you've noticed."

"I have, sir, and it was the certainty I could do nothing to appease this dreadful bent to woe of yours that caused me to lose all sense of camaraderie the last time. I am not an unfriendly person, Mr Degarre. It is not in my nature to withdraw into a despairing heap. That is my father's province, if you wish to know, and I have no desire to emulate him. So pray do not look to me to aid you in turning into a horrid creature who behaves like a bear with a thorn in his paw!"

She stopped, aghast at her own outburst. He sat blinking under the hail of words, as if he was ready to flinch from a whirling flail.

Silvestre let out a sighing breath, dumped her elbows on the table and sank her head in her hands, muttering a curse. In a moment, she heard Joss clearing his throat and sat up in a bang, meeting his gaze with only half-conscious challenge.

"Well, sir?"

He spread his hands, a rueful look creeping into his face. "What can I say? Any apology appears superfluous."

Frustration leapt in Silvestre's breast. "I don't want an apology, Joss!"

"What, then?" He sounded bemused, altogether uncertain, like a colted youth on the threshold of life, rather than the mature man he was.

A rush of warmth superseded everything else and Silvestre let out a conscious laugh. "I don't know. I just wish … I wish you would not close down in the way you do, shut me out. I want to be friends, Joss. Is that so impossible?"

His lip twisted. "I am hardly adept at friendship, especially with a female."

"But you have friends? Surely you must have someone."

"One or two. Stanford Wingley. Did you meet him? We were up at the university together and have remained close. Aubrey too."

"Who is Aubrey?"

"One of my brothers. He is next in age and in the military. We forged an alliance of sorts in childhood."

She embraced these snippets with eagerness. "Like my twin and I, perhaps? What of your other brothers? Your sisters?"

He shrugged. "I see little of them, though I get on well enough with Peregrine and Rupert when we meet. I can't abide Tristan, and my elder sister can't abide me. The other girls were too much my junior."

She drew a determined breath and held out a hand. "Then it is high time you learned to be friends with a female. This one, if you will. Is it agreed?"

A sheepish sort of grin appeared as he took the hand, his grip firm. "It appears I have little choice — Silve." His brows snapped together and he released her fingers. "No, that does not work."

Disappointment flooded in. "You mean you won't be friends?"

He wafted a quick hand. "Not that. *Silve*. It doesn't suit you. It doesn't feel right. I think I will stick with Tyro."

She was curiously touched. That he should prefer his own name for her suggested something more than mere liking. No, she was getting ahead of herself. She presumed too much. But at least he was willing to attempt a cosier relationship. Even if she had forced it upon him. She smiled. "That is settled, then."

Joss made a face. "Is it? You do realise I will fall from grace in an instant, I hope. I fear my tendency to gloom is ingrained. My mother was wont to complain of it even in my youth."

Silvestre laughed. "Well, but I have licence to tease you out of it since we are to be friends."

That amused smile at last appeared. "Or subject me to a bear-garden jaw. Though you cannot hope to rival my father, however comprehensive your indictment of my character."

A dart pierced her. How he must have suffered! Impulse seized her tongue. "I have no quarrel with your character. Only with not being permitted to bring light into your darkness."

An odd sort of hunger lent intensity to his eyes and his tone dropped. "That you have already done, Tyro."

To her combined astonishment and delight, he groped for her hand, brought it to his lips, and dropped a chaste kiss upon her fingers. He released her hand at once, but the touch of his lips had sent a spark zinging down her veins. She knew not what to say or do, for the impulse of her heart dictated what she could not, must not, dare not do.

The opening of the door spelled rescue as Swarland came back into the room.

"The snow is lying too thick. Tumby thinks we would do better to remain here today."

# CHAPTER FOURTEEN

The walk was an oddly mutual idea, though entirely separate at the start. The tyro had vanished to her chamber after breakfast, leaving Joss both dismayed and anxious. Had he presumed too far? He had succumbed to the impulse of the moment and could not sufficiently regret it. When the waiter came in to remove the debris of the meal, he retired to his own room, there to prowl for a time and gaze resentfully out at the white world.

He ought to set to work. He could do so in here. Better than the parlour, even though the fire had almost died. He was used to the cold, though he had invariably repaired to Catterlen's to write. The fellow never disturbed him in his corner booth, merely providing fresh coffee at intervals and even discouraging anyone from approaching him. He had become a fixture there and the familiarity enabled him to compose without restraint.

But now even the thought of composition was anathema. How could he think, bury himself in the moment, when his stubborn mind persisted in presenting him with images of the tyro? This was what came of allowing himself to be beguiled by a petticoat.

He dug into his portmanteau for his scribbling pocketbook, recipient of the pencilled snippets that came to him as he wrestled with the beginnings of a new project. He flicked the pages, finding little to energise his muse.

Shakespeare, Shakespeare. He would need to consult a copy of his works. No doubt Charlton had a set. He possessed few books himself, relying upon the circulating libraries for his reading.

He took a stub of pencil from his pocket and spent a fruitless few minutes tapping it against a fresh page, as empty of scribble as his head. Frustration seized him and he hurled the pocketbook across the room. The pencil followed it.

Infuriating. He could not work like this. The muse must wait for Devenal. Once he was settled there, he ought to be able to find it in him to delve into the store of words that plagued him day and night when he was in the throes of composition. Not now.

He went to the window and inspected the snowy landscape. His room was on a corner near the entrance arch and beyond the yard he could see a field of sorts. The urge to escape overtook him.

Retrieving his pocketbook and the pencil, which had rolled under the washstand, he shoved them into his pocket and hunted for his greatcoat and hat, thrown off all anyhow when he'd come in last night to prepare for dinner. He added a scarf to his ensemble, pulled on his gloves and exited the room.

Halfway along the gallery he spied Miss Latimer, similarly bundled up in the furred pelisse, but without her cloak. Instinct took over and he called. "You are going out, ma'am?"

She swung about, staring at him from under her bonnet. "Oh! I thought you were working."

He went towards her, frowning. "You did not propose to walk out by yourself, I hope?"

She raised her brows, a trifle of haughtiness in her aspect. "Why should I not? We are not in the metropolis. I have no need to observe the proprieties here."

One of her belligerent moods? He did not propose to argue the point. "I'll come with you."

She eyed him, her head tipping to one side. "Just like that? No request? No, would you care to walk with me, Miss Latimer?"

Amusement took him. He bowed with an exaggerated air. "Would you care to walk with me, Miss Latimer?"

The twinkle was in her eye. "Why, I should be delighted, Mr Degarre. Thank you for asking."

He had to laugh. "Mischief-maker! Shall we go?"

She smiled and turned to trip along the gallery. "How fortunate we both had the same idea."

"I doubt it. Mine was merely to escape a futile effort to set to work."

"On your poetry? I thought you might seize the chance." She threw a glance over her shoulder as she hesitated at the top of the stairs leading down to the hallway. "I, on the other hand, merely wish to make footprints in the snow."

He stopped short. "Make footprints in the snow?"

"Yes. Have you never done so?"

"As a boy, perhaps."

"There you are, then. There is nothing more pleasurable than revisiting one's childhood. Come along, Friend. This will form a first lesson in your re-education." With a giggle and a naughty look, she started down the stairs.

His heart lightened as he followed. "My re-education to what, pray?"

"Need you ask? To re-joining the human race."

Mischievous laughter floated up the stairs as she ran the rest of the way. Joss hardly knew whether to be insulted or elated. The latter won and he joined her in the hall where she waited by the door. He opened it for her. "Lead on, Tyro. I am all eagerness for my lesson."

The yard was busy with a coach that had just come in, its wheels caked with dirty ice-packed snow, the horses blowing steam and restless as ostlers released them from the discomfort of their harnesses and hastened them to warm stables.

"Someone thought to brave the weather," Miss Latimer observed as he steered a path through hurrying servants, shifting trunks and bandboxes into the inn.

"No sign of the passengers now, though," Joss returned.

"If they have any sense, they will be warming themselves before a roaring fire."

"Unlike you."

She glanced at him. "I've not been freezing to death in a coach." She paused as they came through the archway and Joss halted perforce. "Which way?"

He pulled her in the direction of the open country he had glimpsed through the window. "Fields this way. You need fresh snow if you want to make footprints."

She laughed, turning her face to the skies. "Well, I don't want it too fresh, I thank you. It looks too clear to start again, don't you think?"

He made no answer, suddenly wishful that it might snow again, if only to keep her in his vicinity a little longer. This freedom would not come again once they were ensconced at Devenal. "Let's find this field, Tyro."

Within a few moments, he faced a pristine stretch of white and halted at its edge. It was banked with snow-laden trees on the far side and bordered with hedgerows. Beyond, a rolling vista suggested cultivated land, dotted with intermittent dwellings.

The tyro released his arm and, with a crow of delight, lifted the skirts of her pelisse and stomped out into the field, her boots trailing an instant pattern of prints.

Joss watched them appear, smiling at her evident enjoyment of the childish game. She made a wide circle and then turned, crossing it in a diagonal sweep. Halting, she raised a glowing countenance to look across at him.

"Come, Joss! You are not allowed to stand there observing, you know. Follow me!"

Infected by her enthusiasm, he set out in pursuit, making a second set of prints alongside hers as he recreated her path. She pointed at his larger prints, gurgling like a child.

"See! Catch me if you can!"

With which, she set off again, faster, jumping in a criss-cross pattern, making swirls, and dancing across the snow in a fashion he could not hope to emulate. He followed in a straighter path, making his prints cross hers but careful not to spoil them. The creative side of him could not but rise and he began to play with the patterns as she made them, leaping from place to place as if he doodled on a massive canvas. He heard her laughter, though he became too engrossed in building on her patterns to look up. Until her sudden cry of alarm jerked him out of the game.

Freezing in the middle of a twirl, Joss followed the sound, his gaze catching on the coated figure flailing right at the edge of the field. Before he could react, it tumbled, sliding out of sight.

"Silvestre!" Thought fled. Instinct sent Joss thumping across the snow in the direction of her fall. He could hear grunts and movement and a fleeting panic raced through him as he tried to hasten, the thick snow a hindrance now. "Silvestre, are you hurt?" He yelled it just as he gained the edge, perforce slowing as he too found himself unbalanced at the top of an unexpected slope. He saw her struggling up below, but had no words as his foot began to slip from beneath him.

"Look out!"

He heard the shriek, but it was too late. Next instant, he was falling, limbs out of his control. She was half up, directly in his path, and it flashed through his head there was nothing he could do to prevent a collision.

The impact took the breath from his lungs and he heard her protesting grunt as his body flattened her to the ground. For a moment, he was incapable of moving as he fought to drag a breath. He felt the wriggle beneath him and instinct made him use his arms to lift off slightly. His breath returned in a whoosh and he blew it out, gratefully sucking in air again.

He became aware the body underneath was not moving and his gaze focused on the tyro's face. Her bonnet was half off and askew. She was watching him, anxiety in her gaze.

"Better? For a horrid moment, I thought you wouldn't breathe again."

Only then did he take in that her hands were on his shoulders. The last few seconds replayed in his head, re-orienting. He had not wholly shoved himself up. She had pushed him free to give him room to breathe. "Thank you," he gasped. "Quick thinking."

A little smile curved her mouth. "I couldn't very well have you dying on me, Vulture."

The appellation barely registered as anxiety overtook him. "Are *you* all right? Did I hurt you?"

"You squashed me flat."

It came to him he was lying at full stretch, his limbs covering hers. The inevitable reaction took him unawares, heating his blood.

He saw her eyes widen. Hell and damnation! Could she feel it? With an effort he threw himself off her and fell back, his breath shortening all over again, though the cause had altered.

He willed the disturbance down, helped by the cold at his back as it began to seep through his great-coat.

"Joss?"

It was hesitant, a note of uncertainty within it that threw his memory back into the breach at Lady Whittlesford's. He could not let it hurt her again. "Don't fret, Tyro. If you are unhurt, all is well."

Her face appeared above him as she raised herself on her elbow. "I'm an idiot, I'm sorry. I should have been more careful."

He moved his head in a negative motion. "You were having fun." He caught her gaze and held it. "So was I."

Her smile lit up the universe. He could not have looked away to save his life. She leaned down. He felt her lips brush his cheek, a butterfly kiss.

Then she was pushing herself up off the ground, rolling her shoulders, straightening her bonnet and brushing the snow off her pelisse.

Joss watched her, mesmerised, his cheek pulsing where she had kissed him, his world falling apart about his head.

She looked down at him, a laugh in her face. "Are you planning to take up residence there?" She held out a hand. "Get up, lazy bones!"

He took the hand. The impulse to pull her down to him again was strong. To drag her into his arms and tumble her right here in the snow. To make her his forever.

She tugged at his hand. "Joss! Up you come, you brooding poet, you!"

She thought he was brooding? Better so. Reality crashed in on him and the fleeting dream was gone. He let go of her hand and made a business of shoving himself to his feet.

"Gracious, only look at you!"

She began brushing at his clothes. Too much like a loving helpmeet. He thrust away. "I can manage." He knew he sounded gruff. He saw the surprise in her face, the disappearing pleasure. Disappointment? He struggled for a semblance of normality. "Thank you. Are you…?" He cleared his throat and tried again. "Are you sure you are not hurt?"

"Me? I am perfectly fine, I thank you, sir." Her smile looked mechanical. It did not reach her eyes. She turned, contemplating the slope that had tripped them up. "The difficulty now, Mr Degarre, is how to get back up."

Mr Degarre? Oh, Lord, what had he done? A niggle at the back of his mind sneaked into his consciousness. Shock threw him into instant speech, indignant. "Vulture? *Vulture?*"

She swung back, her mouth dropping open. "Oh, no! I didn't actually say it, did I?" An embarrassed giggle came, but defiance entered her voice. "Well, it's your own fault! If you weren't so … oh, you know why, you horrid man! You're just like a bird of prey. And why you must needs turn surly all over again, I really don't know."

He was still struggling with the nickname she had bestowed upon him and hardly heard what she said. "Vulture! That's your secret name for me?"

"Yes, it is! Well, it's hardly secret now, is it?"

He slapped at the remaining snow on his garments, feeling decidedly aggrieved. Vulture, she called him. That was how she thought of him. After what had just passed?

The thought brought him up short. She had no notion what had passed. Within him. She was still in the frame of friendship, as she insisted. That kiss was chaste, innocent. She had no notion of its effect upon him.

"We'll have to try and find a way around the side. I doubt we'll be able to climb back up."

He forced his mind out of his preoccupation. But the word kicked in his breast and lodged there. Vulture. He gave his attention to the problem confronting them and looked from one side to the other. "We've fallen into a field gap. Like a ha-ha, to keep them separated. We should be able to find a way back if we follow the ridge."

"This way, then."

She set off, stomping gamely through the snow, but without the lightness, the enjoyment she had exhibited before. Her pleasure in the expedition had evaporated. He had seen to that. Remorse gripped him, but a warning voice at the back of his mind spoke of common sense and caution. He had started down a road he could not travel. The more he allowed her to light his life, the further he would go. In an impossible direction. Better she thought him irreclaimable. A vulture indeed.

Yet a secret yearning would not be entirely suppressed as he set off in her wake.

# CHAPTER FIFTEEN

Determined to keep from following the wretched vulture's example, Silvestre took her pristine notebook to the parlour, along with her pens and a small bottle of ink in a wooden box. A travelling set Mama had bestowed upon her by way of an early Christmas gift.

"There will be ink and pens enough at Devenal, I am persuaded, but I know how you value your independence, my love. I dare say Hetty will persuade Charlton to supply you with all the paper you need."

But the notebook, the largest Silvestre could find, with marbled covers and clean, crisp pages, had been her one extravagance in the metropolis. She had furnished it with a folded sheet of blotting paper, fondly imagining the inked words appearing that would fashion a new story. What better time to start?

She shed her outer garments, unearthed the shawl from the valise that Martha had re-packed with her overnight requirements — along with the precious writing materials — and made her way to the private parlour, where she found Swarland in possession.

He rose from the table at her entrance, where he was himself busy with a notebook and pencil, and flicked a glance at what she carried, his eyes then rising to her face. "Did you have a pleasant walk, ma'am? The exertion has brightened your cheeks, I see."

"Has it? It is chill out, but not too cold." She set down her burdens. "How did you know we had gone out?"

He coughed. "I saw you and his lordship from my window." He set a chair for her, gesturing towards his notebook. "Accounts, ma'am. I keep a record for their graces, though it is his grace's secretary who peruses these things."

"Oh, yes, I believe I encountered Mr Hathersage at Whisley Park in the summer." Silvestre opened her box and began to set out her accoutrements. "You will not object if I set to work myself?"

His brows rose. "Work, ma'am?"

"I am a novelist."

Swarland's jaw visibly dropped and Silvestre felt a rush of pride. She had never before announced her new calling. It felt inordinately gratifying. She had a life, a purpose of her own. She needed no approval, no friend, temperamental or otherwise. Hooray for Aspatria Glasson! She had it right. No female ought to be depending upon a man's interest. She was self-reliant. She was to be published.

In her mind's eye she thumbed her nose at the image of the vulture and found it immensely satisfying.

"I confess myself impressed, Miss Latimer. I had no notion."

Her innate honesty forced Silvestre to reveal the truth. "Well, that is putting it a little high, perhaps. I have penned one novel. No, two. But the first we may discount. Beardsley & Beak are to publish the second." She found herself quite unable to prevent the note of pride entering her voice.

The steward was shaking his head in a bemused fashion. "It is a most praiseworthy achievement, ma'am." Then his brows drew together. "Ah, this is how you come to be acquainted with his lordship?"

"Just so." His gloom-ridden, brooding lordship, yes. "I was fortunate to be introduced into a literary salon and met several extraordinarily interesting writers." Yet none as interesting, as intriguing, as utterly infuriating as the loathsome Degarre.

"Then you share a common interest."

"Indeed." About as much shared interest as a duck and an elephant. No two people could be more dissimilar. Foolish of her to suppose for an instant she could be friends with a reclusive poet.

"Well, I had best allow you to pursue your labours, ma'am."

Silvestre sighed. "I have yet to begin, sir. At this present, I have no notion what I am going to write next."

He eyed her opened notebook. "Perhaps this enforced interlude may allow you the leisure for inspiration?"

She had picked up one of the pens, but set it down again, leaning back in her chair. "At this moment, I had rather inspire a waiter to bring us coffee. Do you think —?"

"On the instant, Miss Latimer." The steward at once rose to seize the hand bell which had been set on the mantel, and rang it with vigour.

She summoned a smile. "Thank you." She wafted a hand towards his abandoned notebook. "But I am disturbing your labours, sir. Pray do not feel obliged to entertain me." A mirthless laugh escaped her. "If I sit and think for a bit, there is no saying what may not come into my mind."

Not that she had the slightest hope of anything useful, so full was it of the aborted effort to lighten a certain gentleman's tendency to dwell in the darkness of his own mind. She had very nearly succeeded too. Joss had even said he was enjoying the game. That unfortunate fall! She could not begin to imagine what had set him off again.

He had been altogether free and bright, for oh, so short a time. Then came the tangle of limbs, his lost breath. She truly had been frightened for an instant. Then she had let slip the secret name for him. Was that it? Did he deem himself insulted? Oh, why try to fathom his torturous mind? Twisting this way and that. Too obscure for words. Words, yes. He might as well be Shakespeare's plays incarnate, he was quite as deep and impenetrable. The Fossebridge dame had said as much of his poetry. She had as well have spoken of layers with regard to the man himself. One could scarcely hope to dig out the core of him, however many scrapings one attempted.

She became aware of the waiter who had answered the bell and heard the steward requesting a pot of coffee to be brought. Heavens, she had been miles away from trying for inspiration. She sat up, picking up her pen again and absently stroking its feathered end against her cheek. Perhaps she could turn her unruly thoughts to advantage. Write of just such a man. Impenetrable. Brooding. A very vulture inhabiting some lonely castle. Ah, the library of a lonely castle, no? Dark and drear, with no vestige of light but a single candle and no company but the scratching of a mouse in the wainscoting.

With a puff of exasperated breath, she flung down the pen again. That would not do at all. She was no longer a writer in the gothic mode. If anything, she must write of an ordinary man. Unfortunately, the only male in her head was so far from ordinary he had succeeded in driving every other possibility out of her brain.

The click of the door latch brought her head round and her heart sank. The poet himself had entered the room. Her pulse pattered into life and she grabbed up the maltreated pen, staring fixedly at the empty page of her notebook.

Swarland, who had returned to his accounts, was once again on his feet. "Ah, you join us just in time, my lord. I have ordered coffee."

Out of the corner of her eye, Silvestre saw Joss's boots moving towards the table. His voice came, subdued. "Thank you, that will be welcome."

He pulled out a chair and Silvestre forced herself to look up. He did not meet her eyes, instead extracting a small notebook and pencil from his pocket and setting it down.

"I had better make an effort myself, since you are both so industrious."

She brushed the feathered end of the pen across her paper. "Without much result on my part. Mr Swarland is showing the way." Aware her tone was flat, not to say cold, she kept her eyes on the steward's neat figures as Joss took his seat. She ought to make more of an effort. He was at least trying for a change. But the consciousness of the last moments of that ill-fated walk rose uncomfortably to the surface. The escape from the second field had been accomplished with the minimum of words exchanged, and they had walked back to the inn in virtual silence. She had been polite to a fault, he morose.

Only one thing had been said with reference to the blight of the day. As they reached the top of the stairs, just before he turned for his own chamber, Joss had caught her arm. "I did warn you I would lapse fast."

Then he had let her go and walked quickly down the gallery, disappearing through a far doorway and leaving her prey to the well of disappointment that had driven her to mentally abuse him and resolve to attack her writing.

The steward returned to his task and Silvestre found herself listening to the sound of his pencil, a soft scratching. The odd crackle came from the fire and an occasional smatter of indistinguishable talk somewhere outside or a clatter that spoke of normal life continuing beyond the confines of the awkward atmosphere in the parlour.

Normality. Ordinariness. This was supposed to be her forte now. But the point of *Emmeline* was the shattering of normality. The entrance into that ordinary life of extraordinary misfortune. Or, no. What happened around her heroine was the sort of occurrence that many experienced. Only not all at once.

A clink nearer at hand jerked her out of reverie. She looked as of instinct to the poet. He had set down a small sheath and she at once spied the little knife in his fingers. He was paring the point of a pencil, letting the shavings fall into the small open notebook before him.

Caught by the motion of those fingers, she sat riveted. She had not before noticed how slim they were, how long, how delicately they moved, dextrous and agile, like the legs of a spider. Deft they were in the doing, but still oddly awkward in motion, as was everything about him.

The point presumably exposed to his satisfaction, she watched him slide the sheath over his knife and slip it into his pocket. With care, those fascinating fingers lifted the notebook, coaxing the shavings to the central dip. His eyes held on the debris as he rose from his chair, pushing it back as he did so. Only then did he glance up.

Silvestre caught his gaze and saw him jerk. The shavings jumped from the page and scattered across the table.

At once contrite, she leapt from her chair, leaning to sweep them up. "I startled you. I'm sorry."

The steward, who had uttered a hasty exclamation, also rose to help. "If you will hold the notebook close to the table, my lord."

To Silvestre's consternation, Joss's colour was high, embarrassment flooding his face as he set the book in a suitable position to receive the shavings, of which Swarland now took charge. "Don't trouble, ma'am. I will manage it."

She left the little pile she'd made and sat down again, feeling perfectly foul. If she had not been watching him so closely, it would not have happened. Why could she not let him alone? It was all he wanted, clearly.

The shavings gathered up, Joss crossed to the fire and she watched him shake them off to join the ashy wood, still burning though the flames had died down. The steward was flicking at residue on the table with a pocket handkerchief.

"There, that is sufficient, I think."

Silvestre could see the poet blowing on his pages to rid them of any leftover specks. She felt horridly guilty, though she was not responsible for his jumping nerves. Or was she? She had not been friendly towards him. The contrary. Had she not pledged to be his friend? If he had lapsed, she had fallen at the first hurdle. It was her fault.

Before she could think how to make amends, the waiter re-entered on his knock, bearing a tray with the makings of coffee. Silvestre infused an amicable tone into her voice as Swarland immediately took charge to make room for the tray on the table.

"Ah, this will be welcome, won't it, Joss?"

He was still standing by the fireplace and looked sharply round, surprise in his face. A muscle shifted in his cheek. He cleared his throat in the way Silvestre had noticed he did when he was ill at ease. "Very much. Yes."

Dismissing the waiter, the steward took it upon himself to dispense the beverage. To Silvestre's relief, the business of discovering and supplying wants afforded an opportunity to dissipate the discomforts caused by the contretemps with the pencil shavings.

"Just what we need on a day like this," she said as she took her cup. With deliberation, she smiled at Joss as he resumed his seat. "I'm hoping I may derive inspiration somehow while we are thus disengaged." She gestured to the notebook he had laid down, now firmly closed. "Are you any further forward?"

"Afraid not."

Those long fingers curled around his cup, as if he sought to derive both warmth and courage from it. She felt his hesitance and the pull of compassion he engendered in her came flooding back. She spoke without thinking, putting out a hand towards the notebook. "May I see?"

One hand let go of the cup and slammed onto the notebook, pulling it closer to him. "God, no!"

Consternation seized her. "I should not have asked. It is too private, is it not?"

He shook his head with vehemence, still possessively keeping the book under his hand. "It's scribblings. Nothing of value. Snatches. Ideas. My mind at work, no more."

In a bid to undo her error, Silvestre tapped at her own notebook. "Well, it's more than I may boast. See? I've written nothing at all. Nor have I the remotest conjecture of what I may end up writing."

He gave that faint smile, at last releasing his notebook and setting the hand back around his cup. "How should you? These things are not premeditated."

"I dare say you are right. Indeed, when I think of how *Emmeline* came to me, I know you are."

Here Swarland, who had evidently been listening as he drank, took a more cogent interest. "*Emmeline?* That is your novel, ma'am?"

"It is the name of my heroine. I am apt to think of it as that rather than the title."

"What is the story, Miss Latimer?"

It was her turn to be embarrassed. She had not spoken about it in front of Joss before. He had shown no interest in her book beyond the exigencies of publication and she squirmed at speaking of it. She kept it brief and to the point. "I doubt it will be of interest to a male reader, sir. It's just about an ordinary girl who sustains severe changes in her life and must learn to cope."

The steward did not appear to find the plot of particular interest. "Well, I must congratulate you, ma'am, and hope for its success."

"Thank you. To be truthful, I cannot believe anyone will find it of unusual merit, but Mr Beak likes it and Mr Christy believes it is different enough to catch a changing public taste."

The steward acknowledged this with a bow of his head. "I imagine her grace the duchess will be delighted for you."

Silvestre merely smiled. She was scarcely going to reveal her hope of using Hetty's position to help build the list of subscribers. She was glad to see Swarland retire into his coffee again, his eyes turning back upon his accounts. With relief, she looked at the poet again, her tone rueful. "The trouble is I am now faced with the prospect of writing another, and I have no clue where to begin. Can you not advise me? You have produced several works, have you not? How do you follow one upon the other?"

His brows drew together. "I don't know. It happens. A trigger of some kind." A corner of his mouth twitched. "You don't know it, but you sprang the latest."

A disbelieving laugh escaped her. "No, did I? I dare not suppose it for an instant." At last a smile came. She rejoiced, her veins singing.

"You may. You spoke of Shakespeare. It set me thinking. It is but a germ as yet. I have to re-read his sonnets."

She laughed. "Well, that is not the penance that one suffers reading some of his plays."

"I must do that too. You find them difficult?"

"Not all. The histories are obscure to me, for I am ill acquainted with the background. I cannot place the references." She laughed, a trifle self-conscious. "Oh, but I am giving myself more than my due. All his plays have flummoxed me at points. I have often been obliged to ask my father's aid."

A look of interest came into his face, the keenest she had ever seen. "Yes, you said he sees the Bard in the light of a deity. He is no doubt familiar with all his works?"

"Every single one, I believe, though Papa dismisses one or two as lesser efforts. But his understanding is superior. Papa is quite a scholar, you must know, and he leaves me standing."

Joss was sipping at his coffee, but he set the cup down. "Don't denigrate your understanding. You are young yet. Your father has had time to acquire his erudition."

She shrugged. "Perhaps. Though I cannot hope to aspire to his level. Any more than I expect to emulate any one of the literary giants I have been privileged to meet — including the great Gausselin Degarre." She smiled on the words, unable to withstand a teasing note.

A lopsided grin attacked his mouth. "Don't think I'm flattered, Tyro. I know well you mean mischief."

"Not at all. Papa was delighted to know I had met you, though he did caution me not to give you the impression he thinks your poetry quite on a par with Shakespeare's genius."

"Ha! So much for that heady comparison."

She twinkled at him. "Well, but he acknowledges you have a similar knack of delineating the human condition. A statement I have yet to verify."

He eyed her with clear suspicion. "Unlikely you will, since you did not listen when you had the chance."

She lifted her chin. "I prefer reading to listening, sir."

"What you mean is, you prefer scourging the manner of my reading to making any attempt to hear the words."

She could not repress a sheepish sort of smile. "Well, you shall be the first to hear my opinion when I have the chance to read the volume Papa lent me."

He threw up a hand. "Spare me! I have no desire to hear you vilifying my work."

"Why should I vilify it? I am more likely to find it hard to understand. Mrs Fossebridge says it is very layered and one has to dig down deep to find the meaning."

"Does she indeed? Must I thank her?"

She laughed. "I suspect she is not nearly as well-read as she would have us think. But she advised me not to begin with one of your epic works."

"I would not have you begin at all!"

This struck her with an unaccountable pang. "Why not, Joss?"

He shifted his shoulders in evident discomfort. He cast a quick glance at Swarland, who appeared to be frowning over his accounts. Joss's tone lowered. "I couldn't bear it if you hated it."

A little spurt of elation rose in her bosom. He did care. She swallowed. "By the same token, I might wish you won't ever read my novel."

His eyes met hers. Something at the back of them caught at her senses and her breath became trapped in her chest. Then he broke the contact, picked up his cup and drank deeply. Silvestre felt abruptly alienated and her pulse went awry.

Why must he do that? Why could he not let it be? Nurture it. Allow whatever this was between them to grow. In vain she struggled not to let the seed of resentment flourish. It was becoming all too familiar. Frustration seized her. If only Swarland were not in the room!

As if on cue, the steward set down his cup and closed his notebook, rising from his chair. "I fear I must leave you in his lordship's care for a space, ma'am. I have a number of matters to discuss with the staff, such as they are. We must look at the prospect of resuming our journey upon the morrow."

She gave an automatic response from the store of courtesies that accompanied her upbringing. The realisation her idle wish was granted superseded all else and she was horribly conscious of Joss having withdrawn again.

The moment the door shut behind the steward, impulse threw her into speech. "Joss, pray don't poker up!"

The vulture look was pronounced, and he spoke with stiffness. "I'm not."

"Then talk to me! Tell me about your poetry. Please. I am going to read it, but I want to hear what you say of it."

He seemed to shrink away for a brief instant. Then he put out a hand for the coffee pot. "More for you?"

"Yes, if you please. But pray don't fob me off with coffee, Joss."

He did not speak while he poured with evident care, though his hand shook. Silvestre was tempted to retract, to tell him he need say nothing if he did not wish it, but she wanted so badly to be close to him, to hear him talk with ease as he had before, to get under his skin if she could.

When he had supplied her with cream and sugar, he turned to his own replenished black brew and seemed to study it. "What do you wish to know?"

For a moment she was nonplussed. What did she wish to know, specifically? She fell back upon the earlier subject. "Tell me of this notion you have about Shakespeare. If I inspired it, albeit unintentionally, I have a right to ask that at least, have I not?"

He gave her a straight look. "You have a right to ask anything you wish. Just as I have a right to refuse to answer."

A spurt of rage seized her and she saw him flinch. Had it shown in her eyes? She curbed it, breathing slow and even, in and out, until it subsided. She sipped her coffee, afraid to open her mouth for fear of what she might say.

His voice came low. "Forgive me. I did not mean to imply I would not answer."

"Just that you reserve the right to refuse? Well, I suppose that is fair."

A heavy sigh came. "Oh, Tyro…"

She said nothing, feeling all the disappointment at the shattering of the better mood all over again.

"I'm trying, Silvestre."

She could not withstand a wry look. "Very."

His smile showed amusement but there was hurt in his eyes too.

She melted, putting out a hand towards him. "Oh, Joss, you are such hard work, did you know?"

He gripped her hand. "Yes, I know."

His fingers opened abruptly, releasing her. She watched them pick up the cup, recalling her earlier fascination. "You have artistic fingers," she said on impulse. "Slender and long. Delicate. It's like watching a spider move."

He set down his cup in haste, a choked laugh sputtering out. "Fiend! As if vulture is not bad enough! Now I have spider fingers?"

Silvestre beamed at him. "Oh, I can conjure even worse comparisons, if you wish for it."

"I thank you, I am content." But the grim expression left him at once, and he eyed her with that look of relaxed amusement she had not seen in a while. "I ought to give you just what you deserve, you atrocious female."

"Oh, and what is that, sir?"

"I shall not demean you by putting it into words. Besides, I do have some gentlemanly instincts."

A giggle escaped her. "I shan't provoke you into revealing them, never fear."

"Thank the Lord. I wouldn't want to jeopardise our friendship by treating you with the respect courtesy demands."

She broke into laughter. "There, now. I may tease you with impunity."

He smiled but refused the bait. Feeling considerably cheered, not to say triumphant, Silvestre forbore to press the point, instead sipping at her coffee.

After a short silence, Joss set down his cup again. "I am intrigued by how far Shakespeare reveals his inner self in the sonnets. I have some notion of discovering him, of then revealing him in a work that purports to show how his character comes through in the plays."

She was startled, both by the idea and his sudden confidence. She was privileged, she was certain of it. She would swear he did not reveal this sort of intention to anyone, other than his intimates. Who were pitifully few. She wanted to respond in kind, without giving weight to her gratification. "An interesting notion. Is that what drives you? Looking for the inner being?"

He frowned, seeming now preoccupied. "On this occasion. It is not always thus. Sometimes, most times, I think, it's like an itch. I don't know what it means, but it troubles me until I begin to set it out in words. That's when I struggle."

"For the words?"

"For the meaning. For the life that is burning in my gut, begging to be freed. It's painful. Until it begins to flower and grow. If I'm lucky, it soars. If not, it feels like … like a gladiatorial battle, a struggle to the death." He looked at her and Silvestre could see the burn, like a simmering volcano. "When it won't come out, I feel as if it's going to kill me. It eats at my vitals like a cancer. Unendurable. Almost." He shook himself, as if he sought to throw off the reminder of his sufferings. His mouth twisted. "I don't know why I told you."

Silvestre, touched to her core, could not help the husky note. "I am glad you did. Thank you."

The grimace became more pronounced, the vulture look total. "For what? Burdening you with my poison?"

"For trusting me. For giving of yourself." She wanted to say she understood his passion now, a little more at least. But she was afraid of driving him to close in again. The less she said the better. Especially because she felt in danger of saying all too much with her unruly tongue. Of saying what was in her heart. She tried for a rallying note. "Well, Mr Degarre, I am very glad I did not choose poetry."

A wry laugh came. "You may well be. Will you think it fanciful and pretentious if I say I did not choose poetry? It rather chose me."

She gave him her warmest smile. "I would say it was pretentious if you were Pelham Ferneux. But from Gausselin Degarre, no."

He made a dismissive sound. "You've not read him. You can't know if the fruits of his agonies are worth the pain."

"They are to him, and that is all that matters."

His brows rose. "On occasion, Tyro, you sound too good to be true."

"But I believe that. You would not put yourself through it if it gave you no satisfaction at all."

He gave her a measuring look. "Did you derive satisfaction through this *Emmeline* of yours?"

She considered the question, dipping her head on one side. "Do you know, I fear I did not. It was indeed a painful process, though I cannot claim to rival your torturous struggles. And when it was finished, anxiety took over. I dared not believe it was of any great worth, and it was with trepidation that I sent it to Beardsley & Beak. A far cry from the hopes I cherished for my first story. It was in the gothic mode and I wrote it with my tongue firmly in my cheek, to be honest."

"Ah, you were emulating Greta?"

She laughed, throwing up a hand. "Guilty! Though mine was much more restrained. But I didn't care much when it was rejected. Had *Emmeline* been thrown back at me … oh, I would have wept buckets!"

He was regarding her with a half-smile on his face. "You need not enquire into my share of satisfaction, then, since you know it is not to be had."

Consternation seized her. "None at all?"

He bit his lip, frowning. Then a quick shift of discomfort in his shoulders. "Unfair. Yes, there is a point. When the printed volume is in my hands. When I see my words on the page. When I take up my paper knife to cut the pages. Before the critic in me rises again to bemoan the use of this word rather than that, or see a turn of phrase I might have bettered. Yes, I may say there is satisfaction there. Pride, even." A faint smile creased his mouth. "Which rises to the surface again when I must endure the opinions of the likes of Moreton Pinckney. Then you may accuse me of inordinate conceit, for an arrogance of pride overtakes me at once if I am obliged to read his damning criticisms."

Spellbound, Silvestre watched the unaccustomed animation in his face as he talked. Convinced she was hearing what few others had heard, if any. She felt all the force of the compliment. Her bosom swelled with affection, with compassion, and the desire to assuage his demons, to provide comfort where she could, lodged there in a core of unassailable determination. The vulture would not be permitted to lour over his nest, not if she had anything to do with it. She did not have to think how to respond. "I am more than ever eager to read your poems, Joss. I promise I won't judge you."

"Make no promise of the kind. You cannot help but do so."

"Well then, I won't criticise."

"In your head you will. I should hope you will. If there is any discernment in you. Which there is. I know you too well to doubt it."

She made a face. "You leave me no wriggling room at all."

He gave an admonitory shake of the head. "Don't wriggle. Be true to yourself. To your own response. Just as you must be true in your writing."

"You make a stern mentor for a tyro."

He emitted a disgusted sound. "I'm no mentor. Not yours. Not anyone's. If I say these things, it does not therefore follow you must heed them."

"But I need such advice, Joss. If I don't heed you, whom should I heed?"

"None. Heed no one. Write from what is in you, be your own judge. I am no fit model for you to follow."

"Well, if I am to be my own judge, you must let me be the judge of that."

He laughed. "*Touché!*"

Silvestre smiled briefly, but put out her hand palm up. "You have touched me deeply. Take my hand in spirit of fellowship, if you cannot hold to friend."

He laid his palm over hers, his dark eyes roving her features. "I would I might hold to more than friend. It would destroy you, Silvestre." His hand left hers and caught her cheek. A tiny, rueful smile came as his fingers stroked her skin. "I could not endure to author that sorry tale."

# CHAPTER SIXTEEN

As the coach lumbered closer to their destination, Silvestre found her thoughts thankfully turning to the anticipated pleasure of seeing her twin again. At least she had that in store. The core of discontent she carried might dissipate. To a degree. She hoped.

There had been no further opportunity for private speech with the poet and a part of her was glad of it. He could not have sent a clearer message. Or one that would have disturbed her waking hours more. As for sleep, it had been fitful, leaving her tired and as grouchy as was Joss himself.

She managed a spurious sort of surface calm, a social face, a desultory effort at innocuous conversation. Joss saw through it; she knew by his retirement into that impenetrable shell. He was incapable of maintaining the social veneer, smoothing the edges as she was trying to do. Though he did try. She must grant him the effort. But it cost him, she could see it in the vulture look. He found it hard to cope with the banal, the mundane, the ordinary.

The difficulty was, he had ruined them for Silvestre too. The glimpse he'd allowed her into his interior world gnawed at her, beckoning like the devil's messenger. At moments she felt desperate with the longing to follow him there, to be at one with the demon that drove him, or to share it enough to lessen its scourge. For Joss. That he might suffer less for her taking a part of the burden into herself.

Yet he would have none of her. Determined to bear it alone. What, did he think it must contaminate her? Did he suppose her so weak she must succumb rather than support?

Well, perhaps he was right. It was true his moodiness chafed her. He believed himself beyond redemption and he ought to know. But she had succeeded. She had chipped away a little of the ice. Only it was not enough. She was impatient. She wanted it all and she wanted it now. The more fool her. A lifetime's work? She was mad even to contemplate it. And yet … and yet…

*Come, Silvestre Latimer, this won't do.*

She had been warned off in no uncertain terms. She had compensations enough in her own expectations. She was going to see Hetty. She *would* be content.

Devenal Castle loomed out of the mist, a louring turreted monstrosity that at once struck Silvestre as utterly suited to the silent creature at her side. But the steward soon rid her of that fancy.

"Ah, you are seeing the ruin, ma'am. The present house is a little further on, just beyond the village of Ockley Par."

"Not a castle, then?"

"No, indeed, though the appellation still obtains. The Devenal who built the mansion, back in the days of Queen Anne, retained the name for the sake of tradition. There are a few turret-like appurtenances, but otherwise it is as unlike a castle as it could be."

This was soon seen to be true when the coach turned in through wrought-iron gates and entered a long and sweeping drive, at the end of which a massive structure loomed into sight. Devenal Castle proved to be a monstrosity in red brick with two huge wings jutting out to the front, to the sides of which rose a pair of octagonal towers topped with curved domes. A sprouting of chimneys took her eye, together with a distant hint of further turrets behind.

Silvestre's first thought was that she would never be able to find Joss again once he was buried somewhere in this rabbit warren. The pang this brought was swiftly superseded by a rush of feeling for her twin, mistress of all this outmoded grandeur. Poor Hetty. How in the world was she coping?

There was time for no more than a growing desire to see her sister as the coach came to a standstill and the travellers were swiftly overwhelmed with a plethora of servants. But no host or hostess.

"We were not looked for, the snow having been thicker here, I understand," Swarland told her as Silvestre hovered in the lofty hall, aware all the time of Joss holding to the background. "It appears our arrival has anticipated expectation by several days. They did not think we would get through so quickly. Someone will have gone to inform their graces. In the meantime, allow me to lead you above stairs. Ninebanks informs me her grace the duchess is in her private sitting-room. Mrs Fadmoor will inform Martha where your chamber is situated and she will see to your trunk, ma'am."

Silvestre started up a grand central staircase which divided in two at the halfway point, buoyed by the knowledge she was going to Hetty, but she halted on reaching the landing, looking back. Where was Joss?

"Mr Degarre is not joining us?"

The steward indicated the next flight up the left fork, inviting her to continue. "Ninebanks will lead Lord Joscelin to his grace the duke."

So it began… A leaden weight settled in her stomach as she followed along a confusing series of corridors, well-lit by candles in wall-sconces along the way.

This was not how she had anticipated her reunion with her twin. But then, the entire journey had been utterly unexpected with the entrance of the vulture, snow, intimacy of a sort, and the destruction of every raised hope. She thrust it all down. She was going to see Hetty in a moment, and that was all that mattered. The present reality did not admit of the joy she had hoped for, but a flitter of excitement ran through her nevertheless.

But when Swarland at last halted, in a wider corridor than any other, and knocked on a door, the voice within that bade him come in threw a choking sob into her throat.

The steward ushered her inside, uttering words she scarcely took in. "We are here at last, your grace. And here is Miss Latimer."

A domestic scene met her eyes. A pretty young woman seated in a sofa placed to catch the heat from a substantial fire, upon her lap an infant, beside her a little girl snug in the other arm, in her hands a book from which she had evidently been reading.

"Silve!"

With a leap in her heart, she heard the joyful note in Henrietta's voice and the little picture broke up. Her twin threw aside the book, released the child and rose from the sofa, thrusting the babe into the arms of a female who rushed to receive her.

"Oh, Silve, Silve, I am so happy!"

Silvestre wept with her sobbing sister as she embraced her, holding her close, all the stresses of the past few days rising up and then melting away. Laughing through her tears, she pulled back so she might look into her shorter twin's tear-drenched features. "Hetty, Hetty, you haven't changed a bit!"

Her twin hugged her again and slid her hands down to grasp Silvestre's fingers. "You have! Gracious, I believe you've grown!"

"I haven't at all. You've forgotten." She sniffed, giggling uncontrollably. "I'm quite the watering pot, though."

"Oh, how could you not be at a time like this? Oh, Silve, I am so very happy! I thought you would never get here!"

A voice piped up close by, in a childish treble. "Softy, you'll have to give her a handkerchief. She's crying fit to bust herself."

Hetty stooped over the little girl. "Not that indelicate expression, if you please, my love."

Silvestre could not help laughing. "Hetty, you sound exactly like Mama."

"No, do I? Ellie, you remember my sister Silve?"

"'Course I do. How do you do?"

The child put out a hand and Silvestre shook it with solemnity. "Very well, I thank you, Lady Ella, although I am a little tired."

That was enough to set Hetty off, clucking with concern. "Gracious, yes, you must be exhausted! Take off that pelisse, dearest, and your bonnet too, and be comfortable." She waved at the female now nursing the infant. "Gatty, pray ring the bell. Or no, let me have Pru and you may run and tell one of the footmen to bring tea at once. It will be quicker. Then come back and take the children to the nursery."

Silvestre, divesting herself of her pelisse and bonnet, understood the nurse to say it was nearly time for the children to visit their mother.

"Oh, yes, of course," said Henrietta, who had taken possession of the infant. "Ring the bell then, Gatty, and you may take the children straight away."

"Story," the infant whined.

Hetty gave her a peck on the cheek. "Not now, darling. We will finish the story another time. See, my sister is here and I want to talk to her. Silve, this is Lady Prudence."

The infant stuck a finger in her mouth and stared at Silvestre with big eyes.

"She don't like strangers," offered Lady Ella. "Only you look like Softy, so she won't mind you."

"Hello, Lady Prudence, I am very pleased to meet you."

Her elder made a scoffing sound. "You won't be soon. Pru is very demanding, Mama says."

"Ellie, what have I told you about repeating what your mama says? Besides, you mustn't be horrid about your little sister. Take her, Gatty. Now, Ellie, listen to me, if you please."

"Oh, not a lecture, Softy!"

"I'm not lecturing you, silly. I only want to remind you to behave when you go to Mama. She is not yet fully well and you must not fidget her."

Ellie grimaced and protested, but was at length persuaded to promise good behaviour before the nursemaid was allowed to remove the two girls.

Amused, Silvestre marvelled at how completely her twin had taken up the mantle of mentor to the dowager's daughters. She set down her bonnet on a convenient chair and ran a hand through her crushed locks. "Is the dowager unwell?"

"Poor Cecilia suffered a bout of influenza," said Hetty, coming to join her by the fire. "She is better now, but still keeps to her room."

"Ah, that is why you have charge of the children, I suppose."

Hetty drew her to sit on the sofa, keeping hold of her hand. "I don't have charge of them precisely, you know, but I do like to take time with them. Miss Jurby is strict with Ellie and it does not answer. Besides, Theo thinks it is good for them to be with me."

Silvestre squeezed her fingers. "Of course it is, my dearest Hetty. I remember this Cecilia of yours only too well. How do you go on with her? Has she forgiven you for marrying Theo?"

Hetty sighed. "She is resigned, I think. But she doesn't approve of me, Silve. She is forever telling me what I must do and what I must not and what is due to my position."

Hetty cast up her eyes and Silvestre laughed. "About which you care not one jot."

"Well, I would try to conform to what she says, but Theo forbids me to turn myself into a copy of Cecilia, as he phrases it. He swears he will divorce me if I dare to become like her. Moreover, I have Isobel, if I wish to emulate anyone."

"Isobel?"

"Lady Lionel. You must remember Theo's mama?"

"How could I forget?"

But her mind darted to the object consuming her deepest thoughts. Joss was here only because of Lady Lionel's interest with the duke. Had not he said his aunt had arranged his librarianship?

"Isobel visits often and will be here for Christmas, thank goodness. Though that is not nearly as wonderful as you being here." Her twin again flung her arms about Silvestre and hugged her, the tears once more standing in her eyes when she sat back. "Oh, I'm crying again!" She whipped out a pocket handkerchief from her sleeve and wiped her eyes, laughing. "Theo complains he is running out of handkerchiefs all because of my wretched sensibility."

All her erstwhile apprehensions leapt to the fore in Silvester's mind. "But you are happy with him? He is kind to you?"

Hetty threw up her eyes. "Kind? Gracious, no, the beast! He is perfectly autocratic and far more demanding than poor little Pru. But if you ask me if I am happy…" She drew a deep breath and let it out in a bang. "Silve, I adore him and he loves me deeply. I desire no more. But it's hard being a duchess. I'm still trying to adjust, but I can't get used to it, Silve. Your grace this and your grace that until my head is spinning."

"Poor Hetty. But you see a deal of Theo, I hope?"

"Oh, yes. He has much on his plate, but whenever he is with me, I am utterly content. Besides, I have grown to love the children. Theo likes me to take them under my wing, for he thinks Cecilia is hankering to go to London for the season and they won't go with her."

This was of immediate interest. "Will you go, Hetty? I hope to be there when my book is published, but —"

"Your book!" Hetty threw up her hands. "Silve, I knew you would find success. You must tell me everything. I have been agog ever since you wrote, and I must tell you I have persuaded Cecilia to write to her acquaintance. Only she has been ill, and I thought it best to wait until you came to tell us just what the book is about."

At this point, a knock on the door brought in a footman armed with a tray. "Oh, it is Jonas with the tea. Mrs Fadmoor guessed it, did she, Jonas?"

"Yes, your grace."

Henrietta had leapt up, moving to pull a small table into place. "Set it here, Jonas, if you please."

The fellow Jonas did as she asked, but took on severity. "I'd have done that for you, your grace."

"Oh, pish!" Henrietta was already upending cups. "I am not so delicate I cannot move a table. Oh, the tea is already made, that is excellent."

The footman, apparently determined to do his part, lifted the pot and poured the brown liquid into two cups.

"Thank you, Jonas, I will do the rest."

The man set out two small plates and pointed out a silver dish. "Macaroons, your grace."

"Well thought of, Jonas, but you need not wait upon us. Thank you, thank you."

Hetty's friendly dismissal produced a benevolent sort of smile and Jonas bowed and retired with obvious reluctance, rather to Silvestre's surprise.

"You seem to have made a hit with the footman at least, Hetty."

Her twin, busy at the tea tray, gave a little giggle. "Oh, they would not have me do a single thing for myself. It is perfectly ridiculous."

"Drilled into it by your predecessor, I suppose?" Silvestre rose, the easier to reach the tray.

"Cecilia was born to all this, Silve. Her father is an earl."

"Have you met her family, then?"

Hetty handed her a cup, already larded with a little cream and the two lumps of sugar she customarily took. "Not yet. Cecilia took the children to visit their grandparents for a month in October, but I have not heard when they will come to Devenal in their turn." She ushered her sister to the chair nearest the fire. "Sit here, dearest, where you will be warm. Take a macaroon. You must be hungry and dinner will be a while yet."

"We took a little refreshment at the last change," said Silvestre, nevertheless accepting one of the little almond cakes.

Henrietta took one herself and plonked down in the corner of the sofa near the fire, the table between them, and beamed across. "This is cosy. I can feel myself almost back in the den."

Silvestre cast a glance about the room, taking in the unexpected elegance in a more modern setting than the corridors she'd traversed had indicated. The walls were done out in a pretty striped paper decorated with leaf tendrils and tiny flowers. A neat little bureau, inlaid with an ivory design, stood by one wall alongside a small glass-fronted bookcase, and the set of chairs grouped about a worktable were upholstered in the same striped chintz as the sofa and the chair she was occupying. "I gather this is a sort of den for you here. Mr Swarland said the duchess was in her sitting-room."

Henrietta made a face. "Oh, Swarland. He is too punctilious for words. I cannot get through to him. Theo tells me I am wasting my time."

"I should think you are. I found him so too, although he is exceptionally efficient."

"Cecilia says she could not manage without him."

For some while, Silvestre listened to her twin's garbled and meandering account of the exigencies of her new life, putting a question now and then when the recital became a trifle muddled. But at length, Henrietta set down her cup and wafted a hand.

"But your book, Silve. How did you come to abandon your gothic novel after all?"

Silvestre laughed. "*The Old Priory* found no favour with the publishers, so it is as well I did so."

"Yes, but what made you change?"

An echo of the feelings that had caused her to write *Emmeline* rose up, but so much had occurred since to plague her, it had little resonance now. "To tell you the truth, Hetty, it was losing you that did it."

Her twin's face puckered. "Oh, Silve, no."

"Don't fall into melancholy. It was salutary, I believe, for I wrote a story with much more truth and feeling in it than I managed with the gothic tale. And really, it has set me on a path I never expected. I feel like a real writer now."

Her sister sniffed and smiled. "In that case, I shan't feel guilty for loving Theo and letting him sweep me off."

"Never feel that, dearest. Besides, I…" She faded out, not yet ready to confess to the very different sort of attachment to which she had succumbed. She had even less hope of a happy outcome than Hetty had had in the whirlwind summer that saw her fall irrevocably in love with a duke.

A tiny frown crossed her sister's face, but before she could query Silvestre's hesitation, the door opened and the duke himself came in.

"Aha! I should have known I should find you monopolising my wife, Silvestre."

She had to laugh. "And I ought to have expected so typical a greeting. How do you do, Duke?"

The young, handsome creature who had won her twin's heart cracked a grin, throwing an affectionate look across at his wife. "How do you think I do, with your disastrous sister plaguing my life out on a daily basis?"

"Theo, you horrid beast! Stop it at once."

He laughed, moving across to throw himself down on the sofa. "Is that tea? I'm gasping."

"Well, you will have to ring for another cup." Her spouse instead seized her empty one and poured from the pot even as she protested. "It's probably cold by now." He drank it in any event, unheeding. "You won't like it, Theo. It's had sugar in it."

"Ugh! How you can stomach it, I don't know." He set the cup down. "As if you aren't sweet enough already. Come here, wife of my heart."

A pang smote Silvestre as he slipped his hands under his wife and lifted her onto his lap, cuddling her close and setting his lips to hers. Such warmth. Such open affection. How fortunate was her twin.

But Henrietta, though she returned the kiss with fervour, pushed him away the instant he released her, her cheeks flying colour. "Theo, we are not alone."

"It's only Silvestre." His grin was wry. "It's not as if she hasn't seen us intimate before."

Silvestre struggled to respond in kind, her bosom thick with a jealousy she could not control. Fortunately her twin chose to berate her husband, relieving her of the necessity to answer.

"Let me go, Theo! I have not seen Silve this age and —"

"I've not seen you this age either, and if a man can't cuddle his own wife —"

"You saw me less than a couple of hours ago, Theo."

"But in company, where I couldn't do this to you … and this…"

Silvestre had to drop her gaze to her cup, unable to bear the evidence of a domestic felicity that could never be hers. Even if her secret, darkest dream came to pass, the vulture would never conduct himself in such a fashion. So openly affectionate. So warmly engaged.

Stifled giggles erupting from her twin brought her gaze back up, and she became aware Theo was whispering in Hetty's ear. It would not do.

"If I knew where to go, I would retire instanter."

At this, Henrietta gave a gasp and pushed herself off her spouse's lap, slapping at his chest as she did so. "There now, you see? Behave, or I shall make you go out."

The duke grinned across at Silvestre. "You'll soon pardon me when you hear how I've had to put up with the worst of my cousins for the last half hour. How in the world did you endure a whole journey in his company, Silve?"

Silvestre stiffened, hot words flying to her tongue which she was obliged to quash. She knew she sounded clipped. "I did not find it in the least bit difficult, sir." Which was an outright lie, but she was not going to abuse Joss to the duke.

Theo's brows rose. "Didn't you? I find him as morose as bedamned."

To Silvestre's relief, her twin took this. "Of whom are you talking?"

"My cousin Joscelin. I told you Mama foisted him onto me for a librarian."

"Oh, yes, I forgot he was to come as well. Was it a trial to you, Silve? Theo said he is not an easy man."

It was too much. "No, he is not easy. But his erudition, his depth of mind and his genius more than make up for that."

Hetty's mouth fell open and Theo stared in patent disbelief.

Silvestre drew a breath. "I am — I am a little acquainted with him. Perhaps you don't know, Hetty, but he is Gausselin Degarre."

Her twin blinked at her. "Who?"

"Gausselin Degarre, the poet. Surely you must remember Papa singing his praises?"

Light entered her sister's face. "Oh, the man he speaks of in the same breath as Shakespeare?"

"The very one."

Astonishment was writ large on Henrietta's face as she turned on her husband. "Theo! Why did you not tell me your cousin is the famous poet?"

The duke grimaced. "Is he so famous? The family are apt to bemoan his poetic leanings. If he's successful, I can't think why he wished to be my librarian."

"He didn't wish for it," said Silvestre before she could stop herself. "He was forced to it by his father. He told me his mother and yours arranged it."

"Well, why the deuce did he agree?"

A sigh escaped her. "I'm not sure. To please his mother, I think." She looked across at Theo. "Joss can't imagine you have need of a librarian. Have you?"

Theo shrugged. "According to Hathersage, yes. He claims there is a mountain of work, enough to keep a fellow busy for a twelvemonth."

Henrietta was regarding her twin with a good deal of speculation. "How did you come to be acquainted with him, Silve?"

She tried for a lighter note. "Oh, I am become quite the bluestocking, Hetty. I met him, and several others, at a salon given by Lady Whittlesford. She is a patron of a literary circle. Felicity came with me and Degarre read some of his work there."

"But you met him? You spoke with him?"

This became both embarrassing and dangerous. She could not bring herself to confide all, especially before the duke. She played it down. "I spoke to him briefly. But we met again at a dinner and happened to be seated side by side, so we conversed a little then."

"How did you find him?"

Must Theo ask such an impossible question? She prevaricated. "Find him? What do you mean?"

"I mean he doesn't talk! You can barely get a word out of the fellow. I'm damned if he said as many as ten words while I was showing him the library. I left him to Hathersage in the end." Theo turned to his wife. "You'd best put him by Silve at dinner. At least she can blab on about this afflictive poetry or some such thing."

A prospect which left Silvestre feeling decidedly apprehensive. As if Joss would respond to any overtures of hers. After what had passed, he was more likely to revert to the nervous staccato of his vulturish moments.

# CHAPTER SEVENTEEN

The task before him appeared at first utterly overwhelming. Had it not been for the tyro's presence in the house, Joss believed he would have turned tail and hastened back to his familiar attic, his mother's disappointment notwithstanding.

But whenever he thought of taking himself out of Silvestre's vicinity, the deep pull inside him drove excuses into his head. It would insult his aunt's generosity. Mama would be grieved and his father furious. He had given his word. His absence would burden the secretary, who had made no secret to Joss of the heavy load he carried.

"You have relieved me of a great weight, my lord. The necessity of this work has been eating at me and I have had no leisure to begin. Some of these volumes are falling to pieces and the disarray and dust is despicable."

Visions of being buried in clouds of dust and moth-eaten pages crossed Joss's mind, until Hathersage relieved them.

"I will assign a fellow to assist at need, but it will take a discerning eye to reorder this shambles and decide what may be disposed of."

Joss had glanced around the tall shelves, stacked floor to ceiling with leather-bound volumes, shapes and sizes set higgledy-piggledy. "Has the duke — my cousin — no preference?"

"There is a smaller library in his grace's private apartments where he keeps those volumes of interest and use to him. His predecessor used it also. Indeed, I believe the greater part of this one has not been touched since the place was built in Queen Anne's day."

His heart sinking, Joss contemplated the place which was to be his headquarters. The library was cavernous, with a gallery holding additional shelves down one end and along the whole of the interior length. Below this, a ladder contraption ran along a specially constructed rail to afford access to the higher shelves underneath, but Joss spied a moveable set of steps for use with the shelving across the way on the window side. A glass-domed roof over a seating bay cut into the outer wall promised to let in more light on sunny days, but candle-sconces protruded from several points about the room and above the mantel in the far end where an inadequate fire failed to provide sufficient heat for a space this size. Two massive desks occupied the open area at either end, with several leather-bound chairs around them. Under the gallery at the near end, the shelving was interrupted by a couple of recessed nooks with seats where, Joss reasoned with a degree of hope, a poet might hide away to indulge in occasional composition.

"I have a list of the particular books that are likely to interest his grace, which I will give to you, my lord. These might perhaps be set together in one area. Otherwise, it would be useful if those volumes remaining after a thorough shake-up could be shelved by subject, as far as possible."

Provoked into producing a wry smile, Joss eyed the man. "You realise my sojourn here is likely to last for years?"

The secretary laughed. "As I understand it, that is entirely in your lordship's hands. Personally, I shall be glad if you succeed in making any sort of inroad into the task. Once begun, I may persuade his grace it must be finished."

"Even if I run away?"

The secretary surprised him. "I cannot imagine your lordship will be content to waste too long upon this work. I am familiar with the fruits of your lordship's calling. Indeed, I trust you may find opportunity to continue to write while you are here."

"So do I, Hathersage, so do I." But he was gratified and rather touched by the fellow's comprehension of his dilemma.

No inroads were made that first day, however, the task of settling into his allotted chamber taking him too close to the dinner hour. A footman, despatched by Swarland, brought hot water and a warning of half an hour's grace for him to wash away the stains of travel and change into appropriate raiment.

The footman did not retire after delivering his message and Joss raised his brows in enquiry. "Anything else?"

"Mr Swarland says I'm to assist you, my lord, as you've brought no valet."

Consciousness of the dichotomy of his position in this house returned and his ill mood dropped the more. "I don't have a valet. I manage on my own."

The fellow bowed. "I'm Peter, my lord. I'll lay out your evening attire, shall I?"

"If you can find it."

It seemed he was to have Peter's services willy-nilly. He felt even more unlike himself and awkward. He'd not had a personal servant wait upon him for years, except when he was staying at the Rotherhythe mansion in Berkeley Square while he waited for this appointment. Such assistance as he received there had been discreet, however. This sop to his rank could not but chafe.

On the other hand, at least he would not make a poor showing in front of the tyro and his robust cousin. He had forgotten, or perhaps not really known, how brisk and energetic was Theodore Devenal. Joss was the duke's senior by a few years, but the man's vigour and dynamism far surpassed his own.

At dinner, attended by both Swarland and the secretary as well as a female of middle years introduced as the dowager's companion, Joss was placed next to Silvestre, who was on the youthful duchess's left. Was it deliberate? He was at once tongue-tied, all the stresses of the journey rising to the fore.

He managed to maintain an appearance of sangfroid when the tyro took it upon herself to present her sister. The latter's sunny smile and kind welcome bore out what Silvestre had said of their father's opinion of him.

"I was astonished, sir, when Silve told me who you are. Papa has often spoken with high praise of Gausselin Degarre, but my husband did not think to mention your poetry."

At this, the duke produced a wry grin. "It's not in my line, Joscelin, or I'd have remembered."

Joss was not deceived. His cousin clearly partook of the attitude embraced by all his family, except his mother. Even Aubrey, the best of his brothers, was inclined to tease him for his preoccupation with 'versifying'.

Swarland, clearly determined to ensure he was fully primed, explained in an aside that the dowager duchess was still keeping to her room on account of a bout of illness but that she had sent a greeting by her companion. Joss wondered if he was supposed to return the compliment and chafed the more at the necessity to bend his mind to the very social niceties he hated.

He struggled for anything to say as they dined, all too aware of the tyro. To his relief, she spent the greater part of the meal talking to her twin, who chattered inconsequently of the Lord knew what. It was plain the pair were close, breaking into frequent laughter at remembered incidents and often finishing each other's sentences.

The duke, evidently impatient of protocol, threw several remarks down the table towards the sisters, while Hathersage, seated across the table next to the dowager's companion, appeared to be making painstaking conversation with her. Swarland, on Joss's other side, punctilious as ever, divided his attention between giving his employer an account of his activities in London and his plate.

At length, Silvestre turned to Joss with a smile he read as forced. "I beg your pardon, my lord, I am neglecting you. I am so much enjoying my sister's company, you understand."

He sipped at his wine to give himself a moment to think of a suitable response. "It is what you came for."

"True." She cast him an odd look. "I was about to say I ought to mind my manners, but I am aware you have no opinion of *ought*."

A laugh escaped him. "None." He lowered his voice. "Yet I find myself in an unprecedented situation. I don't know the rules."

She matched his tone. "You need not be disconcerted. My brother-in-law has no respect for rules."

He cast a glance at his cousin. "I scarcely remember him. It has been years since we met." If they were alone, he would have added the rider that neither had shown interest in the other, so widely had their temperaments differed. When he looked round again at the tyro, he caught an expression of compassion in her face. It vanished on the instant and she smiled. Forced again.

"Well, you will have ample opportunity to amend that."

She sounded brittle. He could feel the barriers she had planted between them. For which he must take the fault to himself. His hand had wielded the scythe. For her protection or his own? He no longer knew. Suffice it the resulting withdrawal was enough to drive him deeper into his demon-infested depths.

Few more words were exchanged between them. Joss became acutely aware of a growing atmosphere of discomfort, which persisted when the ladies retired. The duke's attempts to engage him in discussion felt spurious. Joss struggled even to make any viable remark when he reverted at last to the library.

"Do you suppose you might be able to do something with it, coz?"

Coz? Was he to be employee or cousin? Intolerable position. And did Theo seek information? Reassurance? He could not bring himself to provide either. "Perhaps."

"A mammoth task, eh? You said as much, Hathersage."

The secretary thankfully took on the burden of response. "To be frank, your grace, it would daunt the hardiest spirit."

The duke threw up his eyes and tossed off his wine. "Well, here's to it. Shall we join the ladies?"

Pleading fatigue and the necessity to be up early to begin upon his labours, Joss retired. He could not have endured any more attempts to converse over the breach.

In the event, over the next few days, as he broached the huge task confronting him, he saw Silvestre only at dinner. The relative informality of that first evening vanished with the appearance of the dowager duchess, whose graciousness even encompassed Joss, but who equally rendered the whole party a good deal less free and easy with one another. It was plain the duchess had not yet managed to establish herself as mistress, despite having supplanted the older woman's place at the foot of the table.

Joss no longer had the tyro for his neighbour, which was a source both of regret and relief. He need not struggle against her barrier. Yet the lack of opportunity to do so stabbed at him. Followed him into his dreams, waking and sleeping. It became a relief to bury his head in the rapidly growing mountains of books cluttering the surfaces of the huge library desks.

He added a title to the heading "History" under the rough map sprawling across a large parchment, set down his pencil and straightened up, rolling his aching shoulders. As he looked up, a figure standing just inside the door caught his eye.

His heart jerked. The tyro. Still and silent, like a ghost. Watching him. How long had she been there?

# CHAPTER EIGHTEEN

The look on Joss's face was not encouraging. Silvestre, her pulse misbehaving in a fashion that sent dryness to her mouth, tried for a neutral note.

"I've come to satisfy my curiosity about your labours."

"Ah." He wafted a vague hand at the piles of books surrounding him. "This."

"Yes, I see them."

She took a few paces into the room, her glance shifting about the enormous shelves, although she took in little of what she saw. Her awareness of Joss was too acute.

She had come because she could no longer endure the distance. A few days spent largely in her twin's company had provided sufficient distraction, but her mind was never far from the poet. How was one to forget, to learn to overcome one's feelings, when each exchange — so brief, so uncomfortable — served only to increase the longing? Hetty was today occupied with the dowager over the question of gifts, and Silvestre had opted to retire to her sister's private sitting-room to write.

Inspiration failed her. There was no doing anything when her obstinate brain presented her only with images of a vulture countenance and her equally obstinate heart would not be quieted. She had stolen down here, impelled, building excuses in her mind. If she was honest, she'd meant to from the first, sneaking the information she needed from Martha, who attended her daily.

"Where is this famous library, Martha? I hear it is quite something."

"Ooh, it's something all right, Miss Silve. Something horrid! Nasty big brute of a place it is. All dark and gloomy. Nor it wouldn't surprise me if his lordship were to see a ghost in there."

Having disposed suitably of this fancy, Silvestre had extracted a firm description of its whereabouts and how to find it. The latter proved relatively easy, the situation of the library being in the central section of the rabbit warren of a mansion, although well at the back on the ground floor. She seized on this now.

"I had not thought the library would be so readily found. I had visions of you slaving in a dungeon from what Martha said of it."

A laugh came and he cleared his throat, emerging from behind the massive desk. "Not as bad as that."

"But daunting. Or don't you find it so?"

"The task, yes. I'm growing used to the inconveniences."

A little shiver shook Silvestre and she threw a frowning glance at the fireplace. "It's certainly chilly. Why don't you have them build up the fire?"

He shrugged. "I'm used to cold. Besides, I'm obliged to move about a great deal. It helps."

The awkwardness chafed at her. Oh, for the freedom they'd enjoyed before. Once or twice, at least. Remembrance of the last part of that fateful journey drove in the hurt. She must not show it.

Throwing her gaze over the shelving, she noted gaps, mainly in those on the outer wall. "You're getting on, I see." She went to the one nearest the fireplace and ran a hand across the near empty shelf. "Is there method in your choosing to begin here?"

"I had to start somewhere."

His voice sounded strained. She looked to where he stood, in the space between the desks, light from a domed window bay falling on his face. Pinched and tight, the vulture look pronounced.

Silvestre's bosom grew thick with feeling, the beat of her heart increasing its pace. Why would he not let her in? She had not known how painful it was to care. Nor, worse, to have one's care tossed away.

*Come, Silvestre, this won't do. You are stronger than this.*

With an effort, she wrenched her gaze from temptation. It flew upwards and caught on an unexpected sight. "Heavens, there is a gallery! There must be a thousand books in here."

Joss turned on the spot. "More, probably."

"You've counted them?"

"Hardly."

She crossed to the other side of the room, abruptly fascinated. "How in the world do you get up there?"

He passed her, heading for the door which she had left open. "There's a stair."

She saw the spiral staircase in the corner. It had been half hidden and therefore gone unnoticed. Not that she would have noticed it in any event. But a trifle of genuine engagement drove her to the stair. "May I go up?"

"If you wish."

He sounded a little less distant, but Silvestre took it in without remarking on it as she gathered her skirts into one hand, grasped the iron rail and began to climb. "It's a little scary."

"Don't look down."

At the back of her mind she was aware he did not enjoin her to be careful. Was that good or bad? Not that it meant anything at all. How ridiculous was she!

As she reached the top, she did look down. Joss was waiting below, his face turned up, watching her. Did she detect a trifle of anxiety? Or was that wishful thinking? She returned her attention to the narrow passageway that led off in both directions from the small landing fashioned into the corner. She set off down the longer wall, sliding her fingers along the books. The shelves up here were narrower in width, housing smaller volumes. Silvestre paused, bending close to read the titles on the spines in the poor light.

"*A Treatise of Human Nature*. I think not. *Candide*."

"Ah, Voltaire."

"You are right. I believe Papa has a copy. But this is different. *The Old English Baron*. Oh, it's one of Clara Reeve's. A gothic tale, you think?"

"Clara Reeve? Undoubtedly."

His voice echoed and she turned, setting her hands on the balustrade and looking down at him over them, sudden mischief rising. "This is promising, Joss. Perhaps I shall come upon a Degarre."

His laugh redoubled with the echo. "Hardly. Hathersage thinks the majority of these books are a century old."

"Not *The Old English Baron*. I wonder why anyone would choose to put novels up here rather than down there for easier access?"

"A secret stash?"

"Because of disapproval? Of course! Let me see if I can find more." Turning back to the shelf, she examined the spines. "Oh, look, Joss! You are right. Fielding is here. Fanny Burney. Smollett. Heavens, there is a host of names I don't know."

"Such as? Read them out."

"Well, let me see. Charlotte Lennox, *Cleone, A Tragedy* by a man called Dodsley. Cornelia Knight, Francis Coventry,

Eleanor Sleath, Edward Kimber. So many novelists. This is quite a collection. I wonder which Devenal had the addiction?" She looked over the rail again. "Shall I bring them down to you?"

He threw up his hands. "Lord, no! I've quite enough to contend with as it is. But I'll make a note they are up there."

Silvestre rejoiced at the easier manner between them. Was this the secret? To keep to impersonal topics? Yet even at the thought consciousness returned. She trod the length of the gallery, no longer seeing the titles beyond catching a word here or there. She turned to come back again and saw Joss was at the book-covered desk, writing on a parchment she could now see spread across the desk between the mounds.

"What is that you have there?"

He did not look up. "A map of sorts."

"Of the library?"

"Yes. I'm registering your find."

Why could it not be like this? She helping him as he went about his work. Not this work. His poetry. He would write, while she either did the same or serviced his needs. She would bring him coffee, see that he ate, keep him warm with banked up fires. Make him laugh. Cuddle him close and kiss his gaunt cheek.

Her fingers trembled on the rail and she looked away, forcing her gaze to the top of the spiral stair ahead.

What thoughts were these? Why inflict this torture upon herself? *It would destroy you.*

Why? Why say that? How could he know? Didn't he see how tenderness might envelop and comfort his demons instead? How she could tease him out of his dismals? Oh, she could. If only he would let her.

She glanced down. Joss had his nose in a book. Had he taken it from one of his afflictive piles? Was he so focused he could not even spare her a glance?

Hurting, she made her way along the gallery to the stair. But she could not bring herself to go down. Not yet. Not if he meant to alienate her in this terrible way.

To give herself time, she slipped into the section along the shorter wall. Perusing the spines, the words making no real sense in her mind. Pretending. What else was there to do? Shakespeare, was it? She halted, her eye catching on the title. *Hamlet, Prince of Denmark.* Next to it, *The Tragedy of Macbeth.* Without thought, she called out. "There looks to be a set of Shakespeare here."

His voice came, abrupt and terse. "The whole? A full set?"

"I don't know. A great many." Aware her delivery was as staccato as his, she amended it. "The binding seems to be uniform, so it may well be a complete set."

He spoke again, an anxious note entering in. "The sonnets? Are the sonnets there, Silvestre? Can you look?"

A sliver of excitement flurried her bosom. She could help him with something at least. "I am looking." She studied the spines in earnest, rapidly scanning each title until at last the words she sought appeared. "Yes, here they are! The sonnets, Joss. There's a volume right here."

"Truly?" He was eager now, his steps loud as he headed for the stair.

She was pulling the volume from the shelf, but she leaned out over the rail. "I will bring it down, Joss."

He was already climbing. "I will need the plays too."

The excitement in his tone was echoed in her bosom. All at once all awkwardness vanished. "It will be a piece of work to take them all down."

He had reached the top. "I can do it in several trips."

Then he was hurrying along the gallery towards her, she holding out the volume of sonnets towards him. Her mind was racing with possibilities. "Here. What if I handed them down to you?"

He took it, turning the book to read the spine. "What a find!" His gaze met hers, the dark eyes almost luminous. "I had no intention of bothering with the books up here for some time. If you had not come in, I might have wasted weeks. Thank you!"

Her bosom swelled with triumph. "I'm glad I did." She grasped his arm. "But do you go down and I will pass you the books. Then you need only come halfway up that ghastly stair."

His smile was balm. "You, Tyro, are a treasure!"

But the moment was fast vanishing as he turned his attention to the shelves. She shifted back as he bent to the spines, muttering titles. She had no words, his closeness half stifling, half energising. His maleness affected her in a way it never had before. She wanted to run her hands across his back, feel his musculature beneath her fingers. She wanted to touch his hair, stroke it away from his face as it fell forward in its customary fashion as he bent to the books. She wished she might run her fingertips over the planes of his dear vulture face and press her lips to his.

She could not prevent the tremors that shook her frame as the effort to hold back took a toll on her nerves.

Joss straightened abruptly, his gaze flying to hers, and she knew he felt it. An answering gleam crept into his eyes and her breath caught in her throat.

The air between them vanished. An eon wore away.

A whisper came on his breath. "No…"

Then his gaze wrenched away. She saw his grasp tighten on the book in his hand. She watched him seize another in the shelf. At random? He tugged it out. Then another, piling them in his arms.

"I will take these. You pass the rest down."

Guttural. Heavy with an emotion she could not identify. Except as a breath of finality.

She uttered no word, watching him go. As he started down the stairs, a sort of machine within her set her fingers working, though her mind was far from what she did. It felt blank, unreal. Volumes appeared in her hands. Somewhere in her head she noted the correctness of the words on the spine. When she had as many as she could carry, she took them to the edge of the stair and set them down.

Joss was already at the bottom again. Had he put down those he had? Silvestre knew not where and cared less. She did not hand the ones she had to him as she had suggested. Too close for comfort. And she would have to look at him.

She scurried back to the shelves and hunted for more William Shakespeare, picking them out the instant she spied them. Her hands full, she again went to set them down by the stair, what time Joss had swept away those she first set down and was already descending.

At last she could see no more titles by the Bard. She spoke, but felt the words came from somewhere outside herself. "That's all. You had best count them." She waited, her back to the room as she leaned against the balustrade, gazing at the empty shelf.

Hopelessness claimed her. There was no future here, no dream. He was determined against it. Despite that, he returned her regard. She knew it. Felt it. But he would not have it so. She had no power to change him. She recalled having said it that night at Mrs Whittlesford's dinner. How little she knew then that she spoke sooth. He cared even then, did he not? But, but … a heavy but.

"I believe we have them all."

His voice startled her, jangling her nerves back to life. She turned and looked over. He was standing by the far desk, near the fire. He gestured to the new pile he'd made, a little separated from the rest.

"If any are missing, I can go up again."

She said nothing, regarding him with growing rebellion in her breast.

He fidgeted under her gaze, dropping his to the books, tapping them. "I have counted them. Thirty-seven. You can come down."

She regarded his bent head. "I feel safer up here."

His gaze shot up, the dark brows snapping together. "Safer?"

"Yes, Gausselin Degarre. Safer."

He stared up at her, speechless. The impulse to scream at him died with the recognition of his pain. She did not move, recalling how he averred he could see her changing thoughts in her face. The words came out without will, the husky note outside her control.

"Is there nothing I can do for you, Vulture? Nothing at all?"

The spasm in his cheek quirked his mouth. Was it the appellation?

"You've already done it, Tyro."

She did not understand. "Finding the Shakespeares?"

He shook his head, whipping his hair about his face in a fashion that sent quivers into Silvestre's fingers. "A bagatelle. Helpful. The other … is not." He flung up a hand even as the arrow hit. "Not your fault. It's me, Silvestre. I can't…"

He faded out, jerking away, moving to the volumes he had set on the far desk, turning them. Absently? She would swear he did not know what he was doing. Compassion warred with the crushing disappointment that squeezed her bosom all over again.

She turned back to the shelves, wandering slowly along them, her gaze taking in the old worn leather, the faded gold lettering. Books! This was *life*. This was flesh, blood and bone, capable of being butchered into a million pieces.

*Oh, fanciful, Silvestre Latimer! Stop feeling sorry for yourself.*

The man did not want her and that was all. Friends? That much he had conceded. Only she wanted more and he did not.

"Silvestre!"

She jumped, turning. "Yes?"

He was immediately below, looking up, his head at such an angle that the lush hair had fallen back, revealing the sharp lines of his features, the stubborn tilt to his jaw. "Come down."

A command? It sounded like one. She hesitated, beset with a plethora of reactions. How dared he order her movements when he would have none of her? What did he want? Had he something to say? Did she care? It was bound to be unpalatable.

"Come down," he repeated, dropping his head and starting in the direction of the stair.

What, did he mean to climb up to enforce obedience? This was a different Joss, if so.

She was tempted to test it, but common sense prevailed. Besides, enough was enough. She did not wish to prolong the impasse. Her feet were moving on the thoughts. Reaching the spiral stair, she gathered her skirts and prepared to make the descent. Only then did the perilous nature of going down affect her.

"I'm not sure I can come down."

"Yes, you can. Take it slow." Reassurance in his voice now. His steps echoed on the iron as he sprang up to the first turn. He halted and beckoned. "Come. Take one step."

She drew a breath and set her foot on the first narrow stair. She felt a trifle giddy as she began the descent and had to grip her underlip between her teeth.

"Good, you're doing it. Gently now, don't rush."

Accompanied by words of encouragement, she reached his level at last.

"A little more and you'll be done." He began to step down himself, going backwards. "Don't look at me. Keep your eyes on the steps. That's it."

Her limbs were trembling, her breathing ragged. It seemed to take forever. At last she stepped onto terra firma and let out a whoosh of relief. Without thought, she reached out to Joss, catching at him. He closed in, grabbing her under the elbows.

"Steady, Tyro."

She clutched his arms. "I'm shaking."

"Yes, I can see. Let's get you into a chair."

"No, just hold me for a moment." She let go of his arms and closed with him, instinct taking over as she flung them instead about his neck and clung, laying her face against his shoulder.

For a moment he stood, unmoving. Then she felt his arms close about her and draw her tight against him. Her heartbeat shot into high gear, her breath became ragged, and a violence of tremors affected her limbs. Until she realised Joss was trembling too, his breathing as uneven as her own.

"Tyro … Tyro…"

A whispering caress. Pricking in her eyes, a lump rising in her throat.

Then he stiffened, putting her from him and setting his hands against her shoulders to keep her away.

She drew a shuddering breath, taking her own weight back. "I'll sit down now."

He shifted to the side, slid a hand under her elbow and guided her to the nearest chair, one pulled away from the big desk covered in mounds of books.

No words came as she dropped into it. No words were possible.

Joss's silence ate into her bosom. What could he say? How say anything without reference to what had just occurred, giving them both away? To her utter surprise, he managed it.

"A salutary lesson, Tyro. You won't go climbing spiral stairs again in a hurry. Though I suspect it was only difficult because you were up there too long."

She looked up. How could he sound so impersonal? Yet there was a look in his face that belied the note. She answered without really realising what she said. "How so?"

"You'd grown used to the height." He gestured to the gallery. "Disorienting. The change, I mean. It's a trick of the mind too. The ground. It looks further away from above."

She eyed him. He was babbling. Staccato fashion again. Nerves? She ought to have realised he was anything but assured. Disconcerted? Embarrassed? Her tongue betrayed her. "What just happened, Joss?"

He shifted away, his glance flitting this way and that. Hesitant? Trying to pretend it meant nothing? At length, he turned back to her. "Silvestre… Don't make more of it." A plea in his voice. "I can't take this beyond friendship."

She hit back. "And I can't take friendship alone."

"It's all I can offer."

Oh, the vulture look again! She was hurt, angry, frustrated. He cared. Did that not matter at all? Defeated, she pushed herself up from the chair. "I had better go."

"Yes."

A clear dismissal. Yet she found it horribly difficult to leave him. The feelings she cherished dictated her words. "You won't brood, will you, Vulture?"

That faint look of amusement crossed his face. "Probably. You must know by now I can't help it."

"Do you try?"

He looked taken aback. "I don't know. Do I? No, I don't think I do."

"Then you can't know you can't help it."

His lip quirked. "There speaks the Tyro I know."

Silvestre found she was smiling. "Well, if you won't let me succour you, there is nothing to do but rely upon your own resources. I wish you luck with that."

"Ouch!"

She laughed, a trifle of lightness patching over the cracks. A prick at the back of her mind made her speak with normality. "My proofs are due soon. Will you help me?"

He gave a smile that seemed to possess a smidgeon of tenderness. "It's the least I can do."

This provided her with an excuse to seek him out again. If she could not have more, she must content herself with what he was prepared to give. Could she, though?

Joss watched Silvestre leave the library, then dropped into her vacated chair and set his head in his hands.

Dear Lord in heaven, how was he to bear it? In the plainest terms, she had offered him all his secret desire and he'd had to reject her. Did she care so much? A fantasy. She had no concept of the depths to which he could sink.

Inflict that on her? He would shatter her brightness and devour her soul.

Already the tease and mischief was visibly reduced. All laid to his account. Somehow she was dazzled. Infatuated. He could not begin to guess what attraction he had that drew her. Vulture! The very word a repellent. Or ought to be. Yet on the tyro's lips it had become a caress. The ache redoubled.

Ah, if he dared succumb! Take her to his lair and keep her captive, slave to his moods, balm to his wounded spirit. It must not be. Even on a practical level, he would be a villain. What had he to offer? He could barely keep himself, let alone a wife.

The word echoed in his head. Is that where his thoughts were tending? Damnation, what had she done to him? He was no prospect for a husband, not to any female. Least of all one whose courage and boldness, whose smile, whose teasing laughter, whose twinkle in those mischievous eyes called to his deeps like a siren star.

In all honour, he must not yield. She cared, but she was young and light at heart. She would recover. Find solace in her writing. That he could pronounce with confidence. Silvestre was not plagued by demons. Setting pen to paper would not be the curse it was for him. A damned curse it was too. Yet one he could not relinquish.

Pushing himself up, he crossed to the pile of volumes the tyro had found. This was what he needed. To bury himself in work. His work. Not the spurious task to which he had been set by his anxious mother. That he must do also. But let him fill his head with the other and oust the burn of imagined bliss he could not afford.

# CHAPTER NINETEEN

Lady Lionel Devenal's no-nonsense approach to life was refreshing after days of pandering to the dowager duchess's studied graciousness. Not that Silvestre had to endure much of the woman's company.

"How do you bear it, Hetty?"

Her sister sighed. "Well, if she becomes too much, I rely upon Theo to rescue me. Besides, he is convinced Cecilia is hankering to marry again and I confess I do need to learn from her while I can."

"What about the children? Won't you miss them?"

Hetty set about pouring the coffee which had just been brought to her sitting-room. "Oh, we are bound to see a great deal of them. Theo is their guardian, don't you recall?"

Silvestre had forgotten, her mind too full of a certain poet to allow for much of anything else. Although she had done her best these last days, if not to oust him, at least to relegate him to things past or unattainable. Determined not to wear her heart upon her sleeve, she adopted a cheerful mien and took such pleasure as she could in the balm of her twin's company whenever Henrietta's duties allowed.

But this morning's comfortable coze over coffee was interrupted when the door opened to admit the duke's mother. Lady Lionel Devenal came in like a whirlwind, trailing a huge and colourful shawl over a gown of figured muslin, her pepper-and-salt flyaway hair framing the lively countenance Silvestre had encountered earlier in the year when the remarkable creature had been instrumental in uniting Hetty with her son.

Henrietta's face lit and she jumped up. "Isobel!"

"My love, I know I am horribly late," said Lady Lionel without the slightest preamble, throwing aside an enormous muff and enveloping Hetty in a perfumed embrace, "but I could not leave my orchids until the hothouse glass was repaired. However, I am in time for the festivities and you will forgive your mama-in-law, I know."

"Oh, Isobel, I am so glad to see you. Theo has been cursing terribly. He thought you might not remember, and the company is too depressing for words."

Lady Lionel was laughing. "Ah, he blames me, no doubt. He is finding my nephew trying, I dare say."

This turn could not but prick at Silvestre's partiality, but she was obliged to swallow upon the impulse to defend Joss as her twin turned Lady Lionel's attention upon her.

"You remember my sister, Isobel?"

"With the strange name? Silvestre, is it not?" An embracing smile was immediately followed by a hug. "We won't stand on ceremony, my dear, and I shall be severe upon my idiot son if he dares to tell me the company is depressing while you are here."

"Oh, he does not mean Silve, ma'am," Hetty said on an anxious note. "Indeed, Theo says she is leaven, especially because she is acquainted with Lord Joscelin from her literary set, and besides, I am deriving so much pleasure from having my twin with me."

"Of that I have no doubt." Lady Lionel dropped into the sofa beside Hetty and patted her hand. "I hope you are not allowing Cecilia to bully you, my love."

"Oh, no, and we are in hopes she may find herself a husband when she goes to town for the Season."

Lady Lionel's tinkling laughter floated about the room. "An excellent solution."

"Coffee, Isobel? I will ring the bell for a fresh pot."

While Henrietta bustled to the bell-pull, Silvestre found herself under scrutiny from the visitor's observant gaze.

"Do you know my nephew well, Silve?" She smiled. "You don't mind the informality, I hope? I can't bear ceremony."

Silvestre had to laugh, though she was wary of the pertinent question. "I remember that, ma'am."

"And Joscelin?"

She drew a breath, trying to speak with lightness. "I met him as Gausselin Degarre. As I did several other well-known names when I was fortunate enough to be introduced into that circle."

"Of course, your book! Hetty told me all about it. Such a triumph. For us all, I may say, to be lauding one of our own. Why should these wretched men of ours have all the fun? Thus far I am in full agreement with that renegade, Aspatria Glasson."

Silvestre's mood lightened. "Oh, I have met her, ma'am!"

"In person? Heavens, do tell! Is she dreadfully mannish and bombastic?"

"Nothing of the kind, though she is an original and most unexpected. She's altogether feminine, very fashionable and quite young. I found her kind, though forthright in her views. But she does not force them upon others. I truly think she lives by her beliefs."

Lady Lionel clapped her hands. "How excessively gratifying. I shall read her again with a great deal more attention. She is of Joscelin's circle?"

How was she to answer that? It was so, but since she knew Joss despised most of that same circle and made no attempt to engage with the individuals within it, she felt a trifle false in acknowledging as much. She prevaricated. "Well, she attended the same salon."

A distinctly penetrating eye was bent upon her, and Silvestre was relieved when Hetty claimed her mother-in-law's attention.

"Did you send to Theo, Isobel, or shall I ask Jonas to fetch him?"

"Time enough, my love. Let us enjoy our feminine chatter over coffee first. We don't need Theo's nonsensical interruptions."

To Silvestre's surprise, her twin became mock severe. "What you mean is you wish to postpone having him ring a peal over you for planting his horrid cousin upon him."

A pang smote Silvestre as Lady Lionel broke into laughing protest. Horrid? How could Hetty misjudge him so? Could she not see how it hurt her twin to say such a thing of him?

For several moments, Silvestre heard little of what passed between the two, feeling unaccustomed resentment towards her sister. Until she was obliged to recognise that it was her own fault. She had been as secretive, as protective of her feelings towards Joss as Hetty had been in the summer when she had fallen head over heels for her duke with no hope of a happy outcome. Nevertheless, she could not help a sliver of distress that her twin was so preoccupied in her new life she failed to see a hint of her own sister's torment. It was all of a piece. The separation, which she had mourned so strongly it had resulted in her writing *Emmeline*, was total. Hetty's love and loyalty had veered to her husband.

Well, it must be so. It ought to be. Would it not be just the same for her if she was privileged to be joined to the object of her affections?

The thought brought her up short. Was she thus far gone? Would she truly put Joss's interests ahead of those of her dearest twin? Of those of Mama and Papa? The answer twisted in her heart, almost depriving her of breath.

"Silvestre?"

She jumped, coming to herself in a bang. The footman Jonas was in the room, the used tray in his hands, and Hetty was busy imparting a plethora of instructions. The softly uttered interrogative had come from Lady Lionel.

Silvestre stared at her, struggling for composure. "Yes, ma'am?"

Lady Lionel gave her a questioning smile. "You were off on another plane, my dear. I would love to ask what took you there, but this is not the time."

She was both gratified and thrown into apprehension. "It — it's nothing."

"A particularly uncomfortable nothing, if I am any judge." She added in a hushed tone, "We will talk later."

With which, she turned to Henrietta as she came back to the sofa, requesting to be told just what arrangements were in place for the festivities.

Silvestre felt exposed, irrationally dismayed to have her distress noticed. Ridiculous, when she had just been bemoaning the fact her twin had failed her in this regard. But then Lady Lionel was from home when she visited at Devenal, like Silvestre. She had not the preoccupations that necessarily took up Hetty's time. No, that was not it at all. *Be honest, Silvestre Latimer.* Lady Lionel had a discerning eye. Lord help her, but would the woman see through Joss too?


"Well, well, so this is your domain, my dear Joscelin."

His aunt's voice, coming out of the blue, startled Joss out of his concentration. He was seated in a chair at the desk nearest the fire, surrounded by the volumes of Shakespeare's plays and so deeply buried in the sonnets he had lost track of both time and his proper purpose in this library. He set down his pencil in the groove of his notebook and rose. "How do you do, ma'am?"

"Oh, now don't you dare treat me like a stranger, dreadful boy!"

Lady Lionel sailed across the room and captured him into a stifling hug. He bore it with uncontrollable stiffness. He ought to have remembered her odd manner. As she released him, he took a grateful step back, flicking his hair out of his face. She was smiling at him with a teasing look that inevitably brought the tyro back to mind, and a kick to his gut.

"Well? Do you hate me, Joscelin?"

"For landing me with this sinecure?"

Her brows flew up. "Is it a sinecure?"

He could not forbear a sigh. "It ought to be."

The remembered laughter came. "That's the boy I recall. Are you itching to be gone?" She looked across to the other desk, throwing out an encompassing hand. "I see you are making inroads at least. Heavens, what a dreadful pile! Hathersage said it would be a mammoth task."

His cousin's secretary had popped in once or twice, ostensibly to enquire if Joss was lacking anything he needed, but he was not fooled. The man was clearly anxious to check on his progress.

"You made the arrangement with him, ma'am?"

She had picked up one of his books and was leafing through it. "I never could get on with *Coriolanus*. Such a gruesome piece." She set down the book and regarded him. "You guessed that, did you? I should have known. Your papa has said often you are more intelligent than the four of your brothers put together."

An unprecedented feeling of gratification towards his parent mingled with his astonishment. "My father said so?"

Lady Lionel smiled. "Oh, not with any favourable inclination, you may be sure. My esteemed brother-in-law does not consider intelligence a virtue. A man must rather be an intrepid horseman or a fierce fighter to win his approval."

The sarcastic note was pronounced and Joss could not forbear a laugh, despite the dribble of disappointment. "No, he was far from thinking this a suitable employment."

"Of course he was. Percival is a traditionalist through and through. I can't think what my sister was about to marry him."

"He is a marquis, Aunt."

"Oh, that did not weigh with Amelia. She married for love, just as I did. Just as my idiot son did in the end, though I was obliged to shake him out of this nonsense about duty. Duty! Really, what is the matter with you men? Honour and duty must come before common sense and common feeling. It is perfectly ridiculous and I have no patience with it."

Joss made no remark. His mother was apt to deprecate her sister's tendency to ride upon her various hobby horses. But such excursions were common in his circle and he never bothered to enter into argument with them. There were distinctions of honour and duty which his aunt was unlikely to appreciate.

But she was smiling again, gesturing to his notebook. "You are managing to find time for your poetry?"

As of instinct, he seized up his notebook and closed it, the pencil inside preventing it from shutting completely. "Notes. Preparation only. Research, if you like."

"Oh, you need not guard your precious notes from me, my dear boy. I shan't pre-empt the pleasure of reading the completed work. What is it you intend? Why Shakespeare? Or shouldn't one ask at this stage?"

He put the notebook down, but kept a hand on it, waving the other in a nebulous fashion. "It is vague yet. I'm looking for the man within the work."

Her features lit with interest and Joss was conscious of a similar glow of warmth to the one engendered by the tyro — when she was cerebrally engaged. Or when she teased. Or when she…

He forced the thoughts away, setting his attention on his aunt's words.

"I like that, Joscelin. How does he reveal himself, is that it? I shall not ask how you propose to build poetry from the idea. That is your province. One should never expect an artist to explain his methods."

"I would more people understood as much, ma'am."

The infectious laughter came. "You cannot expect the layman to fathom the artistic mind."

"You do."

She put up a finger. "Ah, but I am not of the ilk of the layman, I'm afraid. Like that girl Silvestre, I possess a more open mind. And the ability to observe. It's a gift, I think."

But Joss heard little beyond the mention of that name, his mind catching on the instant image that had the power to compress his breast and send coursing need into his loins. The image shifted whenever it lodged in his head, showing the changing expressions that mirrored her changing thoughts. How he missed that! She was become an effigy in his vicinity. He saw her only when the company gathered for dinner, and she smiled and talked of inconsequent things when she had occasion to address him. But she was not his tyro and he had only himself to blame.

"An intriguing girl, don't you find? I gather you met her in some salon or other."

His throat constricted. "Lady Whittlesford. Fancies herself a patron. Made me read. I hate it."

His aunt's penetrating gaze was upon him and he turned his to the piles of books, fidgeting. Lifting a book from one pile and stacking it on another, hardly conscious of what he did. Why must she look at him so? She saw too much. Not like his mother, who worried him with care. Sisters. As unlike as the two young ones now seen together here.

"What is her book like? Have you read it?" Lady Lionel, cutting into his scattered thoughts.

"No. I don't know. Christy took it because Beak likes it. It must be good."

"But not in your line, I suspect."

"Novels? No. But I said I'd help her with the proofs. Show her how it's done."

"Ah, then you'll get a glimpse, lucky man. I am dying to read it. Hetty tells me it is unusual, much to her surprise. When they were together, Silve was writing a gothic tale."

He recalled the animated discussion, so free and open, when he had bared his inner fires, more freely than he had to any other, ever. "The gothic was not her forte. She was emulating when she wrote it. Mocking, even. The other, this *Emmeline*, came from her heart. If she has talent, it will be in the truth of it."

"Then you think she has a future?"

At this, he balked. "How can I tell? It's a lottery at best. I hope she may, if she can do it again."

"Ah, that's the key, is it not? You must repeat yourself."

"Repeat?" No, anathema. His innate intensity for the work forced his tongue. "That is for hacks. You must renew. Find that which begs to be written and struggles to emerge. The impulse comes from within, or it is worthless."

His aunt's brows lifted. "A harsh judgement, Joscelin. I cannot believe every writer is in your mould. Did not Johnson say —"

"That only a fool writes for other than money? We all write for money, ma'am. But for money alone? I had as well follow my brothers into the military."

She laughed at that. "Yes, I can see you! You would be wasted, my poor boy. Amelia knows that, which is why she fought Percival on the subject when he would have forced you into that profession."

This was news to Joss. "Did she?"

"Most strenuously. What, did you think your digging in your heels had weighed with Rotherhythe? My poor deluded boy! Your independence began with the publishing of your first book. Without Amelia's intervention, your papa would have cut off your allowance in a bid to force you to his will."

The cynic in him rose to the surface. "That threat? He has held it over my head many a time. My father knows I would never yield. He would not waste his blunt on a commission for me."

Lady Lionel put out a hand and captured his chin, her smile misty. "Stubborn boy! Miraculous Percival failed to break your spirit. Take care you do not ruin yourself with such obstinacy." She released him and he shifted away from her, as ever disturbed by unwarranted intimacy.

"How should I, ma'am?"

To his consternation, she picked up his abandoned notebook and flourished it in his face. "With this, wretched creature! It is not all of life. There is more. There are other pleasures to be had."

He snatched the notebook out of her hand, clutching it to him. "It's not a pleasure!"

"Oh, tush, if you don't enjoy it —"

"It has naught to do with enjoyment. If you must have it, Aunt, it's more a curse than anything else. For me at least."

"Then more than ever you ought to embrace other aspects of life. My dear boy, you cannot live and breathe this poetry of yours. You will burn yourself out."

Only too likely. "What would you have me do?"

She made no answer to this beyond an enigmatic smile, instead turning on the spot and surveying the shelves. "How are you proposing to re-arrange all this?"

"I'm not. Not yet." He fell with relief into talking of the library rather than himself. "At present, I am checking the volumes and making a map of what is here. There's a fellow who comes to help. He takes away those volumes no longer fit for perusal." He waved a vague hand. "Mice. And moths. Mould too."

"Ah yes, Hathersage suspected as much. It is a wonder any are fit for use."

"A great many. Too many. I should doubt of anyone reading more than ten per cent of the whole."

"Then you will have done my son a significant favour. I have reason to be pleased with myself for thinking of you for the task."

"Thinking of me? I understood my mother had arranged it with you for the purpose of finding me employment."

"Ah, but it was already under discussion as a project to be undertaken. I thought of you because Amelia had been bewailing Percival's tendency to fret over your choice of profession."

The heaviness of obligation lessened. If this was the case, he need not feel guilty about dropping the work. He had a choice. Curiously, this at once made the task less onerous.

His aunt, a little to his disappointment, moved towards the exit. "I must away. I have not yet seen Theo." She turned at the door and waved. "We will meet at dinner, no doubt, by which time I must hope to have furthered my acquaintance with the intriguing Silvestre Latimer." She threw Joss a tantalising look of mischief and left him.

He was instantly prey to apprehension. A manipulative creature, his aunt, though charmingly eccentric. Reflecting on her several mentions of the tyro, Joss became uncomfortably suspicious. What was the woman up to? She could not have divined his interest, could she? Lord help him if she had! Lady Lionel Devenal had no qualms about interfering in matters that were in no way her concern.

# CHAPTER TWENTY

The atmosphere of Devenal Castle had become a deal livelier with the advent of the duke's mother and Silvestre found her spirits much improved. She had not yet, as she half expected, been called upon to discuss her relations with Joss, although she caught the flamboyant Lady Lionel eyeing her in a considering way now and then.

She was cheered to see how Hetty blossomed, conducting herself in her own fashion rather than that of the dowager's expectation. Theo laughed more, his burdens apparently lighter for the radiance of his mother's presence.

"Theo complains of his mama forcing him into this or that," her twin told her, "but he adores Isobel, and I believe he enjoys her berating him."

Silvestre laughed. "Just as he enjoys your doing so, dearest."

Hetty made a face. "Well, he deserves it, the wretch. He delights in provoking me."

"I've noticed."

Her sister threw up her eyes, but reverted to talking of her mother-in-law's influence. "I wish she might live here instead of Cecilia, but she says she values her independence too highly. But I do love her visits, for she is never crotchety, even when she goes off on one of her diatribes, as Theo calls them."

Unlike Theo's Aunt Cecilia, the dowager, her twin might have said. Silvestre refrained from saying it, since her sister had managed to escape for a space. They were walking together in the gardens, well wrapped up for this rare crisp and sunny day, the children gambolling ahead in the charge of their nurses. Christmas was almost upon them and Hetty's duties had multiplied, urged thereto by the dowager's chivvying. Silvestre had offered her services, but her twin would have none of it.

"You are here for pleasure, Silve. Besides, I won't have you badgered by Cecilia too. You may write, if you wish, but you need do no household chores while you are with me."

Not that her twin was occupied with the sort of white work or stillroom tasks that used to engage them at Moss House. Her duties were managerial in the household and charitable outside of it. Visits to the poor and the sick with useful gifts formed a great part of her activities, and Silvestre found her in her sitting-room closeted with the housekeeper more often than not. Occasionally she was obliged to play host to courtesy visits by the local gentry, who were few, much to the duke's preference. Such sessions were enlivened while Lady Lionel was present, her witty and forthright remarks keeping Silvestre in a ripple of welcome amusement.

As for writing, she was no further forward. The germ of an idea had surfaced, but the genus of it was so disturbing she hesitated to probe her mind for its expansion. To write of the wife of a vicar made lonely and bereft by her spouse's preoccupation with the Almighty came too near the secret fear that accompanied her deepest wish. The unwitting prompter of this burgeoning story yet impinged upon her senses, whether she saw him or not. Although even Joss was affected by Lady Lionel's dynamic presence.

He looked more relaxed, she noticed. He even addressed one or two remarks to her reminiscent of their early meetings, when the air between them was not charged. It was hard to remember now. His nearness produced so many discordant notes in her, both physically and mentally, she felt herself unnatural whenever he was present. Yet when he was not, she could never quite dismiss the knowledge of the brooding ghost down in his dungeon library.

So it must be for her vicar's wife, Matilda, she thought, who longed to hear that caressing *Maudie* of their courting days rather than the harder *Maud* which came at her with frequency, in a tone either absent or severe. Both of which brushed at the core of pain with which she lived.

*Oh, stop it, Silvestre Latimer!* She must not make a tale out of this. It would not do. He would recognise precisely from where she drew her inspiration. If, that was, he ever read her work as she did his. In secret, in the confines of her bed at night, she had begun to peruse the volume loaned to her by Papa. Her heart's involvement had rapidly become tinged with awe, with pride, with a conviction she could have no dealings with a mind capable of producing such work. That he suffered in the making of it was no longer puzzling. In these pages she found not Gausselin Degarre as she expected, but the man she was coming to know as Joss.

Did he realise how much he revealed of himself? Was this his truth? This deep recognition of the impulses that drove man? Papa had spoken of Degarre's ability to delineate the human condition with a skill akin to Shakespeare's. He could not know, as she had learned, that his words delineated Joss's own condition. His inner torment tumbled out of his poetry, if one knew him well enough to see into his soul.

Such hope expressed in one of his poems gave flutterings to her own heart's desire, despite the hint of yearning for some impossible freedom:

*Is there a world of mystery and dreams*
*Where dwells no shadow of inhuman toil?*

She longed to give him that world, if only she could. Yet he dwelled also in the deep despair of another poem, which treated of the false promise of a reward in paradise for leading an exemplary life, an effusion that sent her spirits plummeting again:

*Nay, pause we, 'ere in dare we hope to grace*
*The brittle talons of that destined place.*


"Silve?"

She started, turning to find her twin regarding her with an expression of anxiety. She summoned a smile. "Your pardon, Hetty, I was miles away."

"Not for the first time. What troubles you, Silve?"

Silvestre's breath caught. "I did not think you'd noticed."

Henrietta's gloved fingers found hers and clutched them. "Have you forgotten how we thought almost as one? How we used to finish each other's sentences on occasion? Of course I noticed. I hoped you would confide in me without prompting."

Even as the guilt rose, Silvestre had to smile. "You've changed, Hetty."

"Oh, no, but I will not readily forget how I wished to keep my secret when I was so hopeless about Theo. Is it Lord Joscelin?"

The direct question struck home. Silvestre halted where she stood, quite unable to prevent the choking sobs from rising in her throat.

"Oh, Silve! Oh, I'm so sorry!"

Her twin's arms closed about her and her head drooped over the shorter girl's shoulder as she struggled to suppress the grief. She could hear Hetty's snatched breath and knew her sister was succumbing too. Ridiculous!

She freed herself, regarding her sentimental twin with a wet gaze but laughing the while. "I might have known you would turn into a watering-pot just because I weep a little!"

Hetty was groping in her sleeve for a pocket handkerchief. "How could I help it when I see you so unhappy?"

"You must help it. If you set me off again, I'll never forgive you. I thought I had myself so well in hand, and now…" She sniffed the remnant moistures away while her sister wiped at her own cheeks, indignant.

"If you had said something before, I would have been perfectly composed."

"Poppycock! You would have started the instant you learned I had lost my heart to that wretch of a poet."

Dismay grew in Henrietta's gaze. "But have you, Silve? Truly? To such an oddity?"

The urge to defend Joss rose, but she curbed it. Had she expected approval? Hetty had called him horrid. She temporised. "He may be an oddity, but if you knew him better, you would not mind that."

"Yes, I had realised you think well of him. That is why I have tried not to be disparaging. But can you care for such a man? He is so … so…"

"Aloof? Brooding? Reclusive?"

Hetty blenched. "Pray don't be angry, Silve! I didn't mean that. Theo is both aloof and reclusive."

"But not brooding." Silvestre drew a steadying breath. "I'm not angry. I know Joss is difficult. He can't help it. He is like Papa in a way. He feels things deeply. He is tormented. All the time. But he can be different. If one … if one makes him laugh

… teases… Oh, what am I saying? There is no future in it, Hetty. It's impossible."

Her twin had once again found her hand and she squeezed it now. "Miracles do happen, Silve."

"You would say that. Your case was different. Joss is not like Theo. He won't … he won't change his mind."

"You can't know that. Although if I am honest, I hope you may."

"Change my mind? Perhaps I will, in time. When I'm away from here, away from his vicinity."

Her sister shook the hand she held. "That will make no difference, dearest, as I know only too well. Is there no hope at all?"

Silvestre swallowed a lump in her throat. "There is always hope, I suppose. He does care a little, that I will swear to."

"Not enough?"

"Not enough to break out of inhabiting the gloomy world he makes for himself. He won't let me enter there, you see. He says it would destroy me. It very likely would too."

"But you still want him?"

A somewhat hysterical laugh escaped her. "For my sins, yes. I must have taken leave of my senses!"

"Softy, Softy, come and see what I found!"

The shrill demand of young Lady Ella cut into the conversation. Hetty's attention veered on the instant. "If it is a slug like the last time, Ellie, I don't want to see it."

"Not a slug, silly." The child came running up, holding out her hand. "It's a skelington. See, it's all frozen."

"Ugh! Must you be so ghoulish, Ellie?"

"It's a dead bird. I'm going to keep it in my box."

"A skeleton? I thought your box was only for treasures."

"A frozen skelington is a treasure, Softy."

"Not skelington, Ellie. Skel-e-ton. I'm sorry but I cannot admire it."

The discussion became vociferous and Silvestre did not know whether to be glad or sorry to have been interrupted. There was scant balm in talking of Joss when Hetty clearly did not like him, though it felt a little less isolating to have been found out. Except that Hetty was bound to confide in her Theo, which would likely put both herself and Joss under scrutiny.

With an inward sigh, she turned to accompany the party back to the house, Lady Ella having won the argument in favour of secreting her find in her box of treasures and determining to do so on the instant.

"I must find Cecilia," said Hetty on a reluctant note. "She wants to show me how the holly must be set about the grand parlour."

"Why can't you have it set how you wish?"

Hetty lowered her voice. "Because I can't endure her sulks. Besides, it is only to supervise. I won't be permitted to set them up myself, as we were used to do at home."

Once more Silvestre was exercised by the enormity of Henrietta's position. She was glad her fancy had alighted on a man in a far simpler situation, despite his rank. If Hetty's miracle should occur, she was more likely to dwell in a cottage than a mansion. Or an attic. An agreeable vision of sharing Joss's garret crossed her mind, but her sense of humour betrayed her. That was assuredly impossible. He really would drive her to despair if she was obliged to live with him in such a confined space.

The thought gave her pause. Perhaps Joss was right. Did he see more clearly than she? No, for she knew just how it would be, did she not? Or poor Maud, the creature of her invention, she knew.

The story, in spite of her stern reminders to herself, began to weave again in her head. She excused herself the moment they reached the house and headed for her allotted bedchamber. Begin it she would. He would have none of her. Why should she not use the inspiration? She must have a tale in hand in case *Emmeline* was successful. Since no other notion offered, she must use what she had. Let Maudie live that life, if she could not.

# CHAPTER TWENTY-ONE

Obliged to participate in the family celebration on Christmas Day, Joss watched the tyro surreptitiously, inescapably aggrieved to see her brightness, her evident enjoyment. Was he so easily forgot?

Not that she was ignoring him. She had wished him the compliments of the day with a ready smile. Nor did she give off that sense of awkwardness whenever they happened to be close enough for conversation. But her manner was distant, as if she spoke to a chance acquaintance, a stranger.

"Ellie is delighted with those toy soldiers Swarland found, did you notice?"

He found it doubly hard to respond, and merely grunted.

"Even the mechanical doll is approved, though Theo was obliged to prevent her from trying to take it apart to discover how it worked."

He struggled for something sensible to say, feeling perfectly alienated. She was watching the children bouncing for comfits as the duke held them just out of reach, their indignant shrieks drawing laughter from her.

"They appear to be enjoying the day."

"Aren't we all?" She flicked a glance at him, too quick for her expression to register. "It's a treat to see my twin so happily engaged."

She left him then, going across to join her sister. The duchess, who was laughingly protesting Theo's antics on the children's behalf, at once turned with a warm smile, seizing Silvestre's hand and leaning to whisper.

"They make a charming pair, don't you think?"

His aunt's sudden advent shook Joss out of his absorption. He grunted again, feeling both bereft and deserted. Why could she not have stayed by him, talking?

"At least you have the decency to participate in the day, Joscelin. I was afraid you might be churlish and refuse."

Guilt riffled through him. He had been within an ace of so doing at breakfast, but his cousin had made a point of insisting on his presence.

"I won't have it said I am a hard taskmaster, coz. No library today for you, my friend. Even the servants have an easy time of it. Oh, and you must attend their ball tomorrow night."

He had groaned in spirit. "A ball? But I never —"

"No excuses!" The duke had waved a forkful of beef in his direction. "We all attend. You're family and that's that."

"I was given no choice," he said now to Lady Lionel.

"Quite right too."

He regarded her with suspicion. "Was this your doing, ma'am?"

She looked mischievous. "You will never know, my dear boy. Theo can't bear ceremony and he learned a great deal on his travels. He does not need me to prompt him to acts of generosity."

But to acts of deliberate intent? Was she attempting to throw them together? He had not forgotten those hints. Now here she was, doing it again. Forcing his attention upon the twins. Or one of them. Not that it needed force. Truth to tell, he could hardly take his eyes off the tyro.

"Can you not, for once in your life, Joscelin, forget these megrims of yours and simply enjoy yourself?"

It was said with an edge of exasperation which echoed in his breast. He could not prevent his tongue from forming the protest. "What do you want of me, Aunt? Are you my mother's envoy? I don't doubt you've written to report on my conduct."

A ripple of her customary laughter came. "Caught! But not on your conduct, idiot boy. Amelia is anxious for your progress, rather. To know if you are content. If you are happy." Her tone changed. "Though that, as I did not scruple to tell her, is baying for the moon."

A crack of mirth escaped him. "How well you understand me!" He saw the tyro glance round swiftly and was gratified. He was not wholly forgotten.

But his aunt was not done. "I understand you a deal better than you bargain for, my dear Joscelin. If you were my son, I'd have boxed your stupid ears for you before this."

He let out a disbelieving laugh, turning to confront her. "What have I done to merit that, pray?"

Lady Lionel's expression registered satisfaction. "Ah, that pricked you, did it? Capital. It's about time you came out of that torturous head of yours and looked about you."

He regarded her with growing indignation. "What is this? I am at a loss to understand you, Aunt Isobel."

"And you so all-alive? Or so your poetry would have one believe. You men, really!" She made a wild sort of gesture, dislodging one of the trailing shawls she habitually wore. "How it has come about your sex rules the roost is a complete mystery to me. Or no, brute strength gave you the mastery, did it not? A great pity the Almighty conceived it so. Had he troubled himself to supply you with more brain than brawn, it would have been a deal more to the purpose."

Joss waved a hand. "If you are going to mount upon your hobby horse, Aunt, I have done. Had our Maker at least provided women with the ability to talk less in riddles, the world would go round a deal easier than it does."

Lady Lionel burst into a trill of laughter. "*Touché!*" She pinched his cheek. "I did not think you had it in you. There is hope for you yet, my dear boy."

He watched, amusement rising, as she crossed to join her son, who was now arguing with the dowager as to the advisability of feeding the little girls too many sweetmeats.

Joss hovered a moment or two, taking in the other members of the company. The secretary Hathersage was absent, having left a couple of days previously to partake of Christmas with his family. Swarland was in residence, however, and appeared to divide his time between serving the dowager's needs and entertaining her companion, Mary Eddleston. Joss had spoken to the woman only once or twice, of necessity, but Swarland had not again come in his way beyond a word or two when dining.

He was obliged to realise he had made no effort to interact with any of the party beyond what he must. Was the habit so ingrained? Had he become so enmeshed in his own concerns, he had no interest to spare for anyone else?

His aunt's words came back to haunt him. Was he so buried in his head he saw nothing outside of it? Apart from the tyro. She had pierced his armour from the first, forcing him out. He looked over to where she sat with her sister, engaged in animated conversation. Her fingers made a gesture and his attention caught.

Ink stains? She was writing again! Had she begun a new tale? Was that why she had not again sneaked into his sanctum? Aware he had thoroughly discouraged her, Joss was yet disappointed. If she had succeeded in ousting him, he had not been similarly successful. She was a constant at the back of his mind, both waking and sleeping. When he saw her in person, it became a physical ache in the region of his chest. And now she was behaving as if she were indifferent!

Well, had he not wished it upon her? He recalled little of what he'd said that day, his own yearnings roiling his senses. How had she become like an itch under his skin? The yearning that had ever plagued him had become centred on the tyro. As if she was the object it had sought. He refused to believe that was so. The scratchings of his pencil were the cause. Not the tyro. The void could never be filled thus. Could it?

No, never. In the person of Degarre, he strove for that which eluded him, even if he knew not what it was. It could not be this! If it was so, he would be writing and he could not. He toyed with words. Returned again to his store of Shakespeare's words instead, feigning research. But the truth was, he was empty. He had nothing. Into the nothingness, the tyro crept and coiled there, like a talisman to which he held, in a hope too vain to be contemplated.

As if she read his mind, she rose at that instant and came towards him, the bright smile in place. "My sister is eager to play charades. We were always used to do so at home for a Christmas treat. Will you join us?"

Charades! Please God, no. It was of all things what he detested, being obliged to make a figure of himself. As bad as being forced to read his work. But the tyro was smiling at him, engaging him with the warmth he had sorely missed.

"Yes, I will play."

Delight lit her features and he glowed inside, even as the latent horror claimed him. He could scarcely believe he had betrayed himself with ready agreement. But Silvestre was already marshalling the rest, an immediate discussion ensuing of who should be selected to team up together.

With dismay he heard the arrangements planned. The separate parties would have an hour to prepare and must then present their offering to the rest, the whole to be completed before dining on the Christmas goose.

At length it was settled he should be of the party with Silvestre, the duchess and Lady Ella, who had insisted upon being in *Softy's* team, with the addition of Swarland. The rest were to team together under the duke's aegis and — again at the insistence of Lady Ella — include the infant Lady Prudence, known to the company as *Baby Pru.*

"We will repair to the far end of the saloon," said the duchess, adding as she wagged a finger at her spouse, "No cheating, Theo! You are not to spy upon us."

The duke cocked an eyebrow. "I have no need to spy. With you in charge, Hetty, there is no contest. You are bound to make a pig's ear of yours and we will win hands down."

His wife ran back from shepherding her team, for the sole purpose, Joss decided, of delivering a blow to her husband's chest, though laughing the while.

"Rude beast, how dare you! We will beat you, see if we don't! Silve and I are expert charaders."

"If you manage not to fall over the furniture. You should have chosen to have me by you, just in case."

"Pooh! And have you dictating how we should do? I thank you, I had much rather have Silve."

Fascinated, Joss watched his cousin seize his wife in a smothering embrace, laughing and lifting her quite off her feet. Utterly disregarding the presence of so many, he kissed her in full view of them all before setting her down.

"Go to it, Disaster! But don't blame me when your team fails you!" Turning, he clapped his hands. "Come, ladies, we have work to do. Pru, you're with me!" So saying, he swept up the babe and took her to where Lady Lionel, the dowager and her companion were already deep in discussion. No doubt led by Aunt Isobel.

But the duchess was calling out, gleeful and gay. "Come, Silve, everyone! We must put our heads together. Anything to confound my brute of a husband!"

Ribald laughter floated across from the far end where Theo had clearly heard his wife's comment. She had raised her voice at the last for the purpose.

In spite of himself, Joss began to be caught up in the enthusiasm of the group as ideas were entered and discarded. But his attention held on the little piece of interplay between the duke and duchess. Such ease! Such obvious affection. A surge of envy twisted within him and he could not avoid casting a glance at Silvestre's animated countenance.

If he could only bring himself to such a point! It was not in him. Yet he could not help imagining a like scene of domestic bliss. Perhaps not as overt, not as exuberant. But with the freedom to express all he felt.

Then Silvestre turned to him with a look of question that reduced his bones to water. But it proved to have no bearing on the tenor of his thoughts.

"We are agreed on *The Tempest* for our subject. Are you with us, sir?"

The agreeable vision shattered. Joss struggled against the engulfing despair, willing the day to end.

# CHAPTER TWENTY-TWO

A meld of confusion, excitement and trepidation warred within her as Silvestre approached the library, carrying the package containing the sheets of proofs sent up from Beardsley & Beak. While it thrilled her to see her own words printed therein, she found the order of the pages utterly confounding. Four to a sheet and all mixed up!

With a legitimate excuse to beard the vulture, who would undoubtedly be able to unravel the puzzle, she was yet beset with uncertainty and apprehension. She had succeeded in keeping her distance, in the main due to the story of Maud that was tumbling out faster than she could write it down. Indeed Hetty had complained she was become as reclusive as Joss, although her twin had scant leisure to attend her. With Christmas over, a veritable deluge of visits to and fro had begun, led by the dowager, who proclaimed that if the duke, notoriously anti-social, would not do his duty, then the duchess must.

"Theo says I need not, but I am determined to learn my part, Silve."

"As long as you don't chivvy him, I take it?"

Her sister giggled quite in the old way. "I threaten him with it when he makes me cross, but of course I never would make him do what he does not wish, poor Theo. He has quite enough to plague him and relies upon me to keep Cecilia off his back, he says."

"And to cuddle him when he needs refreshment," added Silvestre, quoting the duke and quite unable to refrain from a touch of acidity in the words.

Fortunately her sister, so very much under her spouse's spell, failed to notice, instead sighing in her sentimental way. "Oh, yes, he is so very demonstrative, and utterly uncaring of anyone observing us, the wretch. I do love him so very dearly, Silve."

Swallowing her envy, Silvestre hugged her. "I am glad for your sake, Hetty. You deserve to be happy."

"And you, Silve? You seem a little easier in your mind."

"I am writing again, that's all."

Henrietta's gaze grew awed. "Already? Gracious, Silve, you are keen. Perhaps this Joss of yours is indeed the man for you."

The pang this remark brought was inevitable. She quashed it, finding a smile from somewhere. "Well, likely we shall never know."

Her twin had urged her not to lose hope, adding her satisfaction that the writing was taking her mind off the poet. How little Hetty knew. She had as well be writing a fantastical tale of her own life, inhabiting Maudie's skin as she did. As for the vicar, intense and inward-looking, wholly engaged with his devotions, she need not look far for his counterpart in the real world.

But her pen ran away with her nevertheless, engrossing her in the troubled lives of these two invented persons. Now that Hetty knew what she was at, she made no demur when Silvestre excused herself from joining in with most of the duty visits, although she was obliged to be present when the duke and duchess were the hosts. So also was Joss, she noted, introduced as Lord Joscelin Diggory but then indicated as Gausselin Degarre, the dowager opting to cause the guests to lionise the famous poet.

That he loathed this attention, Silvestre could not doubt. She longed to ease his path for him, seeing how he fell into his habit of staccato speech that signalled the onset of nervousness. But Joss had not granted her that right.

Only once, when she caught an anguished look cast in her direction, did she intervene. Gliding across to where a stout female was gushing at him, she slid into place beside him.

"Lord Joscelin, pray excuse me, but I believe you are wanted." She smiled sunnily upon the stout dame. "Do forgive me, ma'am, for removing him. I believe we have not met. I am the duchess's sister."

She held out a hand, which the woman took in a limp grasp. "Oh, Miss Latimer, is it not? We missed you at my soirée."

"Indeed, I was so very sorry to be unable to attend." Not that she had the faintest notion of when or where it was held. "A slight sore throat, you know, and one cannot be too careful. Now, Lord Joscelin, if you please." With which, she tucked a hand in Joss's arm and drew him away, walking the length of the room and planting him within a stone's throw of his cousin, perforce engaged with a couple of gentlemen. She produced a merry look. "There. I hope you are suitably grateful."

The faint amused look came into his face. "Impressed, rather. You do it so smoothly. I would I had your skill."

"You might, if you chose to cultivate it."

A spasm crossed his face. "God forbid!" He threw a harassed glance about the knots of chatterers. "Dare I slip away, do you think?"

Silvestre would have liked to keep him with her, but she could see her twin beckoning. She touched his arm briefly. "Go. I will cover for you at need."

Something flashed in his eyes. "I think I said it before. You are a treasure, Tyro."

She was warmed, albeit briefly. The next time she saw him, at dinner upon the following day, he proved as aloof as ever. He had begun to look gaunt again and her heart ached for him. But she had some pride. If he wanted her, if he changed his mind, he could sue to her instead. But Joss made no move and she sank back into endurance, taking solace in her writing.

But today was altogether different. Her proofs were come, and he had promised to help her. Indeed, if he did not, she could not manage. Yet the thump at her breast would not be quieted as she approached the library door. She grasped the handle with her free hand, took a breath for courage, and turned it.

One glance across the cavernous space found him, but not at work. He was seated in a chair before the fire, an elbow on the arm supporting his head, in an attitude of dejection. Or it looked so.

Silvestre regarded him from the doorway in silence, tenderness rising in her bosom. What ailed him? Or was this a manifestation of poetic invention? One did go off into a dream world when inspiration struck. Well, she did. Joss was more likely to sit over his notebook, scowling, his hair falling about his face.

Loath to disturb him, yet anxious for him, she crept forward. Her steps nevertheless sounded, but he did not move. Was his reverie total?

She still had hold of the wrapped package that comprised her proofs, but a quick glance showed both desks to be covered in piles of volumes, leaving no suitable space to set it down. How to deal with this? There was nothing for it but to keep them in hand as she moved to the fireplace. What, still no response to her presence?

His hair concealed the greater part of his face, but a certain quality in the rise and fall of his chest betrayed that he slept. Feeling both privileged and guilty, Silvestre watched him. She ought to signal her presence, wake him with a word. But the opportunity to take him in, to enjoy the sight of him without the liability of his knowing it had never before come in her way. She could not relinquish the precious moment.

So still was he, beyond that breath. Silvestre had never seen him so relaxed, even though the pose did not permit of full relaxation. If she was not burdened with her package, she would be tempted to reach out stealthy fingers to touch his hair, stroke it away from his face, and —

"I can see you, Tyro."

Silvestre almost dropped the package. "I thought you were asleep!"

His head lifted and he shook back his hair, revealing the dark eyes that gazed up at her with a piercing gleam. "I was thinking." A grimace. "I may have dozed off for a moment."

Indignation rolled off Silvestre's tongue. "For some time, I should think. You didn't hear me, I know that."

A faintly sheepish look crept into his face. "Well, perhaps not."

She regarded him steadily. "Is this the poet at work, then? Sitting by the fire with his head in his hand?"

"I was cold."

"I am glad to know you can feel something!"

He ignored this, his gaze evidently catching on her package. "Is that what I think it is?"

Silvestre held it out. "My proofs. I wish you will keep your promise, Joss. I cannot make head nor tail of it."

His eye brightened. "Ah, I forgot how they would come." He rose, seemingly unaware of the solecism of remaining seated while she stood. "I'll clear a space."

She watched him cross to the first desk and begin shifting his piles of books to one side. When there was a space large enough for the package to be set down, she crossed to join him. But Joss continued to move books.

"Isn't that enough?"

"No."

So cryptic. "Well?"

He flicked her a glance but continued with his task. "Wait."

Really, he was perfectly irritating. "Why cannot you explain at once?"

"Simpler when I have it prepared. You can set it down."

She did so, feeling distinctly aggrieved. She pulled open the brown paper wrapping to expose the printed sheets. Could he not show a little interest in her work? He called her Tyro, for heaven's sake! He must know how much this meant to her.

It was all of a piece. Even at that first meeting, his intervention had been purely on the basis of the financial implications. Now he was setting about the clerical task at hand with no vestige of question as to her feelings about seeing her words thus displayed. Her very own words! If the proofs were his, it would be a very different matter. He was self-absorbed beyond belief. Must she count herself fortunate he was willing to assist her thus far?

"Have you nothing to say beyond telling me to set the thing down?"

He had moved to the other side of the desk, but his hands stilled on the books he was about to pick up and he lifted his gaze to hers, his brows snapping together. "Attacking me, Tyro? I'm trying to help!"

Abruptly fuming, she struck the thick pile of sheets with her fist. "This, Joss! This is my story! It is not just a pile of paper. My heart and soul are invested here. Have you nothing to say of that?"

He surveyed her, muscles twitching in his face. "I don't know. What should I say?"

Her throat ached and her voice turned husky. "Oh, I have been blind indeed! I thought … I thought you cared a little."

Anguish in his face? She was too wound up to read it. His hands clenched on the books.

"I … you know … Silvestre, I —"

"You can't? You can't even grant me that? Well, so be it. You warned me enough." She threw a wild gesture over the pages. "Show me how to do it and I will leave you to your obsessions."

For several nerve-racking moments he did not speak, his gaze lowering to the desk, his fingers shifting the books in an aimless fashion, his hair falling forward to conceal his face.

Too distressed and angry to have room for his ubiquitous tensions, Silvestre struggled only to contain the hot words rising to her tongue. She had said enough. She knew enough now. She was a fool ever to have supposed she might pierce his armour to his core and draw forth the dream figure she had invented for herself. The one who was learning to encompass the concerns of another as well as his own. He was not Gausselin Degarre.

The fury died out of her, leaving a corrosive disillusionment that threatened to overwhelm her. She spoke, but the dead voice did not seem to belong to her. "It makes no matter, Joss. You are who you are. Let us leave it there."

The words, the tone, so reminiscent of that earlier time, broke through the despairing guilt. It signalled withdrawal. She was pulling away from him. The agony now was a thousand times multiplied from what it had been then. The impulse proved too strong.

"Don't, Tyro! Please don't give up on me!" Without prior intent, Joss went around the table, fast. He caught her unquiet hands and held them in a fierce grip, meeting the clouded gaze. "I do care. You know I do. If I could change for you, I would."

An affecting little smile twisted her mouth and echoed in his heart. "But you can't, can you? You won't let yourself."

"I dare not."

Her fingers moved in his, as if she would release herself. He let them go. The tyro's eyes showed pity and he cringed inside.

"But it's no use, you see, Joss. I've been foolish, a dreamer. If you were the man I hoped was there, you would have thought first of me, not the proofs."

Confusion wreathed his brain. "Why? Proofs are within my experience. I said I would help."

"Yes, and I am grateful for it." Her gaze shifted to the pages and she ran a finger across the type. "I wrote this, you see."

A thick band of pain began to tighten on his brow as he struggled to understand what had made her so alarmingly infuriated. "Yes, I know."

She gave a sigh that pricked at his conscience again. What had he done? Or what had he not done? Her gaze met his, an odd look in her eyes he could not interpret.

"Did not you feel it when you saw your own first proofs? Was it not a wonder to you, to see your very own words looking back at you from the page?"

He fluttered his hands. "I suppose I did. I no longer recall. When I receive my proofs I am only anxious they have not utterly misread my writing and made a plethora of errors."

She nodded. "Yes, you would be. That is how you thought of mine, no doubt. Or at least, you thought only of the necessity to do whatever it is we must do to make sense of them."

"Yes, I fear that is true." He still felt guilty, but without knowing why. He was losing her and he did not know how to prevent her going away from him. Desperation seized him. "What should I have done, Tyro? Tell me. What should I have said?"

"If I have to tell you, it becomes worthless, Joss."

"I want to learn. At least, I want to learn of you." *Keep you. Have you think of me with a better thought than the one you now possess.* But he could not bring himself to say it aloud.

She was touching the proofs, delicately, picking out words, lighting on the name of her leading character. She said it. "Emmeline." She picked up the top sheet and held it in her fingers. "Magic, Joss. It is a process of magic, is it not? I think it up, I write it down and then here it is, in print, almost ready for another to partake of my imagination. It awes me. It excites me. It makes me swell with pride and affection."

He heard it with a rise of grief. He did remember. It was a long time since he had felt it. No, that was untrue. He spoke on the thought. "Yes, I should have realised. There is that first rapture. Until it is overlaid with anxiety."

She smiled and the sun came out for him. "You see!" A tiny frown. "You admitted as much before. When I asked about satisfaction. That was what you said. When you first had the book in your hand."

A laugh escaped him. "Ah, the book. That is different. Then you will feel it indeed."

She waved the sheet at him. "I feel it now, Joss! But you did not think of it, and that is the difference between us."

He was silenced. She had as well have called him selfish. He felt terrible. He had failed her, just when it behoved him to buoy her spirits, to offer praise. Or at least applause for her achievement. Had not his mother warned him? Her words had come home with a vengeance. The one person he desired to please above all others, and he had fallen so far short she despised him now. Knew him for what he was. Had he not over and again enjoined her to do just that? Who had he to blame except himself?

Yet he still had a trick to play. She needed him, if only for this one thing.

"Let me show you how it works."

She had been sifting the pages, but she desisted at this, looking up with eagerness. "Yes, do, Joss. I can see four pages are printed on each sheet, but upside-down and the page numbers higgledy-piggledy. How can I possibly read it?"

He fanned the top few sheets. "See here. These leaves are called signatures, printed ready for folding and sewing, the putting together of the book. Do you see how each leaf is printed on both sides, making eight pages in all?" He took up one sheet and turned it over, folding it back so the printed pages sat together. "This will be folded like so." He made another fold to create the crease as it would be within a book. "Then again, like so. Now you see how the numbers begin to marry up." He grabbed up a paper knife and slit the top fold, holding it firmly together. "When the page is cut, you will see we now have consecutive pages on each side."

She reached to point to the crease. "But these do not go together."

"No, because they will sew three or four sheets together to make a batch. Then the batches are sewn to make a whole and that is the binding done."

"So they are ordered to fit the necessity? No wonder it made no sense."

"It makes sense to the printer. For our purposes, we must cut it up and order it so that you can read it without difficulty. I will cut the pages while you begin to set them in consecutive order." He extracted his pocket knife and slid off the sheath, aware of her watching. Inconsequently, as he set about the first cut, slicing through two or three sheets at once, he recalled her speaking of the motion of his fingers and a flitter of amusement lightened the latent panic. "Don't watch me, Tyro. You make me think of that spider analogy of yours."

A gurgling laugh escaped her. "You remember it?"

"How could I forget?" He made a horizontal cut and collected up the first batch of freed pages. "Take these and you may begin your part."

She took them from his hand, but did not move from the spot. He had begun cutting again, but paused to glance up. Silvestre was reading the text, her lower lip caught between her teeth, her face glowing.

Mesmerised, he watched her concentrated attention. This was what she meant. She was savouring her words on the page. A snippet of remembrance of his early years came back to him. "It is as if it was written by another, is it not? Hard to believe you wrote it?"

She looked up, joy breaking in her face, a flush mounting to her cheeks. "Oh, it's exquisite! I feel … dazed. Privileged. Ecstatic!"

A welter of feeling tumbled through him. Exquisite? She was exquisite! She was everything a man could ever want. She was beyond his deserts. An unattainable dream, a golden butterfly, too delicate for a spider's web. He would crush her wings to powder.

But she must be answered in kind. She must be allowed her pleasure in the triumph.

"Well, they are your words, Silvestre. Yours alone. Whatever comes, no one can take that away from you."

Her beam rewarded him and her eyes shone. The ache of want curled in his breast.

"Thank you, Vulture. I feel like a real writer."

"That you are, Tyro. Or, no. I will have to revise my name for you."

Her lips parted and the mischievous glint appeared. "Don't. I like it. I am a tyro compared to you, to the others I met."

"Not for long, I'll wager." He turned, feeling as if he acted a part, to resume cutting the pages. "You are writing again."

"How did you know?" She was shuffling the pages together as she moved to the other side of the desk.

"Inky fingers."

She laughed, a carefree sound that vibrated in his heart. "I cannot keep them free of it."

"That's why I use pencil. I am obliged to copy in ink, but while I am composing, I use only pencil."

"I did for *Emmeline* in the end, though I held off as long as I could. I like to see the words appearing in ink." She set down her pages and began to sift them into order. "Though I am likely to run out, with the speed at which this story is determined to flow."

Joss was conscious of a sliver of envy. She wrote with facility? Fortunate tyro. Some writers had it. He did not. Nor was he one of those who supposed fast writing necessarily meant bad, as Moreton Pinckney was disposed to believe. He cut into the pages with a touch more ferocity at the thought of the critic who had savaged his words too often.

Without speaking, he handed the cut pages across, noting in passing how absorbed was the tyro in her task, sorting the pages. He was conscious of a smidgeon of pleasure in the act of sharing the work with her.

She glanced across. "It is coming together. I had not thought it would be as many pages as this."

"It is likely two volumes for a novel. You will find where they start and end."

She took the next batch of pages from him. "Two volumes! This is exciting, Joss."

He smiled but made no comment, noting how she was creating little piles of consecutive pages and adding to them. "Wait until you read it properly."

"In book form, you mean?"

"No, like this. I will show you how to make the marks where you find errors. There is a science to it."

She paused in her work, looking at him with an expression he could not fathom. "That is what you were doing when we met, do you remember?"

A spasm gripped him. "I remember it all." How could he forget? Her every word was etched in his mind, her every facial turn, revolving there to haunt him.

She remained unmoving, regarding him steadily, the papers she was about to sort held loosely in her fingers. Her voice came softly. "You won't forget me when I go?"

He could not speak, instead indicating a negative with his head so that his hair whipped about. He tossed it back with an impatient hand and set his concentration back to cutting pages.

The silence as they worked on became oppressive. Joss cut through the last of the pages and began absently to sort them.

*Don't go. Don't leave me. Stay. Be mine.* Live in his darkness, he might as well say. The thought forced words to his tongue, innocuous, necessary. "I'll help you sort them." Necessary, because then he could show her how to do for the printer's edification and be freed from unbearable temptation.

Soon enough the pile of sheets were ready, and her mood became brisk. "There, it is looking more like a book already. What do we do now?"

He found two chairs and set them side by side. "Come. Bring the pages."

She came to take a seat, setting down the now thick pile, what time Joss found one of his sharpened pencils.

"Read," he instructed, "and stop when you find an error."

Beardsley & Beak's typesetter was good at his job, but mistakes crept in nevertheless. There was one on the second page.

"Emmeline is missing the final e."

His professional instincts aroused, Joss showed her how to mark the error, with a stroke in the margin adding in the missing letter. "There are marks to delineate different types of errors. Here, I will draw you up a list as you read on."

He found a fresh sheet of paper and set down the correction marks commonly used in the work of proofing, explaining them as he wrote them in. "If you come across an error for which you have no mark, just write a note in the margin. With clarity. That is the important thing."

He worked with her through some ten or twenty pages, forgetful of his inner demons for the little companionable time he spent doing it. It felt pleasant to instruct her, so apt a pupil as she proved, ready to learn, willing to do as he said without argument. He was struck by her humility in deferring to his better knowledge, humbled himself by her gratitude as she turned at last to look at him rather than the page.

"Well! It is a demanding task. I can see why you were so concentrated that time at the publisher's premises."

His quiescence at an end, Joss felt the now familiar yearning rising again. He forced words to his tongue. "You will become accustomed. Take a break when you tire. It is best to do it in small doses."

She quirked a smile. "You don't. You go at the thing like a demented boar, digging for roots."

He burst into laughter. "I thank you, Tyro. Yet another evil comparison."

The mischief, balm to his affection, was rife in her eyes. "A very helpful boar to me, however. Also decidedly patient with the novice. Thank you."

"You are very welcome." It was not at all what he wanted to say. If he spoke his mind he would say she might count upon his services all the days of his life. That he would cherish and worship her from now until eternity. If he did not know himself too well to dare. Promises, promises. He would fall at the first hurdle. Renege. Abandon. Loose the vials of his pent-up frustrations over her freshness and smash it to smithereens. "You are very welcome."

She had turned back to the proofs, but she glanced round, frowning. "You already said that."

"Did I?"

"Just now." A quizzical look. "Where have your wits gone begging, Vulture?"

He could not look away from her. "I don't know."

She eyed him, her changing thoughts reflecting in her face. If he could only read them! No. They would prick and hurt and cause him to lose control as he had lost the thread.

She dipped her head on one side. "Yes?"

He made a half-gesture of his head. "Nothing."

Her brows lifted. "Why do you stare at me, then?"

Instantly he cast his gaze elsewhere, unseeing, her image yet in his mind's eye. "You … confound me."

"What, like a magician?" A light laugh, but was there a note of pain within it?

Obeying instinct, he turned to her again. "Exactly like a magician. Casting spells."

She did not answer, her gaze roving his as if she sought to fathom his thoughts. Thankfully veiled, he hoped. He willed his tongue to silence for fear of its betraying him into words he must not utter.

Silvestre at last looked away, got up, gathered the pile of proofs and turned the overturned pages back. He watched her with growing dismay, knowing she was going to depart, tear herself away. He rose, shoving his chair back.

"May I keep this pencil?"

He gestured permission. "It won't remain sharp for long."

"I have a knife in my writing box." She moved away from the desk and looked at him. "I enjoyed that."

His heart thudded out of rhythm, beating in his head. *Don't go.* "I too."

She lifted the proofs a fraction. "I shall go and work on these. I must send them back within the week, Mr Christy wrote."

"Yes. If they mean to publish in spring, the time is tight."

She nodded, turned, walked to the door. He willed her to turn back, but she did not pause. The door opened and she was gone.

Joss stood for an endless time, watching the closed door.

# CHAPTER TWENTY-THREE

The rocking of the carriage at length began to soothe Silvestre's lacerated bosom. Like a cradle, with an unseen hand in constant motion, humming the baby to rest. Along with the hush of wheels, the clopping hooves, the jingle of the harness and the shifting miles that carried her out of reach.

She had been free to weep, mingling her tears with Hetty's, who had thrown herself into her husband's arms at the last for comfort. No such embrace for Silvestre.

What, fling herself at the vulture, whose arms, though he was present with the rest for the general farewell, remained firmly clasped behind him? In a fancy of the night before, she had pictured herself stealing into the library to find him, setting her hands upon his shoulders and, ignoring his prohibitions, putting her lips to his. To say goodbye. To let him know her heart. Oh, what? He knew it already. Knew it, and threw it back, unwanted, a burden to him and his confounded poetry.

It had hurt to be allowed only to shake his hand, the skin dry to her touch, the spider fingers clinging for an instant before they let hers go. Balm, of a sort. But then it hurt the more to leave her twin, to feel again the wrench of parting that had spawned *Emmeline*.

She was grateful for Lady Lionel's silence through those first agonising miles. No platitudes, no beseeching her to think of the silver lining, no attempt to turn her mind from grief. Instead, she captured Silvestre's hand, squeezed it strongly, recommended her to have a good cry, and released her to her tears.

They ceased sooner than she might have supposed. It was not in her nature to weep buckets like poor Hetty. Besides, when she noticed how Martha partook of her feelings, sniffing into a pocket handkerchief, a riffle of amusement could not but lighten the gloom. The maid, her services superfluous to Devenal now that Silvestre was going home, was returning to Whisley Park. Like Lady Lionel Devenal's personal maid Miss Melmerby, a dour dragon of a female, Martha was detailed to wait upon Silvestre during the journey. She roused herself to rally the girl.

"You are not sorry to be going back to Whisley, are you, Martha? I thought you said you preferred it to Devenal?"

"Oh, yes, Miss Silve." The maid pocketed her handkerchief with an air of being done with crying. "But it were melancholy just the same."

Her own situation prompted a possible reason for the girl's woe. "Do not tell me you have a beau there?"

Martha's cheeks flew colour under the poke bonnet she wore. "Me, miss? Well, not as you might say, Miss Silve. I don't think as Jonas has an eye to me."

"Jonas, is it? Well, he is a handsome fellow."

A sigh escaped the maid, which drew a disapproving look from the elder woman beside her. "Ooh, that he is, miss. He were kind too."

Miss Melmerby cleared her throat in a marked manner and Martha, blushing again, subsided.

A silvery laugh came from Lady Lionel. "Well, well, let us be done with weeping over him, or any other male. Really, these men are far too idiotic to be worth so many tears from their womenfolk."

That this was directed to herself Silvestre could not doubt. Lady Lionel had not taken the opportunity to quiz her about Joss, and it struck her now that it had been deliberate. Had she then planned to use instead this convenience of travelling together? The suggestion had come from her, had it not?

"Silve, we have solved the difficulty of sending you home," her twin had disclosed on an eager note. "Not that I wish you to go, but you may stop fretting."

Silvestre had been anxious. Not that she wanted to go either, but their godmother had written that she meant to go to London in February and it had been settled Silvestre would go with her to be in the metropolis for the publication of *Emmeline*.

"Mama too has sent to ask when you are going home, Silve, for Papa is anxious to have at least one of his daughters at home for a space before you go gallivanting off to the capital, as he puts it."

"I will hardly be gallivanting."

Henrietta's eyes had filled. "I expect he does not wish you to be too long under Theo's influence."

"No such thing. Dry your eyes, Hetty. Mama says he is coming round. I dare say he will be so reconciled as to meet Theo with complaisance when you come down to Whisley Park in the summer."

The only blight upon Hetty's happiness, as Silvestre knew, was their father's freely expressed aversion to her husband. But she obediently sniffed back her tears and smiled. "Well, I will have the pleasure of seeing Mama again. You too, Silve. Oh, I have loved having you with me! I shall miss you so."

Silvestre replied suitably, but she did not think her sister would miss her for long, so absorbed into her new life as she had become. If she was honest, the thought of the wrench from Joss exercised her more than that from her twin. She focused her attention on the matter at hand. "What is the solution, Hetty?"

"Oh, you will like it above all things. Isobel is going to Aike Manor to visit her sister and it is not too far out of her way to set you down at Sinsham."

"Going to visit her sister? Lady Rotherhythe?"

"Yes, do you know her? Oh, no, I suppose Lord Joscelin has spoken of his mother."

"Once or twice. Does he know of this?"

"I have no notion. I expect she will tell him. He may have messages or a letter for his mama, after all."

The intelligence served to set up a train of speculation in Silvestre's head. Gratified, and sensible of the favour conferred upon her, she still questioned the extent of Lady Lionel's intent. Had she any influence with Joss? Or did she merely seek to discover how Silvestre's feelings lay?

One ought not to be suspicious of a benevolent act, but she had not failed to notice measuring glances cast upon her whenever Joss was present. Try as she would, Silvestre knew she could not wholly conceal her partiality. Lady Lionel was besides a female of extraordinary perspicacity. How much had she divined?

Silvestre was glad of the presence of the maids, which must spare her from any untoward questioning in the carriage. Outspoken as she was, Theo's mother did not lack discretion. She began innocuously enough.

"An exciting time awaits you, Silve. I declare, I could almost be persuaded out of my retirement to partake of your triumph."

"We don't know there will be any triumph, ma'am. Mr Christy warned me in his letter not to expect an overnight success. Especially as my book is something of a departure from the type of story they have been publishing."

Lady Lionel struck a hand on her knee. "I love that! It is high time we readers were offered better choice. I predict you will become a sensation in no time."

A flitter of excitement overlaid the settled ache of loss. "To be truthful, I doubt it, ma'am, but I am happy to be published at all. It was a strange experience reading my own words."

"Ah, yes, proofing. I gather my nephew roused himself to show you how it is done?"

Remembrance of those bittersweet moments with Joss could not but prick at her despair. She spoke as lightly as she could. "He did, yes. I could not have managed without his help. As it was, I was done within two days and sent the proofs back express."

"Capital. Joscelin has his uses."

The tone was mischievous, but Silvestre could not respond in kind. She turned the subject. "Do you make a long stay with your sister, ma'am?"

"I hardly know. We do not meet often, but one should keep up when one can. We correspond regularly and have always done so. Amelia takes solace from it, poor love. She is plagued with so many children, she has been in a constant worry forever. She only has Louise on her hands now, but do you suppose she has ceased to fret over those boys of hers?"

Oh, this was riding close to the wind indeed. But the urge to hear any snippet of Joss's family would not be denied. "Well, I suppose any mother would worry with three sons in the military."

"Three hulking officers, my dear, and all as healthy as they are mutton-headed."

Silvestre could not forbear a spurt of laughter. "For shame, Lady Lionel! How can you say so?"

"With ease, I assure you," said the other, twinkling. "Too harsh, you think? Well, perhaps. But this I will say for the poet: his intellect outstrips them all."

Must she harp on Joss? She made a bid to deflect the emphasis. "What about the daughters?"

"To be frank, I know less of them than the boys. With Louise under her eye, Amelia has only to fret about bringing her out, and not for a year or two yet. Selina looks set to follow her parents, for she has already produced three or four boys. I cannot precisely recall how many, but from my sister's letters, she seems to be forever pregnant. Penelope, however, has yet to bring one babe to term. But she is young yet and may do so in time. I sympathise, for it was much the same with me."

This called for remark, and Silvestre did not hesitate. "I am sorry to hear it, ma'am. You had only Theo in the end?"

"Yes, and he is idiot enough, I thank you," said her ladyship with a merry laugh. "Oh, don't misunderstand me. I adore the boy and he uses his head most of the time. But he was as foolish as any man when it came to love. Really, it is a wonder any of them manage to find domestic felicity, so stupid as they can be upon this subject."

They were back to that, were they? Silvestre refrained from answering, but she need not have troubled in any event, for Lady Lionel held forth upon her favourite hobby horse for several miles, regaling the occupants of the carriage with her unflattering opinions on the vagaries and stupidities of the male sex.

Tinged with wit as they were, her observations kept Silvestre in a ripple of amusement and she could not but suspect it was a deliberate ploy to divert her mind. During the one short break taken, there was time only to snatch a little refreshment before the horses were put to and the coach set off again.

Lady Lionel travelled with her own coachman and groom, along with a single outrider who acted as her courier, smoothing her path at the various halts. "I leave all that to Brigsteer. A capable fellow. He accompanied Theo upon his various travels, much to my peace of mind. But he was my husband's man and did not wish to transfer to Devenal. He serves me well."

This was soon seen to be the case. It was already dusk when the carriage drew up in the yard of the inn where they were to stay the night, but at sight of the inn sign designating a crown, recognition and remembrance leapt in Silvestre.

Brigsteer was awaiting them with the landlord ready to usher them into the Crown.

"I am Postwick, my lady. Allow me to conduct you to your private parlour. Your dinner will be ready within a half hour, and my wife will see the maids to your rooms."

Silvestre followed in Lady Lionel's wake, dismay rising at the flood of images flitting through her mind. Of snow, of precious shared confidences, of the vulture in his moods. Worse yet, she found herself in the very same parlour the party had occupied on the journey up.

She removed her cloak and bonnet at Martha's urging, undid the buttons of her pelisse and went to warm her hands by the fire, unheeding of Lady Lionel's instructions to the maids, who disappeared in the landlord's wake.

Here had she sat, Joss showing anxiety about her condition. Even then was it thus between them? Here in this room they had called friends. Friends! A convenient alternative to what ought to have been. Might have been, but for his obstinacy, his obsessive insistence that he would do more harm than good. Really, Lady Lionel had it right. Men were unutterably stupid!

"Are you desperate, my dear Silve? I carry a bordaloo, but I hate using the things in a carriage. So undeedy and apt to spill."

Startled out of her abstraction, and not a little embarrassed by Lady Lionel's candour, Silvestre felt her cheeks grow warm. "I am comfortable enough for the moment, ma'am, I thank you. But I can do with freshening up before dinner."

Lady Lionel gave a peal of laughter. "Freshening up? How we women love our euphemisms!"

Silvestre had to laugh. "Not you, Lady Lionel. You call a spade a spade."

"I do, for I can't bear such namby-pamby nonsense. As if the necessary functions of our bodies were taboo. Ridiculous." She joined Silvestre by the fire, dropping into the opposite chair. "Speaking of names, I wish you will call me Isobel, my dear. I loathe formality and it quite makes me feel a stranger to hear you address me as Lady Lionel. Heaven knows we are well enough acquainted."

"Are we?"

"Well, if not, we are going to be, so there you are."

The prediction was faintly alarming, but her charm was irresistible. "Very well. Isobel it shall be."

Isobel smiled. "Now we may be comfortable together and chatter away like old friends."

More alarming still. With the memories in her head, Silvestre could not but fear the potential topic that might well be broached. She spoke at random, anything to effect delay.

"Your fellow Brigsteer is indeed efficient. We had Mr Swarland to order things."

"Cecilia's steward? A dour man, but indispensable to her, she says. Which is true, I expect. When one has no husband, it is comfortable to have a man about for such purposes."

"They have some value for you then, ma'am?"

Isobel burst into laughter. "There's for me! Oh, I don't deny they have their uses. The world would not run without them, the dear creatures. If only they would use their heads to better purpose. Yet no one will persuade me of the truth of this nonsensical notion that women have smaller brains and cannot rationalise. A convenient excuse to keep us in our place. My husband — an exceptional man, I'll have you know — never subscribed to that science. Indeed, I suspect he had more of woman in him than most, his understanding was so superior."

"You were fortunate."

"I was, and I am ever sensible of it. I would never marry again. I could not hope to find his like."

A sentiment that echoed in Silvestre's bosom. Spinsterhood was preferable to marrying any other man than the vulture.

She caught an intent look on Isobel's face and at once recalled how Joss would say her thoughts were mirrored in her face. She must veil them. Lady Lionel needed no ammunition.

Thankfully the maids came in before Isobel could remark upon it and she followed Martha to her allotted chamber. By the time she had made use of the chamber pot and washed away the travel stains, she was so hungry she forgot the possible trend of the conversation and was relieved to see a waiter setting out dishes on the table when she returned to the parlour.

Isobel hailed her from the fireplace. "Ah, good, you have not changed. I meant to say you need make no alteration in your dress."

"I had not thought of doing so, I confess. Besides, it is a deal too cold to be wearing an evening gown."

"Come and warm up by the fire, my dear, while the waiters are making all ready. It would be foolish to stand upon ceremony when there are only the two of us."

The frisson of expectancy rose up again and Silvestre was glad of the excuse to keep her face averted as she leaned to the fire, rubbing her hands. But in a very few minutes, she was seated at the table opposite Lady Lionel, who was lifting the lids off dishes.

"Roast fowl, cutlets and beefsteaks in mushroom. Ah, and a dish of broccoli. Well, it all looks well enough prepared. You don't mind that I dismissed the waiter? So much cosier to serve ourselves."

Her look was mischievous and Silvestre braced. The moment had come, she was convinced. Isobel meant to tackle her about Joss.

She partook of chicken and a cutlet, her appetite quickening as she began upon the meal. When nothing untoward was said, Isobel confining her remarks to the food, she began to relax. In vain.

Lady Lionel rang the bell with vigour when both plates were clean. "We will have all this away and sit to our wine like the men, shall we? Brigsteer will have commanded cheese and fruit, but would you wish for sweetmeats? Or tartlets, if they have any prepared?"

Silvestre declined, feeling hollow with rising dread at the thought of the coming *tête-à-tête*. Before long, the table was cleared, a cheeseboard laid together with a bowl of pears and grapes and a dish of walnuts and Isobel was refilling her glass from the claret bottle.

"There! At last we have a little time to ourselves, my dear, and high time it is too."

Silvestre felt a tremble at her lips. Instinct threw her on the defensive. "If you mean to quiz me, Isobel, I must warn you we tread on marshy ground and I may sink."

A warm look of sympathy came her way. "Do you suppose I did not know it? My dear child, your heart is in your eyes."

Those same eyes pricked and Silvestre had to blink the wetness away. "Don't, ma'am!"

"Weep if you wish, my dear, though I had far rather you talked freely. You have given yourself a rocky road, falling in love with my terrible nephew."

Indignation rose, superseding the urge to weep. "He is not terrible! You misunderstand him. Everyone does. He can't help his nature."

"Oh, pish! Does he try?"

Having accused him in the self-same way, she was hard put to it to find excuses. "Well, if he does not, it is not really selfishness. He is … he is self-absorbed, yes, but not vain. There is no arrogance in it. It is more that he is caught up in his own head, in the struggle within."

"You defend him with vehemence, Silve. I wonder if he deserves it?"

Between unwarranted fury and her innate honesty that had forced her to such appraisals on her own, Silvestre sputtered in reply. "That is not … whether he does or not… Oh, can't you see, Isobel? I don't care for that. What he deserves is immaterial. He is who he is. How could I wish to change him? He drew me as he is. Yet I do — or I have tried. He likes me to tease him, I know he does. I can bring him out of his shell and make him laugh, and he likes that. But he's afraid of … of hurting me. He thinks he will crush my spirit, and I fear he's right."

Lady Lionel set down her glass and put her hand over Silvestre's, clasping the fist she'd made without realising. "You love him deeply, I can see that, my poor child."

For once, in this little parlour that had seen the burgeoning of her feeling, and of his, Silvestre let the truth flow at last. "I love him so dearly, I had rather let him go than try to net him, only to satisfy my own desire to be with him. It would hurt me to know he took me against his better judgement."

Releasing her, Isobel threw her hands up in a wild gesture. "Heavens, you are as obstinate as Joscelin himself!"

"Well, if I am, it is for his own good."

"Do not talk flummery to me, girl! I have no patience with it. What, will you condemn yourself to misery — and Joscelin too — merely for lack of a good shove? It is of no use expecting any man to take the plunge without being kicked into it, you know, and my nephew is no exception."

"But I don't want him to be kicked into it! If he were willing, if he wished to offer marriage…"

"My dear, if we were to wait upon men being willing, there would be few marriages at all! Why do you suppose these poor females, unfairly designated matchmaking mamas, are driven to throw their daughters under the noses of suitable men? Nary a one of them, unless desperate to catch a fortune or in need of an heir, will set themselves one foot towards the altar unless their womenfolk thrust them in that direction. They love their untrammelled lives too much. Why take on the burden of a wife if they need not?"

This could not but rouse Silvestre's debating instinct. "Oh, you exaggerate, ma'am. Moreover, you make no allowance for those so desperate to marry the woman they love they will even run off to Gretna Green."

"Pooh! It's not marriage they want, my dear. But in order to get what they want with a respectable female, they have no choice but to offer marriage."

"You are too cynical, Isobel. I don't believe men are as wholly to be despised as you say."

That drew a feathery laugh from the older woman. "Naturally you don't. You are head over heels in love, and that, as I know only too well, is apt to colour one's judgement."

"Yet you would have me shove poor Joss into going against his conscience."

"Conscience forsooth! He's afraid of losing his independence. They all are. Wives are an encumbrance and a spur to doing things he would far rather leave undone. Indeed, I was astonished he consented to partake of the Christmas festivities."

"Theo insisted. Hetty told me."

"There you are, then. Left to himself, he would have hidden in that mausoleum of a library and brooded all alone. As it was, he enjoyed himself a great deal. I can vouch for that. I was watching him, as I don't doubt you were too."

"I was not!" Silvestre drew a breath and back-tracked. "Well, I tried not to."

"With scant success, my child, and who shall blame you? Take comfort from the fact he was watching you quite as assiduously."

Silvestre's breath caught and her heart felt as if it stopped in her chest. She stared at Isobel. "Was he? Truly?"

A mischievous smile creased Lady Lionel's mouth and she took up her glass again and sipped.

Silvestre balked. "Pray tell me! I need to know!"

Isobel's brows rose. "Oh, now you need to know? But a moment ago you were ready to renounce the creature."

"Oh, ma'am, don't tease me, pray!"

Her companion laughed and put down her glass. "My child, he could scarcely take his eyes off you. I have no doubt he is at this moment bewailing having held his tongue and missing you like the devil."

# CHAPTER TWENTY-FOUR

The emptiness yawned at him. Though the mansion bustled, never free of its plethora of master, mistresses and servants going about their business, the absence of one individual made the place barren. Joss threw himself, demon-like, into his library work, keeping himself and his appointed helper scouring away the hours.

Yet no amount of scurrying up and down ladders, no weight of books, books, books to sort, no scribble of pencilled notes in his makeshift maps served to eradicate the images. Nor the constant ache as the days turned into weeks.

Worse at table, when the twin was present, so like and yet unlike, tormenting him with a trick of similarity which brought the tyro into sharper focus. Once, when Henrietta set her head on one side to ask a question of him, he stared at her blankly, beset with the impossible notion that it was Silvestre sitting there. Then she shifted and the illusion was gone.

Worse yet, the duchess had begun treating him with a sympathetic air. He found his seat moved to her left at dinner, forcing him to converse with a creature all too apt to call her sister into play. That she was in Silvestre's confidence he could not doubt. Why else feed him bulletins of her doings?

"Silve tells me her new book is growing fast, Lord Joscelin. She is in hopes it may be done by the time she goes to London with our godmother."

He knew not how to reply. He cleared his throat. "Some writers can. Write fast. Useful."

"You don't, sir?"

He shook his head. He wrote in spurts. Or slowly. Not at all of late. He was devoid of inspiration and willingness both. He was dry, unable to settle to the task beyond reading Shakespeare, only to be reminded by some twist or turn of plot or speech. The fellow wrote too much of the curse of loving.

"But will the publishers wish for a second book so soon?"

A nuance in Henrietta's voice struck a pang into his breast. It might have been his tyro speaking. He answered at random. "Hard to say. Likely they'll wait."

"To see how the first book is received? I am dying to read it! I am so proud of Silve. She is much more capable than I am, you must know. We were always used to say she is the practical twin."

"While you, my sweet disaster," came laughingly from the other end of the table, "are the twin all sensibility and utterly impractical."

The duchess threw her husband an admonitory look. "You shouldn't be listening, Theo! It's rude to talk across the table."

"It's my table. I'll talk across it if I like."

A degree of informality had obtained the last couple of days in the absence of the dowager duchess, who was keeping to her room on account of some trifling disorder. Leaves had been removed from the dining-table when the duke's mother and Silvestre had left, giving a cosier arrangement. It did not suit Joss, obliging him as it must to join in the general conversation.

"It happens I was talking to your cousin, not to you, my lord duke."

Well used by now to the banter between the young couple, Joss was nevertheless conscious of the twinge of envy and loss that never failed to strike him. In their case, it was his cousin who teased, just as the tyro teased Joss. He missed that. Yet he missed her serious mien as much. He missed the way her features showed her changing thoughts. He missed the tell-tale affection in her eyes. He even missed the way she berated him when he did not respond as she wished.

"It is a pity you cannot be in London when the book comes out."

He came out of his thoughts in a bang. London? Longing swept into his breast. Yes, he missed that too. He had thought he despised his literary set, but this exile from it was punishing. The tyro would be in the thick of it while he was incarcerated in this northern retreat. He would know nothing of her success or failure. He would not be there to comfort or advise. Or to applaud.

"Yes, I wish I might be there." He said it without thinking. Then instantly regretted it as the duchess gave him a look brimful of anxious question.

"Do you think it will be a success, my lord? I can't bear it if poor Silve is disappointed. It is bad enough to see her —" She broke off, flushing.

Guilt swamped him. He had no difficulty in completing the sentence. To see her despairing? Miserable? As despairing and miserable as he was himself? But moodiness was habitual to him. He alone was responsible for Silvestre's clouded mien. What comfort could he offer? None to the twin who ached for her sister's pain. But the book he could speak about. "Beak likes it. His judgement is sound."

"Beak?"

"The publisher. I don't speak of Christy. He's a mere cypher. Beak knows his business. His predictions are invariably correct."

"Does he predict a success?"

"A change in public taste. This *Emmeline* is different enough. Beak thinks it may take."

The duchess beamed, lighting up in a fashion that could not but bring the tyro to life in his head again. In just such a way had she smiled at him in the snow. And turned his life upside down and inside out.

"Then there is hope for her. I am so glad."

"Hope, yes."

Henrietta gave him a straight look. "For the book."

Her meaning pierced him. No hope for the other. No hope from him. He fell back upon the reasoning that was keeping him sane. "She is resilient. She will weather it."

The sister eyed him, her eyes brimming with moisture. "You think so?"

He ignored the husky note. Tried to. "I believe so."

She gave him a sad little smile. "I don't think you know Silve very well, Joscelin."

Not as well as he wished he might. But the rebuke was just. His mother had warned him and he had paid no heed. He ought to have been more caring. He ought to have given…

Given what? The question haunted him through the ceremony of passing the port when the duchess and the dowager's companion had retired. Joss left Hathersage and Swarland to bear the burden of conversation with his cousin, sitting in a brown study as he nursed his glass.

"Don't hog the bottle, coz."

He looked up at the duke. "What?"

Theo jerked his head and Joss realised the decanter was at his elbow. He passed it along with a word of apology. The duke filled his glass and set the decanter down before Hathersage, but his eyes were on Joss.

"Nothing to say this evening, coz? We're talking books, you know."

Joss frowned in an effort of concentration, his question still revolving in his head. "Books?"

"The things you write? That my sister-in-law writes? Bluestocking fodder, my friend. Hathersage here is all for Smollett, but I've had adventure enough of my own, I thank you. Swarland favours histories. Who's that fellow you mentioned, Swarland?"

"Stanford Wingley, your grace."

"That's it. Wingley. You know him?"

Joss blinked to attention. "He's a friend of mine. We were up at Oxford together. A good fellow."

"There you are, Swarland. I thought my cousin must be acquainted with these literary types."

Obliged to answer a series of enquiries from the steward, Joss lost track of his question for a while. But it came back to him when he took to his bed, causing him to lose sleep, tossing and turning. He ought to have given what?

It came to him at last in a dream. He was walking, his mother at his side. There was snow, and strange heat, and a smattering of birdsong in the air. Somewhere his brothers shouted in their rough and tumble fashion, pelting each other with snowballs. A coach rumbled past and he caught a glimpse of her face. Silvestre. Looking out at him, a passing ghost with sad eyes.

"You should have given of yourself, Joss." His mother's voice. "You're a miser, my son. You kept yourself inside and you would not let her in. See the bright sunshine? See how your brothers play?"

"I can't," he replied, anguished.

"You can, but you won't. There is nothing to stop you. It is all you have to give. You should have given of yourself."

*You should have given of yourself … of yourself … given of yourself…*

The snow blinded him. He could not see her, his tyro, out there in the blizzard. He became lost, hunting, desperate, and woke in a sweat in the dark confines of his curtained bed.

His aunt's letter, arriving hot on the heels of the disturbance of the night, fell on his senses like water on a barren desert.

# CHAPTER TWENTY-FIVE

It was done. Silvestre gathered the ink-spattered sheets of hasty writing into a pile, impossibly untidy. There was no creating a neat block of it, try as she might. The pages were creased here, crumpled there with blotches where her tears, Maudie's tears, had fallen on the paper as she wrote. It was a question if the copyist would manage to read the scrawls she made as the story hastened to its end.

A hopeful end. She had given Maud what she could not have herself. A turning of her Oswald, a realisation of his neglect, imparted to him when he found his Maudie softly weeping as she sewed his shirt. A scene that had brought forth a welter of grief so that she was hard put to it to write even though the words flew from her pen, dulling its point and blotting from the frequent dips into the lowering level in the inkwell. The sun set in Maudie's story on a comforting reconciliation, with promise of a better future than Silvestre had any right to expect for herself. In terms at least of loving well and truly for a lifetime.

But she had her writing and she was determined to take more than solace from it. She would take what happiness she could, if indeed *Emmeline* opened a path for *Maudie*. Would Mr Beak like it as well?

She packed for London in a state of nervous excitement, tinged with dread and the blight of loneliness etched in the core of her heart. The precious new manuscript she tucked into a leather case, a gift from Papa, who, upon learning how far along she was with the new story, had astonished her with an unprecedented act of generosity.

"You must have it professionally copied, my dear Silve, and send me the reckoning."

Silvestre had blinked into her father's usually austere countenance. "Send it to you? But, Papa, I began writing so I would not be a charge on you."

He leaned to place a kiss upon her forehead. "So I understand. Yet until your first book is out, you will not be in funds. Allow me to do this much for you, my dear, though I cannot do as a father ought for his daughter."

Her eyes pricked. "Oh, don't, Papa! You will turn me into a watering pot like poor Hetty."

"Poor Hetty is well settled, and she is happy, which is all I ever wished for my girls."

"Yes, but —"

"No, do not argue with me. I applaud your industry and this I can do for you." His eyes clouded and he frowned. "Alas, I cannot bring the bloom back into your cheeks, but this much I can and will do."

Aware of how she must have given notice of her state of mind in so many little ways, despite every effort to appear cheerful, Silvestre tried to smile. "I will come about, Papa. It is only a matter of time."

Papa embraced her then, and the hug was cruelly gentle, throwing her instantly into the memory of those other arms, holding her perforce and tightly for a brief instant of balm. "I trust so, my child," he said as he released her. "I hoped you might confide in your mama, Silve."

She had. Up to a point. There was no concealing the depth of her unhappiness from those all-seeing eyes behind the spectacles. "Did she tell you, Papa?"

"She would not break your confidence, Silve. Even to me. But I have eyes in my head. I will not ask, though I may guess,

I suppose." He hesitated, eyeing her with a sort of odd diffidence she had never seen before.

A rush of affection loosened her tongue. "It is Gausselin Degarre, Papa. But he won't … there is no…"

"Say no more, Silve. It is a pity. I might have respected such a man for you."

Her bosom swelled with feeling. Ironic, that she had lost her heart where Papa approved, but without a vestige of hope, and to a man virtually a pauper. Whereas poor Hetty had been swept off her feet into a fairy tale with a princely creature of means whom Papa utterly despised.

The interview brought it all back, churning in her head as she prepared to depart with Mrs Summerhayes for the metropolis. Her talk with Mama had been far longer and more painful, coming as it had within a few days of her return to Moss House. She had been writing when Mama's voice interrupted her.

"I know I intrude, my love, but I hope you will forgive me this once."

Silvestre turned on the chair in the den of which she was now the sole occupant, buried there, bent over her growing manuscript like the vulture in his dungeon library. Her mother was hovering in the doorway, her spectacles agleam, and there could be but one answer.

"Of course, Mama. What is it? Do you need me?"

"No, no, my love." Mama came into the room, softly closing the door behind her, and approached almost upon tiptoe. "I don't like to disturb the writer at work, you see."

"Oh, Mama! I am still your daughter."

A smile came. "You are, and I have been hoping for a chance to talk since you returned."

Had she not known it? Certain careful remarks and odd looks were notice enough that Mama knew. Ignoring the patter of her pulses, Silvestre set down her pen and got up, moving to the sofa where Mama gestured for her to sit.

"Dinah is bringing coffee."

Silvestre gave a little sigh, but forced a smile. "I can do with a break. I've been writing so hard my hand hurts."

She flexed her fingers. Mama took the hand in hers and gently massaged the aching joints. Her voice remained matter-of-fact. "It is not all that hurts, is it, my love?" The anguish rushed to the fore and Silvestre could not speak. Mama's fingers tightened on hers and then released them. "My poor darling. Come to Mama then, my dearest girl."

Her arms opened and Silvestre sank into their embrace, letting the tears fall, her mother's crooning murmurs soothing her lacerated heart. Presently she was able to sit up, hunting her sleeve for a handkerchief.

"There, that is better, my dearest. Dry your eyes. Ah, and here is Dinah with the coffee." The knock was followed by the entrance of the matronly maid with a full tray. "You timed it well, Dinah, thank you. Set it down, if you please."

The maid did so, bringing the little table closer to the sofa, tutting, her eyes on Silvestre. "Now, you drink up and stop your fretting, Miss Silve. You'll have us all down in the dumps."

"I'm sorry, Dinah. I am trying to be cheerful."

"And succeeding very well. That will be all, Dinah. Ask Cook to make tarts for dinner. Miss Silve's favourite."

The maid nodded with determination. "That I will and tell her so too, if she starts complaining as she has enough to do already."

Silvestre poured the coffee while Mama urged the maid out of the door, and found herself laughing. "Cook will have a fit, Mama. You know she hates making pastry."

"Because she says it takes too long to prepare. Never mind. It will give her something to fret about instead of gossiping over your megrims."

Guilt rose up. "I never meant to make everyone miserable, Mama."

"Of course you did not, my love, and you may be sure they are all concerned only for your welfare. As am I."

"Papa too?"

"Well, he's noticed, of course, but he will never pry, as you know. Such a good man as Henry is. He believes we women have rights too, and one is to keep our secrets."

"Joss is like that," Silvestre said without thinking. Conscious of Mama's surprised look, she caught her breath, adding with difficulty, "At least, he — he makes no distinctions between men and women. He sees only people. He never … he does not disparage one's opinions, or suppose one is … is less able for being female."

Her mother retook her seat, taking up her cup. "Drink your coffee, my love." Only when Silvestre had taken a sip or two did she speak again. "This Joss of yours sounds to be a man of sound judgement."

"He's not *mine*." It escaped her lips without intent, ragged and bitter.

Mama said nothing, but the calm of her regard worked its magic. Silvestre nursed her cup in her hands, lowering her gaze to the dark liquid therein.

"He will not yield to me, Mama, though he is touched."

"How deeply? Or can't you tell?"

"Oh, I can tell. He admits to it. I can see it, feel it. He yearns for me as I yearn for him."

"But? What withholds him from you?"

She sighed out a calming breath and glanced at her mother. "It is balm to talk to you, Mama. You understand so much." She sipped at the coffee, needing the warmth as the icy regions of loneliness crept back. "He fears his inner torment will affect me badly. He said he would destroy me. Destroy my lightness with his dark. That's why."

Mama considered for a moment, sipping her drink. "Do you think that is true?"

Silvestre shifted with discomfort. "I don't know. Sometimes, yes. I can see too clearly how his brooding might bring me down." She gripped the cup. "But his rejection has done that, Mama. He does not want me. At least, he does, but he won't allow himself the luxury of what I can do for him. Or give me the chance to do it."

Mama set down her cup and folded her hands, her troubled gaze glinting through the spectacles. "My love, could you truly endure a lifetime of such a man? Let me give you fair warning. It is not easy, living with a person who feels things very deeply."

Silvestre met her eyes, both touched at the confidence and pained by the implication. "Papa. I know you have had much to bear."

"Oh, I bear it well enough, Silve, and I consider Henry to be worth the effort." She put up a finger. "Yes, I know you will say the same of Joss, but be clear, my love. If you commit to him, it will be for better or for worse. He will not change. It is a fallacy that love changes a man. A romantic conceit."

This was hard to take. "But you have changed Papa, I know you have. Your influence with him is strong."

Mama's lip quirked. "He has mellowed a little under my care. But at heart, he is what he is. I have learned to manage him, at the expense of myself upon occasion. That is marriage, my dearest. It is always the female who makes the sacrifices. Remember that. Read your friend Aspatria Glasson. She has it down pat. That woman has wisdom, let me tell you."

She could not hear her mother's words unmoved. So much had she divined for herself. Witness *Maudie*, the recipient of all her inmost fears. Yet the hopelessness rankled. "It is well for you to say it, Mama, and I do believe you are right. But the decision is not mine. I am not to be given the choice."

At this, Mama laughed, surprising her. "Oh, my love, you are too young to fathom the hearts of men! Believe me, they are quite as susceptible as those of women, and as likely to abandon all for the sake of love. You just wait and see."

But Silvestre had no faith in any such miracle. She knew the vulture too well. Her absence would relieve him. He was likely buried in his new work as she was in hers, his mind wholly occupied with his muse. No, it was foolish to indulge the hope. She must learn to live her solitary life. She was not going be called upon for sacrifices of the kind.

It was time to look ahead. *Emmeline* was on the horizon and she was going to London. Besides, she had a new novel to finish. To the devil with the vulture!

# CHAPTER TWENTY-SIX

There was no denying the virtues of dwelling in the capital, to begin with at least, where distractions were sufficient to quiet the devils of memory and longing. They came back at night when Silvestre's defences were down. But one could not be wholly in a slough of unhappiness when there was the visit to Beardsley & Beak and the first sight of those printed pages, bound in tooled leather with the title embossed in gold lettering: *Emmeline, or A Girl Most Ordinary* by *A Lady*.

Silvestre ran a fingertip over the embossed lettering, feeling its roughness along with the rising thrill. The pages of the sample were already cut and she opened it, her eye falling upon a random paragraph.

*Emmeline watched, straining her eyes after the coach as it carried the last of her dreams away to an unknown destination.*

Her heart swelled. Joss had been right. To hold in her hands the very book that contained the story of her devising was an instant precious beyond anything.

"Oh, Mr Christy, it is beautifully done!"

The fellow beamed his pleasure. "I am glad it meets with your approval, Miss Latimer. We have made two volumes of it, and the list is growing, thanks to Lady Whittlesford and the names you supplied."

"When will it come out?"

"Ah, a few weeks yet. Our printer is a little behind, but we must hope to send you an author's copy shortly."

It was disappointing not to be able to take the book away with her, but Silvestre left the place on a cloud and with the promise of receiving her due bank draft within a few weeks. She had dared to make casual mention that she had been writing a second novel, but Mr Christy had pursed his lips at the news.

"Early days, Miss Latimer, early days. But good to know. Let us hope I will be asking to see it."

"But will you tell Mr Beak, sir?"

"Certainly, certainly. He will be glad to hear you have wasted no time."

This was scarcely encouraging, but when Silvestre went to visit Aspatria Glasson, that lady put her mind at ease directly.

"You may depend upon it Christy will tell him. He would not dare withhold such a piece of news."

"Why not? I am very much a beginner."

"So you may be, but a beginner who has produced two works within the space of a few short months. Beak will wish to secure your second book before you are tempted to take it elsewhere. He cannot risk losing a promising new author."

But Silvestre had been in Town for over a week and nothing had been forthcoming from the publishing house. She was restless and anxious, feeling unsettled now that *The Vicar's Wife* had gone to a copyist and she had nothing to do. The Season had not begun, but her godmother was busy with preparations and visits to friends already resident in the capital as Parliament came together again after the Christmas break. Felicity had not yet arrived, though Lynchmere was in attendance.

"She did not wish to leave my sister alone too soon," he told them when he called upon his cousin.

"But you have persuaded her to come for the Season, I hope, Raoul? She must establish herself if she is going to bring Lucille out next year."

Lord Lynchmere had given her one of his enigmatic looks. "Felicity is relying upon your good offices, Angie. She may not be in a condition to come to Town next year."

"Good heavens, why not?" Then Mrs Summerhayes uttered a shriek. "Raoul, is she enceinte?"

He smiled and nodded. "We think so. Not a word mind, Angelica. It is not yet certain."

This was a matter for celebration, and the subject occupied her godmother's conversation for some time after her cousin's departure. It set up a train of unwelcome thought in Silvestre's head, however. In her wildest dreaming she had never considered the inevitable accompaniment to a domestic life in the vulture's company. Children? How could he cope? How afford the luxury? The very idea would terrify Joss.

*What are you doing, Silvestre Latimer?* Such speculation did not belong in the present. She had put all hope of that outcome behind her. Or tried to.

No, she must stop this. Lady Whittlesford had not yet come to Town, Miss Glasson had told her. But soon the literary salons would resume and she might further her acquaintance with those she had met. She toyed with calling upon Greta Fossebridge, but balked at it. Mrs Fossebridge cherished a liking for Gausselin Degarre and was bound to speak of him. How in the world could she answer suitably when she was guilty of securing his affections? No matter that he would have none of her. No, it would be too embarrassing altogether.

As for Aspatria Glasson, though she had welcomed the visit with all her usual kindness, she had confessed she was engrossed in her latest work and needed to spend more time interviewing women of a less fortunate class for the purpose. All of which left Silvestre in a hovering limbo after the first week in George Street. At length, she sat down at the bureau in the Yellow Parlour to compose a difficult letter to Hetty. Difficult, because she knew not how to refrain from asking about Joss.

In her mind the questions multiplied. Was he growing gaunt again in her absence? Was he brooding? Did he seem to miss her at all? Had he begun his poems of Shakespeare?

She shook her mind free of such pointless enquiries and began to write, laboriously, of her visit to Beardsley & Beak, dwelling on how it felt to hold the volume in her hands and see her words on the page. Oh, and could she mention Felicity's possible condition? No, too soon. Lynchmere had enjoined their silence until it was confirmed. What else? Papa's generosity, yes. That provided a paragraph more.

She sat back, teasing the feathered end of the quill against her cheek. What more was there to say? Hetty would be anxious for her distresses, but Silvestre could not set them down. She had begun with saying she was doing well and that must suffice. How speak of the deep gaping wound that would not heal? The ache in her breast that never quite lifted, though she laughed and smiled when opportunity offered?

"Silve, are you fit to receive a visitor?"

Her godmother's voice, cutting into her thoughts, made her jump. "Aunt Angelica! You gave me such a fright."

She turned on the chair. Mrs Summerhayes was standing in the doorway, one hand about the handle, a frown creasing her forehead. Her words penetrated.

"Visitor? What visitor?"

Her godmother jerked her head towards the gallery behind. "Maunder says he's waiting in the hall."

A shocking presentiment leapt in Silvestre's bosom. "Who is he?"

"Gausselin Degarre, the poet fellow. Do you wish to see him? Shall Maunder tell him to come up?"

Her mind whirled. Was it a dream? Had she conjured it? Joss here? What was he doing in London?

She had no notion if she spoke, nor what she did, but she found herself standing, moving. Mrs Summerhayes slid out of the room and her voice came clearly.

"Show the gentleman up, Maunder."

The butler's tread going downstairs. Aunt Angelica coming in again, moving towards her.

"You look like a ghost, Silve! What in the world is happening? What am I missing? Why has he come?"

She stared at her godmother's face, mesmerised, dazed. "I — don't know."

"Good heavens, Silve, are you faint? Sit down, do!"

"No!" She thrust out her hands, waving the menace away. "Wait! I am … I am all right."

Footsteps on the stairs. Hasty. Thumping as they came at a rapid rate.

The door was wide. Silvestre, her pulse humming, heating both body and mind, kept her eyes glued there.

A figure hurtled through the doorway and came to a stumbling halt. The vulture. Hair wild. Eyes piercing her. Out of breath.

"I ran all the way."

Disorientation seized her brain and she spoke it without thought. "From Devenal?"

"From Berkeley Square. My father's house. I came down to Whisley Park by the night mail. To find you. You weren't there."

His voice as ragged as his breath. Her confusion total. "Whisley Park? No, I'm here."

"Moss House. Your sister gave me your direction."

"But I left there a week since."

"Yes, they told me. I followed you."

His breath was still short, his gaze roving hers in a hungry fashion that spoke to her deeps. Only half knowing what she did, Silvestre opened her arms to him. He staggered towards her like a drowning man and then she was caught in a fierce hold, the beat of his heart vibrant at her breast.

The miracle of his presence invaded all her senses, her body heating to his breath on her skin. Her face buried in his shoulder teased a masculine aroma into her nostrils, causing her fingers to writhe in the hair she'd yearned to touch.

Her godmother's voice threw sanity into the maelstrom. "I appear to be *de trop*. Propriety dictates I remain, however, before this goes too far."

Silvestre broke free in a bang. Her limbs water, she nearly fell, seizing at the nearest chair back for support. One glance served to show Joss in a similar condition, shaking. He was staring at Aunt Angelica, his cheeks rather paling than showing the red of embarrassment. The reason struck Silvestre on the instant.

Heavens, he had not even realised Aunt Angelica was in the room! She hastened to smooth his path. "Aunt, this is Lord Joscelin Diggory. He is Lord Rotherhythe's son."

"I know very well who he is, I thank you."

The tart note flurried Silvestre, but she persisted, turning to the assailant of her heart. "Mrs Summerhayes, Joss. My godmother."

He jerked a bow. "Ma'am."

Aunt Angelica's brows rose. "That is all you have to say? After such an exhibition?"

To Silvestre's dismay, her love dropped into his nervous staccato.

"Bad, yes. Should not have. Wasn't thinking. Just wanted…" He gestured wildly towards Silvestre, throwing her a desperate glance.

She responded at once, going to his side. "Don't scold, Aunt Angelica, pray. You don't know all."

"I don't know anything! Are you betrothed?"

"No!"

But Joss grabbed her hand and faced her godmother. "Yes!"

Indignation leapt in her bosom and she turned on him, wrenching her hand free. "You have not even asked me! How dare you say so? After all that has passed? After everything you said? You can't just waltz in and announce —"

"As well he did after your conduct, my dear Silve!" But Aunt Angelica's eyes were brimming with amusement. "It seems to me I had best leave the two of you to thrash the matter out." She sailed towards the door and paused there. "Mind, I shall be satisfied with nothing less than the whole story, Silve. And for heaven's sake, don't go looking a gift horse in the mouth. He *is* the son of a marquis."

With which, she left the room, closing the door behind her. Silvestre was left confronting the man who was threatening her with precisely what she had desired. Only it was all wrong. She seized upon her godmother's ridiculous assumption.

"Gift horse? She clearly knows nothing of you, Vulture!"

He met her gaze, consternation in his own, a tremor in the hand he held out towards her. "I'm no gift, I know it too well. You'll teach me to be better. Show me how to treat others."

She backed away from the hand, still hurting. "How have you changed? Why are you here?"

He looked anguished. "Does it matter? You know I want you. Is that not enough?"

"No, it's not enough, Joss! The last time I saw you, spoke to you, you were adamant. There was no future for us. You said you would destroy me. Now suddenly you come after me and tell my godmother we are betrothed. What happened? What changed?"

He withdrew his hand, brought it up to press at his brow, rubbing it. "You'll be angry, I know it."

"Never mind that. Tell me."

He moved, restless, crossing to a chair by the mantel, turning there, seizing its back as if he needed the support. "Aunt Isobel wrote to me. There's a house. Entailed on the sisters — she and my mother — by my grandfather so no husband could touch it."

Bewildered, Silvestre eyed him. "A house. What of it?"

His glance met hers and lowered again, looking into the bowl of the chair. "My aunt says they wish me to have it. If I need it. For you."

Shock ripped through her. Isobel had acted. Without consulting her. On purpose to coerce him into this. "They forced you to it!" Her heart plummeted. "You don't want it, do you? You feel obliged to offer."

His head came up. "No. No, you don't understand."

Fury rippled in her veins, fuelled by hurt. "I understand only too well. Oh, Joss! I would have lived with you in a cottage. In your attic, even! Do you suppose I needed a bribe?"

His grip on the chair back intensified. "It's not like that. I knew you would be angry."

"Well, and you know why too!" She confronted him across the chair. "I love you, Joss. There, I've said it. I love you and I would have taken you just as you are, if you'd let me. Now you come to me with a house? It's insulting!" She swept away again, seething. She heard his step behind her and her shoulder was seized, his hand pulling her around to face him. Dark eyes burning at her.

"Why do you doubt me, Tyro? I've been dying by inches since you left. Look at me! I can't eat. I can't write. Not a word. I tried drowning in that damned hideous library work, but it was no use. You haunt me, Tyro! When the letter came, I seized on it."

She was melting at the underlying passion to his words, but not yet ready to believe. "A convenient excuse. You could have followed me before the letter came."

His threw up his hands, clutching at air. "It was a spur, don't you see? What had I to offer you had I come before?"

"Yourself, Joss. You could have offered me yourself."

"Yes, that's it!" He sounded eager, his gaze becoming intent. "That is it exactly. I knew it, realised it, before the letter came. A little before, I can't remember precisely."

"What? What did you realise?"

"That I should have given you of myself. It took me a while to get there, I'll tell you. I'm not adept at such things. I puzzled over it. But it came to me at last. I should have given you of myself. I want to, Tyro. I need you to teach me how."

She was conscious of a quiver beginning inside her. A tiny rise of the mischief that had been missing for so long. "I've never heard you so eloquent, Vulture."

His faint smile came. "Your influence, Tyro." He waited, trepidation warring with hope. Had he yet done enough? She did not look to be wholly appeased. Joss wished he knew what he ought to say, what would cause her to put him out of his agony.

She was eying him askance. Waiting for something more? He ventured a question.

"Will you?"

Her features mirrored change and his heart sank.

"Will I what?"

Goaded, he caught her hand and held it in a grip that made her wince. Joss ignored it. "Take me. Will you take me? Marry me, Tyro!"

For an instant, her lip aquiver, he thought she was going to say yes. Her fingers moved in his grip and he loosened it, but did not let her go. She spoke. Husky and warm. "You've still not said it, Joss. I won't marry you if you can't say it."

Frustration invaded his breast and he released her, rearing back. "Say what? I've said it all! What more do you want me to say?"

Her eyes rimmed with moisture and he was riven with the guilt she could so readily raise in him. The whisper was anguished. "Love, my darling vulture. Will you never speak to me of your affections? A woman likes to hear these things."

He wanted to weep with her. "I don't know how."

"Just say it, Joss. Just say the words."

He swallowed, drew courage from somewhere. "I … I love you."

A smile trembled on her mouth. "There, that wasn't so hard, was it?"

To his own astonishment, it was not. His mouth formed the words as they rose in his head. "If it is that which tells me I cannot live without you, then yes, it is love. It is affection. It is passion, and yearning and desire and the wish to be showered with your sunshine forever, my golden butterfly."

Silvestre's tears spilled over. "I knew you had it in you, Gausselin Degarre. You are a romantic poet after all."

This time she stumbled into his arms and felt them close about her, strong bands that told her the truth of his words. She wriggled and his hold loosened. She shifted back enough to be able to look at him. She raised her fingers to the dear face she had longed to touch, stroking his gaunt cheek.

"You have lost flesh, you terrible man. Is it to my account?"

He was shaking again and an instinct in Silvestre divined the cause. Her breath hushed in her throat and she caught his gaze, looking deep into the eyes that burned with the hunger she might now fulfil.

"My vulture," she whispered. She leaned to him, held his face between her hands and pressed her lips to his.

For a moment they trembled there together, and then Joss took her mouth and the world exploded.


"What is this house then?"

She had made him sit on the sofa, placing herself upon his lap, relishing the way he abandoned himself to her will, holding her close and letting her touch him as she would. Astonished and gratified at the passion she had unleashed, Silvestre determined to keep him affectionate. At this moment, she experienced no difficulty. He kissed her, lingeringly, before he answered.

"I have not seen it. My aunt speaks of a modest place. The best is that it is within easy reach of the capital."

"You mean we may still attend the salons?"

"If we must."

She tapped his chest. "You may be sated with them, but I am not. Don't sigh! I won't let anyone bully you."

He hugged her. "I will depend on you utterly."

She submitted to the embrace, but her mind ran on the future. "How will we afford this house, Joss?"

"There are rents from surrounding farmlands which ought to sustain it."

Silvestre's housewifely instincts became aroused. "We might keep a servant or two there, do you think?"

"I don't know. We must, I suppose. I can't have you scrubbing and slaving at menial tasks." He frowned. "You could not have managed in a cottage."

She gave him one of her teasing looks. "I could not have managed *you* in a cottage, Vulture. As for that attic, I would likely have been driven to climb on the roof and throw myself off it."

The faint smile she loved twitched his mouth. "I will likely drive you screaming from this house in any event."

"All too probable, brooding spider that you are."

"You won't permit me to brood, Tyro." He traced her lips with his finger. "If I do, you have leave to tease me out of it."

Silvestre kissed the finger and took his hand in hers, caressing it with her mouth. "I shall close the door on you and get on with my writing until you behave."

"You won't. You'll nag and badger me into behaving."

She laughed. "I shan't, because I write best when I'm distressed." A horrid thought struck her and she gazed at him in consternation.

He put up a hand and stroked her brow as if he would smooth away the frown. "What? Have I said aught amiss?"

Silvestre drew an anxious breath. "You're going to hate me when you read my new book."

"I could never hate you. Why, is it to vilify me? I wouldn't blame you for that."

"Not vilify. But the vicar is a man like you, brooding and enclosed, and he makes poor Maudie's life a misery."

He picked up her hand and brought it to his lips. "I'll take it for my lesson." But a tiny smile crept into his face. "Although such a lesson might be taken two ways, Tyro. If treating you to my demons makes you write better…"

Indignant, she wagged a finger in his face. "I didn't tell you so you might take it for licence."

He drew her to him, nuzzling her neck. "I mean to be good to you, but I fear I'll fail miserably."

She sat up, smiling at him. "You won't fail. I won't let you. We will both have our writing places and we may bury ourselves separately. If you become impossible, I will escape to mine and let you simmer in yours. Then you may recover and come out and be good to me all over again. There, is it a bargain?"

He gave a sigh and she saw him relax in a way he never had before, a smile creeping into his eyes. "It is anything you wish it to be, my golden butterfly. You brighten my world. Henceforth, I am in your hands."

Silvestre's overburdened heart quietened. Serene, contented, as if it had come home.

# A NOTE TO THE READER

Dear Reader,

One of my habits stolen from Georgette Heyer is to use a map to garner surnames for my characters. You can find them dotted across England. When I was hunting for names for the literati, I struck lucky. Several offerings gave me not just a surname, but the whole name for these individuals.

If you check out a detailed map of the United Kingdom, or just go to Google, you will find towns for Moreton Pinckney, Aspatria Glasson, Carleton Rode, Stanford Wingley and Pelham Ferneux. I have tampered with the spelling here and there, but I took those names wholesale from the map as the characters jumped out at me.

Lord Joscelin Diggory, AKA Gausselin Degarre, was a different matter. For that, I had to check my trusty Oxford Dictionary of English Christian Names. A useful tome that informs me of rough date usage of the name, together with its derivatives, surnames, nicknames and versions in other languages, if any. I was able to take Gausselin for Joscelin and Degarre for Diggory from this invaluable resource. I can't write a book without consulting this one.

In fact, I can't start a story without knowing the names of my principal characters. Names are a personal identification. They conjure up an immediate picture in the mind. It's unfortunate if the name of a main character happens to be one you associate with someone in life you had rather not remember, but in that respect I think we are luckier with historicals as current names were not necessarily common in the Regency.

The other pertinent aspect of this particular story is that I made my heroine a novelist and my hero a poet. I've written a poet hero before, but a much lighter character than this one. This poet suffers all the angst commonly attributed to writers. It can be a painful process, but I doubt if most writer friends go through the inner torment Joss puts himself through. Nor did his counterparts of the literati.

I did enjoy creating different writer types. The nature of the individual dictates how they go about their labours. I suspect if Joss had been instead a clergyman or, Heaven forbid, a soldier, he would have suffered just as much if for different reasons. But poetry gave him real scope for his torment, so I hope he is grateful to me for supplying him with the perfect calling!

I hope you enjoyed the tale. If you would consider leaving a review, it would be much appreciated and very helpful. Do feel free to contact me on **elizabeth@elizabethbailey.co.uk** or find me on **Facebook**, **Twitter**, **Goodreads** or my website **www.elizabethbailey.co.uk**.

Elizabeth Bailey

**Sapere Books** is an exciting new publisher of brilliant fiction and popular history.

To find out more about our latest releases and our monthly bargain books visit our website: **saperebooks.com**